Acclaim for Alice Hoffman's
Skylight Confessions

"*Skylight Confessions* is classic Alice Hoffman: a magical, melancholy love story."　　　　　　　　　　*— Redbook*

"One of Hoffman's very best. . . . *Skylight Confessions* has all the hallmarks of a Hoffman novel: well-wrought and empathetic characters, love gone awry, interstitial magic, ghosts real and metaphoric, familial dissent, and emotional fractures. *Skylight Confessions* also has the beautifully wrought language and compelling imagery that make each Hoffman tale come alive. . . . *Skylight Confessions* is a beautiful, intricate, lush, and ineffably sad novel of one family's arduous path toward wholeness. Hoffman is one of our great storytellers and one who knows the American family in all its many facets. In *Skylight Confessions,* she has once again written a story and characters that are truly unforgettable. A novel to be savored."
　　　　　　— Victoria A. Brownworth, *Baltimore Sun*

"Wholly original and haunting."　　　　　　　*— Parade*

"Hoffman's brand of magical realism squeezes caring out of hard-to-reach places and ends up being a celebration of love."
　　　　　　— Margo Hammond and Ellen Heltzel,
　　　　　　　　　　　　　　　Good Housekeeping

"This is one of Hoffman's best. . . . Even when these characters are shadowed by the ghosts anchored in their past, it is obvious they are in the hands of a loving creator, a woman who continues to write with amazing grace."
　　　　　　　　　— Steve Duin, *Portland Oregonian*

"Hoffman has done it again, superbly this time, echoing and subverting fairy tale themes. . . . Her latest novel is a compelling story that is heartbreaking and poignant."
— Nandini Bandyopadhyay, *Tampa Tribune*

"An enchanting novel about destiny, true love, and a family haunted (literally) by heartbreak."
— *Hallmark*

"A gloriously spooky ghost story about a dysfunctional family trying to deny its past. . . . Hoffman's touch is so deft, her tone so austere, that the paranormal — china that breaks itself, strange scents, red-headed specters — seems normal. . . . Hoffman's restrained, elegantly plain prose recalls Eudora Welty's fairy tales. . . . Like Welty, Hoffman can be sly, black-humored, and startlingly powerful. . . . Hoffman's night-dark fairy tale offers no panacea from the pain of being human except a sense of the wonder of the world. That's what literature is for, after all."
— Diane Roberts, *Atlanta Journal-Constitution*

"Haunting. . . . Achingly beautiful and filled with heart-wrenchingly real characters: one of Hoffman's best."
— *Kirkus Reviews*

"Hoffman's most spellbinding, accomplished novel yet. . . . Although this is her nineteenth book, it feels utterly fresh. Hoffman's voice — touched by the cadences of fairy tales — buoys us through the novel's saddest currents."
— Andrea Chapin, *More*

"Hoffman has attempted something admirable here, and she largely achieves her goal. . . . Improbably, somewhere in this tangle of sorrow and blighted relationships, she finds the magic of human connection."
— Ellen Emry Heltzel, *Minneapolis Star Tribune*

"Arresting. . . . A haunting meditation on the curse of bottomless grief, a wickedly hard spell to break."
— Andrea Simakis, *Cleveland Plain Dealer*

"Because of the arduous demands of our so-called real lives, every society needs fairy tales, and Alice Hoffman, over the years, has excelled at producing them for us."
— Carolyn See, *Washington Post*

"An absorbing novel. . . . In another of her captivating modern fairy tales, the prolific Hoffman pulls the reader in, too. Arlyn's saga of an unfulfilling marriage, her early death, the fate of her two children, the angst of her husband and other survivors covers a lot of territory. Yet it flows along almost effortlessly in Hoffman's limpid prose. . . . Hoffman never settles for a cheap solution to the complex demands of imperfect love. And some of her characters are drawn with great vividness. . . . Arlyn is the one who haunts the family, and haunts the reader, too."
— Steve Raymond, *Seattle Times*

"Among the many pleasures of *Skylight Confessions* is a sense of continuous corner-turning, a chain of surprises. . . . At the end of this book I didn't know myself how its people and places had gotten such a hold on me. But there it is. There's magic in it. . . . *Skylight Confessions* is about the unresolvable contradictions that lie at the heart of life."
— Ann Harleman, *Boston Globe*

"Alice Hoffman remains a literary sorceress par excellence. She has spun yet another haunting, fairy tale–like fiction for grown-ups. . . . In a novel that unfolds like a dream, Hoffman reminds readers that love and family create the most potent magic of all."
— Martha Woodall, *Philadelphia Inquirer*

"Hoffman's shimmering, multigenerational melodrama bewitches with supernatural imagery while imaginatively dramatizing all-too-common heartaches."

— Donna Seaman, *Booklist*

"A natural storyteller and a romantic at heart. . . . *Skylight Confessions* is a fairy tale imbued with the intense emotional undercurrents of adolescence and haunted by loss and failures of love. . . . Hoffman gives us the heartbreak of a dying young mother and her love for her son, the solace of the green days of May, and the possibilities of art and of love winning out."

— Jane Ciabattari, *Los Angeles Times Book Review*

"*Skylight Confessions* presents life as something full of overwhelming wonder. . . . There is plenty to learn from Hoffman's ability to observe the everyday complications of life."

— Ken Foster, *Time Out New York*

"Haunting. . . . *Skylight Confessions* isn't just Hoffman's best recent novel; it's one of the best of a distinguished list that includes *Turtle Moon* and *Practical Magic*. . . . Long after the last page is turned, the characters and their stories are impossible to forget."

— Gail Pennington, *St. Louis Post-Dispatch*

"*Skylight Confessions* is the luminous story of a family haunted by love. Simple in construction and elegant in execution, Alice Hoffman's seventeenth novel is at its heart a modern fairy tale, replete with doomed lovers, wicked stepmothers, and even an itinerant ghost. . . . In the end, this redemptive story about love is transformed into something larger: a powerful deliberation on the exigencies of fate."

— Hilary Black, *Tango*

Skylight Confessions

SKYLIGHT CONFESSIONS

a novel

ALICE HOFFMAN

BACK BAY BOOKS

Little, Brown and Company

New York   Boston   London

Back Bay Books / Little, Brown and Company
Hachette Book Group USA
237 Park Avenue, New York, NY 10017
Visit our Web site at www.HachetteBookGroupUSA.com

Originally published in hardcover by Little, Brown and Company, January 2007
Back Bay international mass market paperback edition, February 2008
Back Bay trade paperback edition, February 2008

The characters and events in this book are fictitious. Any similarity to real persons, living or
dead, is coincidental and not intended by the author.

Allen Pierleoni's interview with Alice Hoffman, which appears in the reading group guide
at the back of this book, originally appeared in the *Sacramento Bee* on January 29, 2007.
Copyright © 2007 by The Sacramento Bee. Reprinted with permission.

Library of Congress Cataloging-in-Publication Data
Hoffman, Alice.
    Skylight confessions / Alice Hoffman. — 1st ed.
        p.   cm.
    ISBN 978-0-316-05878-0 (hc) / 978-0-316-00533-3 (int'l mm pb) / 978-0-316-01787-9 (trade pb) /
978-0-316-02662-8 (Scholastic edition)
    1. Architects — Fiction.   2. Spouses — Fiction.   3. Life change events — Fiction.   I. Title.
PS3558.O3447S59   2007
813'.54 — dc22   2006001391

10 9 8 7 6 5 4 3 2 1

RRD-C

Printed in the United States of America

Skylight Confessions

Ghost Wife

SHE WAS HIS FIRST WIFE, BUT AT THE MOMENT when he first saw her she was a seventeen-year-old girl named Arlyn Singer who stood out on the front porch on an evening that seemed suspended in time. Arlyn's father had just died and the funeral dinner had ended only hours earlier. It was a somber gathering: a dozen neighbors seated around the heavy mahogany dining-room table no one had used for over a decade. Now there were pans of macaroni and cheese and a red velvet cake and a huge platter of fruit, food enough to last a month if Arlie had had an appetite.

Arlyn's father had been a ferryboat captain, the center of her world, especially in his last years; the captain had burned brighter in the grasp of his illness, a shining star in the dark. A usually silent man, he began to tell stories. There were tales of rocks that appeared in the dark, of mysterious reefs whose only purpose seemed to be to sink ferries, of the drowned men he'd known who had never come back. With a red crayon, he drew charts of stars that could lead a lost man home. He told of a tribe who lived on the other side of the water, in far-off Connecticut, who could sprout wings in the face of disaster. They looked like normal people until the ship went down, or the fire raged, and then they suddenly revealed themselves. Only then did they manage their escape.

On his night table there was a collection of stones the captain said he had swallowed when he was a young man; he'd gone down with a ship and had been the lone survivor. One minute he'd been standing on deck, and the next, he'd been above it all, in the sky. He'd fallen hard and fast into the surf of Connecticut, with a mouth and a belly full of stones.

When the doctor came to tell the captain there was no hope, they had a drink together and instead of ice the captain put a stone in the cups of whiskey.

It will bring you good luck, he'd told the doctor. *All I want is for my daughter to be happy. That's all the luck I need.*

Arlyn had sobbed at his bedside and begged her father not to leave her, but that was not an option or a choice. The last advice the captain had given her, while his voice still held out, was that the future was an unknown and unexpected country, and that Arlyn should be prepared for almost anything. She had been grief stricken as her father lay dying but now she felt weightless, the way people do when they're no longer sure they have a reason to be connected to this world. The slightest breeze could have carried her away, into the night sky, across the universe.

Arlyn held on to the porch banister and leaned out over the azaleas. Red and pink flowers, filled with buds. Arlyn was an optimist, despite her current situation. She was young enough not to see a glass as half empty or half full, but as a beautiful object into which anything might be poured. She whispered a bargain, as though her whispering could make it true.

The first man who walks down the street will be my one love and I will be true to him as long as he's true to me.

She turned around twice and held her breath as a way to seal the bargain. She wore her favorite shoes, ones her father had bought her in Connecticut, leather slippers so light she felt as though she were barefoot. Her red hair reached her waist. She had seventy-four freckles on her face — she had counted — and a long, straight nose her father had assured her was elegant rather than large. She watched the sky darken. There was a line of ashes up above, a sprinkling of chimney soot. Perhaps her father was up there, watching over her. Perhaps he was knocking on his casket, begging to be let out. Or maybe he was here with her still, in her heart, making it difficult for her to breathe whenever she thought about her life without him. Arlie felt her aloneness inside her, but she was hopeful, too. The past was done with. Now she was made out of glass, transparent and clear. She was an instant in time. One damp evening, two stars in the sky, a line of soot, a chattering gathering of neighbors who barely knew her in the dining room. She had convinced herself that her future would arrive on the street where she'd lived her whole life if only she'd wait long enough. If she trusted in fate.

In the living room, people spoke about Arlyn as though she had died right along with her father. She wasn't a pretty girl, after all, just plain and freckly. She had a high-school diploma and, as far as anyone could tell, no particular skills. One summer she'd worked in an ice-cream shop, and in high school she'd had a dog-washing service, shampooing basset hounds and poodles in the kitchen sink. An ordinary girl all alone in a house where the roof might blow off in the next big storm. People felt pity, but as everyone knew, that wasn't an emotion that lasted long.

A low horn sounded as the ferry came across the water from Bridgeport; the fact that there would be fog tonight was discussed as the women cleaned up, wiping off the table, putting away the pound cakes and the casseroles before going out to the porch to say good night to Arlyn. It was a heavy, salt-laced fog that had settled, the kind that circled lampposts and street signs and made folks lose their way. A damp, soft night. The neighbors assumed that once they'd left, Arlyn would go inside her empty house. Surely she would walk along the hall where her father's coats still hung on the rack, then take the flight of stairs the captain hadn't been able to manage for the past six months. She would edge past his silent room. No more coughing all night long. No more calls for water.

But Arlyn stayed where she was. She was so cold her skin felt like ice; still she remained on the porch. Her father had said to prepare for the future, and Arlyn was ready and willing. Her destiny was sure to come to her in her darkest hour. That was now, this damp, sad night. It took some time, but after three hours Arlie's faith was rewarded. By then the fog had turned to a light rain and the streets smelled like fish. A car stopped; there was a young man inside, lost, on his way to a party. When he got out to ask directions, Arlyn noticed he was taller than her father. She liked tall men. His hair was combed back. He had beautiful pale eyes, a cool gray color. As he approached he shouted, "Hello." His voice was not what she expected — flat and nasal. That didn't matter. Anything could happen now.

Arlyn took a step back in order to study him. Perhaps the young man thought she was afraid — a stranger stopping to talk to her in a banged-up old Saab his dad had given him. He could have been anyone, after all. A murderer, an ex-con, a man who would rip the heart from her chest.

"I'm lost," the young man explained. Usually he would have kept on driving; he had never in his life stopped to ask for directions. But he was late, and he was the sort of person who was usually on time. Veering from punctuality made him anxious; it made him do stupid things. For instance, he had circled around this particular block twice. Before leaving, he'd forgotten to check to make sure his gas tank was full and now he worried that he wouldn't be able to find a service station before he ran out.

The young man's name was John Moody and he was a

senior at Yale studying architecture; he recognized Arlie's father's house as an Italianate worker's cottage, built, he would guess, in the 1860s, common in these North Shore towns on Long Island. Not kept up, of course — the roof looked like flypaper, the shingles were badly in need of paint — but charming in a run-down way just as the girl with the long red hair was charming despite her dreadful clothes and the freckles scattered across her pale skin.

Arlyn was wearing an overcoat though it was April.

"You're freezing," John Moody said.

Arlyn took this as concern rather than mere statement of fact. The truth was, she was shivering in the cold light of her future, the light that had been cast by this tall young man who had no idea where he was.

Arlyn felt faint. Fluttery, really. Her whole life had been spent in a cocoon; she had been waiting for this hanging globe of an evening. *This is when everything else begins. Whatever happens next is where my life will lead me.*

John Moody came up the porch steps. Rickety. In need of repair. John took a moment to catch his breath, then spoke.

"I've never met the person having the party. My roommate Nathaniel's sister. I don't even know why I'm here."

His heart was pounding uncomfortably hard. His father had had a heart attack earlier in the year. Was he having one, too? Well, he'd never liked speaking to strangers; he'd never liked speaking at all. John Moody was a champion of quiet and order. Architecture meant rules one could depend upon. He was a devotee of the clean line and of truth in form, without frills or complications. He didn't like messes of any sort.

Arlyn looked over the directions John's roommate had

given him. They were all wrong. "If you want to go to Smithtown, you turn at the corner by the harbor and keep going west. Four towns over."

"That far?" John Moody had been working hard at Yale throughout the semester, trying to distinguish himself; all at once he felt exhausted. "I didn't realize I was so tired."

Arlyn understood. "Sometimes you don't know how tired you are until you close your eyes."

There was no rush, was there? Time was suspended; it wasn't moving at all. They went inside and John Moody lay down on the couch. He had long legs and large feet and he fell asleep easily. He could not remember the last time he'd had a dream. "Just for a minute," he said. "Until I get my second wind."

Arlyn sat on a hard-backed chair, still wearing her overcoat, still shivering. She watched John fall asleep. She had the feeling that whatever happened next would be the true test of whether or not they were meant to be. John's eyelids fluttered; his chest rose and fell. He was a beautiful sleeper, calm, unmoving, peaceful. It felt so right to have him there. The room was littered with chairs that had been pulled into a circle by the visiting neighbors. When Arlyn's father had been at his worst, in such pain he had to be sedated into sleep, he had moaned and thrashed in his dreams and tore at the bedsheets. Sometimes Arlyn would leave him, just for a short time, for a breath of air, a moment alone. She'd walk down to the harbor and look into the darkness. She could hear the water, but she couldn't see it; she couldn't see anything at all. All she'd wanted, then and now, was a man who could sleep. At last he was here.

Arlie left John Moody and went into the kitchen. She hadn't eaten for three days and she realized she was famished. Arlie went to the refrigerator and took out nearly everything — the tins of baked beans, the homemade strudels, the ham, the sweet-potato pie, the last piece of red velvet cake. She sat at the table and ate three days' worth of food. When she was finished she went to the sink, filled it with soapy water, and cleaned the pots and pans.

She was so full no one could accuse her of being lightheaded. She was rational. No doubt about it. She knew what she was doing. She took off her coat, her black dress, her slip, her underwear, even the soft leather shoes her father had bought her. She turned out the light. Her breath moved inside her ribs like a butterfly. In and out. Waiting. *If he walks through the door, my life will begin.* And indeed, when John Moody came into the kitchen, time hurtled forward, no longer suspended. He was walking to her, shocked by his good fortune and by the dreaminess of the evening, the extreme weirdness of setting out from Yale as a bored college boy and ending up here, in this kitchen. Arlie looked like a ghost, someone he'd imagined, a woman made of moonlight and milk. The neighbors who thought she was too plain to notice would have been surprised to know that all John Moody could see was Arlie's beautiful nakedness and her long red hair. He would never have imagined they thought of her as ugly and useless.

As for Arlyn, if nothing ever happened to her again, this would be enough. The way he circled his arms around her, the way the dishes in the dish rack fell to the floor, the good white china in shards and neither one of them caring. She

had never been kissed before; she'd been too busy with bed-
pans, morphine, the practical details of death.

"This is crazy," John Moody said, not that he intended to
stop. Not that he could.

Would he hold this against her, years and years later, how
waylaid he'd become? Would he say she tricked him with a
rare beauty no one had noticed before? All Arlyn knew was
that when she led him to her bedroom, he followed. It was a
girl's bedroom with lace runners on the bureaus and milk-
glass lamps; it didn't even seem to belong to her anymore.
The way time was moving, so fast, so intense, made her
shudder. She was about to make the leap from one world to
the next, from *the over and done* to *the what could be.*

Arlyn went forward into time and space; she looped her
arms around John Moody's neck. She felt his kiss on her
throat, her shoulders, her breasts. He had been lost and she
had found him. He had asked for directions and she had
told him which way to go. He was whispering, *Thank you,* as
though she had given him a great gift. Perhaps she had
given him exactly that: her self, her future, her fate.

HE STAYED FOR THREE DAYS, THE ENTIRE TIME SPENT IN
bed; he was crazy for her, hypnotized, not wanting food or
water, only her. She tasted like pears. How odd that was,
that sweet green flavor, and even odder that he should notice.
John didn't usually pay attention to people, but he did now.
Arlie's hands were small and beautiful and her teeth were
small and perfect as well, but she had large feet, as he did.
The sign of a walker, a doer, a person who completed tasks

and never complained. She seemed neat and uncomplicated, everything he admired. He did not know her name until the first morning, didn't learn of her father's death until the second. And then on the third morning John Moody awoke suddenly from a dream, the first dream he could remember having in many years, perhaps since he was a child. He'd been in the house he'd grown up in, a renowned construction his architect father had built outside New Haven that people called the Glass Slipper, for it was made out of hundreds of windows woven together with thin bands of polished steel. In his dream, John Moody was carrying a basket of pears along the hallway. Outside there was an ice storm and the glass house had become opaque. It was difficult to see where he was going at first, and then impossible.

John was lost, though the floor plan was simple, one he had known his whole life. His father was a great believer in minimalism, known for it, lauded for his straight lines stacked one upon another, as though a building could be made purely from space and glass. John Moody looked down to see why the basket he carried had become so heavy. Everything was odd: the way his heart was pounding, the confusion he felt. Stranger still: the pears in the basket had become flat black stones. Before he could stop them the stones arose without being touched; they hurtled up through the air as though they'd been fired from a cannon, breaking the windows of the Glass Slipper, one after the other. Everything shattered and the sky came tumbling into the house. Cloud and bird and wind and snow.

John Moody awoke in Arlyn's arms, in a room he did not recognize. There was a white sheet over him, and his chest was constricted with fear. He had to get out. He was in the wrong place; that was all too clear to him now. Wrong time, wrong girl, wrong everything. Next to him, Arlie's red hair fell across the pillow. In this light, true morning light, it was the color of the human heart, of blood. It seemed unnatural, not a color that he, who preferred muted tones, would ever be drawn to.

Arlie raised herself onto one elbow. "What?" she said sleepily.

"Nothing. Go back to sleep."

John Moody already had his pants on and was searching for his shoes. He was supposed to be in class at that very moment. He was taking conversational Italian, planning to travel to Florence during the summer between graduation and his advanced-degree program in architecture. He would stand in great halls, see what the masters had accomplished, sleep dreamlessly through still, black nights in a small hotel room.

Arlyn tried to pull him close. But he was bending down, out of reach, retrieving his shoes from beneath the bed.

"Go back to sleep," John told her. All those freckles he hadn't noticed in the dark. Those thin, grasping arms.

"Will you come back to bed?" Arlie murmured. She was half-asleep. Love was stupefying, hypnotizing, a dream world.

"I'll watch you," John said.

Arlyn liked the sound of that; she may have smiled. John waited till she was asleep, then he left her. He hurried along the stairs Arlyn's father hadn't been able to get down, then went through the empty hall. There was dust in every corner, black mourning ribbons still tied on the backs of the chairs, bits of plaster trickling from the ceiling. He hadn't noticed any of that before; everything fell down and fell apart once you looked closely.

Once John got outside, the fresh air was a jolt. Blessed air; blessed escape. There was a field behind the house, overrun with black-eyed Susans, tall grass, and weeds. In daylight, the cottage had very little charm; it was horrible, really. Someone had added on a dormer and an unattractive side entrance. The paint was a flat steamship gray. Disgraceful what some people thought of as architecture.

John prayed his car would start. As soon as it did, he made a U-turn and headed back to the ferry, counting to a hundred over and over again, the way men who avoid close calls often do. *One, get me out of here. Two, I beg of you. Three, I swear I will never stray again.* And so on, until he was safely on board the ferry, miles and leagues away, a safe and comfortable distance from a future of love and ruin.

When Arlyn woke all she heard was the silence. It was a while before she realized he was truly gone. She looked through the empty rooms, then sat on the porch, thinking maybe he'd gone to the coffee shop to fetch them breakfast, or to the florist for a dozen roses. No sight of him. No sound. At noon she walked down to the harbor, where Charlotte Pell in the ticket office was quick to recall the man Arlyn described. He had taken the nine-thirty ferry to Bridgeport. He'd been in such a hurry, he hadn't even waited for his change.

It took two weeks for Arlyn to think the situation through.

Another woman might have cried, but Arlyn had cried enough to last a lifetime during her father's illness. She believed a bargain was a bargain and that things happened for a reason. She was a planner and a doer, just as John Moody had suspected from the size of her feet. She found out where he lived by calling the Yale housing office and saying she was a shipping service ordered to deliver a basket of fruit. It was not a lie exactly; she planned to bring pears with her. John had said she tasted like pears, and she imagined just the mention of that fruit was now meaningful to them both.

Arlyn was not a liar by nature, but she was a dreamer. She believed there was an ending to all stories, a right and proper last page. Her walk back from the ferry ticket office was not the ending. Not yet.

It took two weeks to settle matters. She cleaned out the attic and the basement, selling odds and ends at a yard sale, then put the house on the market in order to pay off her father's outstanding medical bills. In the end she had very little: a thousand dollars and so few belongings she could pack them into a single suitcase. Her neighbors threw her a goodbye party at the coffee shop across from the ferry terminal. Those same neighbors who had imagined she had no prospects were happy to drink to Arlyn's new life. She was a good girl, after all, and everyone deserved a chance, even Arlie. Over a lunch of oysters and macaroni and cheese and egg-salad sandwiches the neighbors all wished her luck. Exactly where she was going, no one asked. That was the way the future worked. People often disappeared right into it and all anyone could do was hope for the best.

*   *   *

ARLYN TOOK THE FERRY TO BRIDGEPORT, THEN THE TRAIN to New Haven. She felt sure of herself at the start of her travels, anxious by the time she reached the university. When she got out of the taxi, she went behind some rhododendrons and vomited twice, then quickly put a mint in her mouth so that her kiss would be fresh. There was nothing to go back to, really, so being nervous wasn't an option.

John Moody was studying for exams. He had the feeling Arlyn might track him down and he'd had the jitters long before his roommate Nathaniel came to tell him he had a red-haired visitor. Ever since John had returned from Long Island he'd been dreaming. That in itself was a bad sign. He couldn't get rid of his nightmares; therefore, he refused to allow himself to sleep. He was flat-out exhausted; if he wasn't careful he'd ruin his grade-point average. His dreams were filled with disasters, wrong turns, and mistakes. Now one had come knocking at his door.

"Tell her I'm not here," he said to Nathaniel.

"You tell her. She's waiting in the hall."

John closed his books and went downstairs, and there she was, shockingly real, flesh and blood, nervous, freckled, carrying a basket of fruit.

"John," she said.

He took her arm and led her away. They stood in the hallway, near the mailboxes. "Look, I've got exams. I don't know if you understand how difficult my courses are."

"But I'm here. I took the ferry."

John thought she really wasn't very bright. And she had a suitcase with her. John picked up the suitcase and signaled to Arlyn. She followed him outside, around to the rear of the dormitory, so no one would see. The fact that she wasn't angry with him made him feel he was the one who actually had a right to profess some injury. If you looked at the situation from a certain point of view, he was the wronged party. Who the hell did she think she was, appearing this way? Screwing up his study hour?

"I haven't got time for this," John said, as though speaking to a cat that had strayed into the yard. "Go home, Arlyn. You have no business being here."

"We're supposed to be together." Arlyn tilted her face up. She had such a serious expression. She hadn't yet turned eighteen. There was hope all over her; she smelled of it.

"Oh, really? How did you come up with that one?"

In the shadows of the rhododendrons John could barely see how freckled her skin was. She was so young, after all, and it was flattering that she'd come after him this way. She'd chased him down, hadn't she? She had that lovelorn look on her face. He couldn't remember ever having seen such certainty.

"Only until tomorrow," he said. "Then you have to go home."

She picked up the suitcase and followed him back inside. She didn't tell him she had sold her father's house and everything in it. She didn't announce that all of her belongings had been packed into that one suitcase. All right, John didn't seem as happy about their future together as Arlyn had thought he'd be, not yet. But he wasn't the sort to be rushed into anything.

Once in his room, he did let her sit in the easy chair and watch while he studied. She understood he needed quiet; she even went out to get him some supper, a corned-beef sandwich and some hot, black coffee. When he was through with his books, she was there for him in bed, so sweet, so much like a dream. He gave in to it one last time. A good-bye to her, that's what it was. The sex was even hotter; he was in a fever, he was acting like a man in love. But as soon as he fell asleep there were those nightmares again, houses falling down, broken windows, streets that never ended, women who held on and refused to let go. Nothing good could come of this. John got out of bed and quickly dressed, though it was dark, hours before his classes. He didn't care whether or not his socks matched. The basket of fruit on his desk smelled overripe, rotten. He left a note on his desk — *Gone to take exam. Have a good trip home.*

Frankly, when he did go to class later in the morning, he did terribly on his Italian exam. He could not think of the word for *water* or *book* or *bowl.* His heart started pounding again — the heart-attack feeling he'd had the last time he was with Arlyn. Maybe it was panic. He simply had to get away. He was afraid she would be waiting for him, there in his bed, and that somehow he'd be mesmerized into want-ing her again. Because of this he never went back to the dorm. He went straight from class to his car. He stopped at a bar on the way out of town and had some beers; his hands were shaking. He'd made an error in judgment, nothing more. Nothing he had to pay for for all eternity. He got back into the Saab and headed toward his parents' house, outside Madison, counting all the way: *One, no one will find me. Two, I am free. Three, I owe her nothing. Four, it will all disappear like a dream.*

The roommate, Nathaniel, was the one who told Arlyn that John often went home on the weekends. Nathaniel had found Arlyn back in the hall, late in the day, her suitcase beside her, in tears when she realized John had disappeared. Arlyn explained that she'd sold her father's house and had nowhere to go. Nathaniel had never liked John Moody, he thought of him as a selfish, spoiled prick, so it was a pleasure to give Arlyn a ride to John's family's house. In fact, they made such good time taking back roads that Arlyn was dropped off in the driveway half an hour before John Moody arrived, a bit more drunk than he'd thought.

Arlyn was in the kitchen with his mother, chatting and cutting up carrots for the salad. John spotted her as he walked across the lawn. It was just the way he had dreamed it. The glass house. The woman who wouldn't let go. He felt as though everything that was now happening had already happened in some dark and dreamy otherworld over which he had no control. There were thirty windows in the kitchen and all he could see of Arlyn was her red hair. He thought of pears and he was hungry. He hadn't eaten all day. Just those beers. He was tired. He'd been working too hard and thinking too much and he'd hardly slept. Perhaps there was such a thing as fate. Perhaps this was all part of the natural order of things, the rightness of the future, a grid of devotion and certainty. He went around the back, just as he had when he was a little boy, in through the kitchen door, shoes clattering on the tile floor, shouting out, "Anyone home? I'm starving."

THEY LIVED IN AN APARTMENT ON TWENTY-THIRD STREET, in a large studio with a sleeping alcove five floors above the street. The baby's crib was in a corner of the living room/dining room; a double bed filled up the entirety of the tiny ell of the alcove. It was never fully dark, which was probably just as well. Arlyn was up at all hours, feeding the baby, walking back and forth with him so as not to wake John, who was in graduate school at Columbia, and so she noticed things other people might not. Dark things, sleepwalker things, things that kept you up at night even if there happened to be a few moments of quiet. Two in the morning on Twenty-third Street was dark blue, filled with shadows. Arlyn had once seen a terrible fight between lovers while she nursed the baby. The baby hiccuped as he fed, as though Arlyn's milk was tainted with someone else's misery. The man and woman were in a doorway across the street, slugging each other with closed fists. The blood on the sidewalk looked like splatters of oil. When the police came roaring up, the couple had suddenly united and turned their venom on the officers, each swearing the other hadn't done anything wrong, each willing to fight to the death for the partner who had moments ago been cursed and abused.

Arlyn's baby, Sam, had dark hair and gray eyes like John. He was perfect. Small perfect nose and not a single freckle. He had a calm disposition and rarely cried. It wasn't easy living in such close quarters when John had so much studying to do, but they managed. *Hush little baby,* Arlyn whispered to her son, and he seemed to understand her. He stared at her with his big gray eyes, her darling boy, and was silent.

John's parents, William and Diana, were discriminating and somewhat reserved, but Diana was thrilled with her grandson; because of this the elder Moodys came to accept Arlyn. She wasn't the daughter-in-law of their dreams — no college degree, no talents to speak of — but she was sweet and she loved their son and, of course, she'd given them Sam. Diana took Arlyn shopping and bought so many outfits for Sam he outgrew most of them before he ever managed to wear them; Arlie had to stack them on the topmost shelf of the closet, still in their wrappers.

No matter how good the baby was, John had little patience for him. Diana assured Arlie that the men in their family were all like that when it came to children. That would change when Sam could throw a baseball, when he was old enough to be a son rather than a baby. Arlyn was easily convinced of things that she wanted to believe and her mother-in-law was so sure of herself that Arlyn assumed John's attitude would indeed change. But as Sam grew, John seemed even more annoyed by his presence. When the baby came down with chicken pox in his eighth month, for instance, John moved into a hotel. He could not bear to hear the whimpering, and he himself was at risk, having never had the disease. He stayed away for two weeks, phoning once a day, so distant he might have been millions of miles away rather than thirty blocks uptown.

It was then, alone in the darkened apartment, bathing the fretting baby in the kitchen sink with oatmeal and Aveeno to soothe his red, burning skin, that the bad thought first occurred to Arlyn. Maybe she'd made a mistake. Was it possible that on the night of her father's funeral she should have waited to see who was the next person to come down the street? She felt guilty and disloyal for thinking this, but once it had been imagined — this other man, this other life — she couldn't stop. At the park, on the street, she looked at men and thought, *Maybe it should have been him. Maybe I have made a terrible error.*

By the time Sam was two, she was quite sure she had. Her fate was out there somewhere, and she had wrongly stumbled into another woman's marriage, another woman's life. John was finished with graduate school and now worked at his father's firm, complaining about being the low man despite his talent, a junior partner called upon to do everyone's dirty work, never given the freedom to truly create. He was often gone, commuting in reverse, back and forth to the office in Connecticut, staying overnight at an old friend's in New Haven.

Arlyn was teaching Sam his ABCs. He was a quick learner. He studied her mouth as she made the letter sounds and didn't try himself until he could repeat each letter perfectly. Sam clung to Arlyn, never wanting to play with the other children in the park. When his father came home, Sam refused to speak; he wouldn't show off his ABCs, wouldn't sing his little songs, wouldn't answer when John called his name. John had begun to wonder if they should have him looked at by a doctor. Something was wrong with the boy. Maybe he had a problem with his hearing or his vision. But Arlyn knew John was mistaken. That wasn't the problem. She and Sam were in the wrong place with the wrong man; she knew it now, but how could she say it out loud? The wrongness of things had grown from a notion to the major fact of her life. She should have waited. She should have stayed where she was until she was truly sure of the future. She shouldn't have been so foolish, so hopeful, so young, so damn sure.

Every month or so, Arlyn took Sam on the train out to Long Island. Sam was refusing to eat anything but peanut-butter-and-jelly sandwiches, so Arlie always made several to bring along. Sam loved the train; he made choochoo noises and chattered all the way. Arlyn thought about recording him, and presenting John with the tape, saying, *So there! There's nothing wrong with him. It's all you!* But she had the strange feeling that if John reversed his opinion and discovered that his son wasn't worthless, he might try to steal him in some way and cut her out of Sam's life, so Arlie never made that tape. She never encouraged John to spend more time with Sam. She kept her one bit of joy to herself.

When the train reached their station, they walked down the hill until the harbor and the ferry were in sight. On windy days there were whitecaps and the water hit against the wooden pilings. On clear days everything looked like glass, the blue sky and even bluer sound, and the hazy outline of Connecticut, so far away. There was another family living in Arlyn's old house. She and Sam would often stand on the corner and watch the new children play. A boy and a girl. They played kickball in the street and climbed up the maple tree and picked azalea buds when they bloomed and stuck the red and pink blossoms in their hair.

Sometimes the children's mother called them in for dinner. When she came out to the porch, she would notice a red-haired woman and a toddler staring. The new owner of the house would then hurry her children inside; she'd stand behind the curtain, watching, making sure nothing funny was going on. A stalker or a kidnapper or something like that. But no, the strangers just stood there on the corner, even on cold, windy days. The red-haired woman wore an overcoat she'd had for years, thick, gray wool, very unstylish. The child was quiet, not one of those squirming, yowling types. A dark-haired serious boy and his loving mother. Sometimes they'd be there for over an hour, the woman pointing out the catalpa trees, the sparrows, the streetlights, the porch, the little boy repeating the words. They laughed as though everything were a marvel in this run-down neighborhood. All common objects no normal person would bother to take note of, unless she was a woman who thought she'd made a terrible mistake, someone who came back again and again, hoping that if she just walked down the same street fate would whirl her backward in time until she was once more seventeen, when the future was something she had not yet stepped into, when it was just an idea, a moment, something that had not disappointed her yet.

MAY IN CONNECTICUT WAS LUSCIOUS, SO GREEN IT WAS like a waking dream. Oriole, mockingbird, mock orange, birdsong. In a glass house the green was everywhere. There was no need for carpets, only bare ash floors; no curtains, only the lilacs, the rhododendrons, and yard after yard of boxwood, a hedge of nubby velvet. They had come to live in the Glass Slipper after John's father had had a second heart attack and the older Moodys had moved to Florida. When William Moody passed, Diana stayed on there; the warm weather was better for her arthritis.

How odd that nearly two years later Arlyn still missed her mother-in-law. Someone who cared about her child. Someone who understood that a person living in a glass house could easily become obsessed with the oddest things: stones, birds mistaking windows for thin air, deer running into the sliding doors, hail, windstorms. Glass needed constant care, after all. Rain splatters, sticky sap, falling leaves, pollen. John had hired a service to wash the windows once a week. Arlyn always did it wrong, at least in John's opinion. There were smudges when she did the cleaning herself; she could not reach the tops of some windows even when she dragged out the longest ladder from the garage.

The window cleaner came in a truck marked *Snow Brothers*. Arlyn often watched — it was always the same man, short, stocky, serious about his work. She could not help wondering what had happened to the other Snow brother, if he'd died, or run away.

Arlyn wore her red hair twisted, put up with tortoiseshell combs. It was an old-fashioned style; she believed that her mother, who died when Arlie was a toddler, wore her hair this way. At twenty-four, Arlyn herself felt old. After she sent Sam off for the morning, walking him down the lane to the bus stop so he could go off to nursery school, she usually came back to the house and slipped into bed with her clothes on. Sometimes she didn't bother to take off her shoes, the old leather slippers her father had bought her, which were by now falling apart. She'd had them resoled twice, but the leather itself was shredding. Whenever she wore them she remembered that the entire time her father had been a ferryboat captain, nearly twenty years, he never stayed a single night in Connecticut. *It's a far-off country,* he would say of the place where she now lived. *Those people with wings keep them folded up, under their suits and dresses, but at the right moment, just when they need to fly, the wings unfurl and off they go. They never go down with the ship — they lift off at the very last moment. When everyone else is sinking into the sea, there they go, up to the clouds.*

Wherever she went, Arlyn found herself searching for such people, in the treetops, at the market, on telephone poles. She felt light in some strange way; disconnected from roads and grass, from everything on earth. She herself would have chosen a raven's wings, deep blue-black feathers, shimmering and strong. Once she went up to the roof of the garage and stood there, feeling the wind, wishing that her father's stories were true. She closed her eyes until the urge to jump passed. She had to remind herself that her child would be getting off the school bus at two, that he'd expect her to be waiting, and that no matter how she felt inside she must be there, holding a bunch of lilacs she had picked as she walked down the lane.

Sam continued to surprise her with how special he was. Today, for instance, when she picked him up at the bus stop he said, "I hate school."

"No, you don't." Had she made him feel too special, as John often accused her of doing?

"Everyone has to stand in a straight line or we can't go to recess and I'm not everyone."

"Well, everyone is someone special," she told Sam.

"But the rules don't bother everyone."

"We all do things we don't want to do." Was this what she wanted her son to believe?

They walked home hand in hand.

"Daddy doesn't like me." They had reached the turn where the largest hedge of lilacs was. They could see the roof of the Glass Slipper. You had to know it was there to see it, otherwise you would look right through it into the clouds.

We could hide here, Arlie wanted to say as they passed by the hedges. *We could never come out again. Not till our wings grew. Not till we could fly away.*

"Every daddy loves his little boy," Arlyn said.

Sam looked at her. He was only five and he trusted her, but now he didn't seem so sure. "Really?" he said.

Arlyn nodded. She certainly hoped so. When they walked up the driveway, Arlyn was thinking about how tired she was. All the while her father was sick she didn't sleep through the night and then when Sam was a baby she had sat up to watch over him. The exhaustion hadn't left her.

Every time she'd heard her father cough or moan she was on her feet, ready before he called for her. She knew her father loved her; he showed it in the way he looked at her when she brought him water, or his lunch tray, or a magazine to read aloud. She had always been certain of her father's love; the same wasn't true for Sam and his father.

Maybe tonight Arlyn would dream about her father and he would tell her what to do. Stay or fly away. Tell John what she truly wanted or go on as they had been, living separate lives under the same glass roof, pretending to be something they weren't, pretending that all little boys' daddies were too busy to care.

She and Sam continued down the drive until the Glass Slipper was right in front of them. All at once Arlie realized how much she hated it. It was a box, a cage, a trap that couldn't be pried open. *It's not an easy place to live,* her mother-in-law had told Arlyn when she first moved in. *It seems to attract birds.* True enough, there on the steel-edged roof a cadre of blackbirds called wildly. Oh, they would surely make a mess. John would be able to see their shit and feathers from the living room whenever he looked up and he'd be furious. One more thing that was imperfect, just like Arlyn herself. Arlyn guessed she would have to drag out the ladder so she could climb up and clean the glass, but then she saw something odd. A man with wings. One of the Connecticut people her father had spoken of. Such creatures were real after all. Arlie felt something quicken inside. The man on the roof was standing on one leg, like a stork. One of the Snow brothers, not the usual one, but the younger brother, flapping his coat thrown over his shoulders, scaring all the blackbirds away. He was tall and blond and young.

"Boo," he shouted. Scallops of sunlight fell across his face. "Get into the sky where you belong!"

Arlyn stood on the grass and applauded.

When the window washer turned to her he was so surprised to see a red-haired woman grinning at him, he nearly slipped on the glass. Then Arlyn would have seen if he really could fly, or if like any mortal man he would simply crash and splinter.

JOHN MOODY LEFT THE HOUSE AT SIX IN THE MORNING AND didn't come home again until seven thirty or eight in the evening, often missing dinner, just as often missing his son, whose bedtime was at eight. Not that Sam was necessarily asleep; after being tucked in, he often lay in bed, eyes wide open, listening to the sound of tires on the gravel when his father came home. John was usually in a foul temper at the end of the workweek, so Arlyn had a standing arrangement with Cynthia Gallagher, their new neighbor and Arlyn's new best friend, to come over on Fridays for drinks and dinner. Cynthia was having her own problems with her husband, Jack, whom she referred to as Jack Daniels, for all the drinking he did. Arlyn had never had a best friend and she was giddy with the intimacy. Here was someone she could be real with.

"Oh, fuck it all," Cynthia was fond of saying when they went out shopping and something was particularly expensive and she wanted to encourage Arlyn to loosen up. Cynthia had delicate bone structure; she was attractive and dressed well, and she certainly knew how to curse and drink. "If we don't have a good time, who will?"

Cynthia had a way of cheering things up. She wore her brown hair straight to her shoulders and she looked young, even though she was several years older than Arlyn. Maybe it was the fact that Cynthia was free. She had no children, and had confided she didn't think Jack Daniels had it in him to produce any progeny, though he'd sworn he'd been to the doctor to be tested; he vowed that he was, as Cynthia put it, positively filthy with sperm.

Cynthia was daring and fun. She could snap John Moody out of a bad humor in an instant. "Get yourself a glass of wine and get out here," she'd call to him when he came home from work on Fridays, and he would. He'd actually join them on the patio and tell stories that had them laughing about his idiot clients whose main concern was often closet space rather than design. Watching John in the half-light of spring, with his jacket off and his sleeves rolled up, Arlyn remembered how she had felt the first time she saw him, back when he was lost and she was so dead set on finding him.

John went to the kitchen to fetch some cheese and crackers and freshen their drinks. "And olives, please!" Cynthia called after him. "God, I love your husband," Cynthia told Arlie.

Arlyn blinked when she heard that remark. There was a scrim of pollen in the air. She stared at Cynthia: her pouty mouth, her long eyelashes.

"Not like that!" Cynthia assured her when she saw the expression on Arlyn's face. "Stop thinking those evil thoughts. I'm your friend, honey."

Friends as different as chalk and cheese. They disagreed on politics and people, on fashion and homemaking. More than anything, they disagreed on Sam.

"You should have him tested," Cynthia always said, just

because he liked to be alone and preferred playing with blocks to making friends, because he didn't speak in the presence of strangers, because of the look of concentration Cynthia mistook for an odd, troubling detachment. "Something is off. And if I wasn't your friend I wouldn't bother to tell you."

Well, Arlie had finally had him evaluated and it turned out Sam had a near-genius IQ. There was some concern over one of the tests; Sam had refused to answer the series with the pictures, he'd just put his head on the psychologist's desk and hummed, pretending he was a bee. What on earth was wrong with that? Sam was imaginative and creative, too much so for silly personality tests. And a little boy had a right to be tired, didn't he?

"You're going to have problems with him," Cynthia warned. "He's pigheaded. He lives in his own world. Wait till he's a teenager. He's going to drive you crazy. Trust me, I know big trouble when I see it."

It was the beginning of the end of Arlie's friendship with Cynthia. She didn't let on that she was disenchanted for quite a while, not even to herself. But the damage was done. Arlyn could not value someone who didn't value Sam. And now that the blindfold was off, Arlie couldn't help noticing how flirtatious Cynthia was. All at once she saw the way John looked at their neighbor during their Friday evening drink time. People thought because Arlie was young and freckled and quiet that she was stupid. She was not. She saw what was going on. She saw plenty.

They were playing a game around the table when she first understood what was happening. *I spy with my little eye.*

John had gone first and Cynthia had guessed correctly. John had "spied" the tipped-over pot of red geraniums. Then it was Cynthia's turn. She was looking at John's tie, a pale gray silk, the color of his eyes. She spied something silver. Something that was very attractive, she said. Cynthia had sounded a little drunk, and much too friendly. She had a grin on her face that shouldn't have been there, as though she knew John Moody wanted her.

Arlyn glanced away. Even if nothing much had happened yet, it would. Arlie stared upward and noticed Sam at his window. He waved to her, as though they were the only two people in the world, his arm flapping. She blew him a kiss, up into the air, through the glass.

Maybe that was the day when Arlyn left her marriage, or maybe it happened on the afternoon when she ran into George Snow at the market. He was buying apples and a sack of sugar. Her cart was full of groceries.

"Is that what you eat?" Arlyn said to him. George was ahead of her in the checkout line. "Don't you have anyone who takes care of you?"

George Snow laughed and said if she came to 708 Pennyroyal Lane in two hours she would see he didn't need taking care of.

"I'm married," Arlyn said.

"I wasn't asking to marry you," George said. "I was just going to give you a piece of pie."

She went. She sat outside 708 for twenty minutes, long enough for her to know she shouldn't go in. At last George came out to the car, his collie dog, Ricky, beside him. He came around to talk to her through the half-open window.

Arlyn could feel the mistake she was about to make deep in her chest.

"Are you afraid of pie?" George Snow said.

Arlyn laughed.

"I didn't use anything artificial, if that's what you're worried about," George said.

"I'd have to know you a lot better to tell you what I'm afraid of," Arlyn told him.

"Okay." George just stood there. The dog jumped up and barked, but George didn't seem to notice.

Arlyn got out of the car. She felt ridiculously young and foolish. She hadn't even brought the groceries home before she went to Pennyroyal Lane; she'd just driven around as though she were looking for something and couldn't quite recall what, until she found herself on his street. By the time she did get home, half of what she'd bought at the grocery was ruined; the milk and the cottage cheese and the sherbet had leaked through their containers. But George had been right. He made a great apple pie. He listened to her when she talked. He fixed her a cup of tea. He did all those things, but it was Arlyn who kissed him. She was the one who started it all, and once she had, she couldn't stop.

Sometimes Arlie would go to his house on Pennyroyal Lane, but she was afraid of getting caught. More often she drove out to meet George at a public landing at the beach while Sam was at school. She never let it interfere with Sam; never let her affair with George affect Sam in any way. It was her secret life, but it felt realer than her life with John ever had.

George's collie loved nothing more than to run at the

beach. They'd chase the seagulls away, running and shouting, then George would throw stones into the sea.

"I'm afraid of stones," Arlyn admitted. She didn't want things to break and fall apart any sooner than they had to. She thought of the stones on her father's night table from the time he'd almost drowned. She thought of the house she lived in now, made of a thousand windows.

"Afraid of a stone?" George had laughed. "If you ask me, it makes more sense to be afraid of an apple pie."

George had the blondest hair Arlyn had ever seen and brown eyes. His family had lived in town for two hundred years; everybody knew him. For a while, he had left window washing to start a pet store, but he was too kindhearted. He gave away birdseed and hamster food at half price, he was bad at figures, and the business had failed. Reopening the pet store was his dream, but George had a practical nature. He did what needed to be done. He was a man who fulfilled his responsibilities, and his brother had asked him to come back to the family business. That was why he was up on her roof the day Arlie met him, working at a job he hated, although Arlyn secretly believed it was fate that had put him there. Her true fate, the one that had gotten misplaced on the night John Moody got lost, the future she was meant to have, and did have now, at least for a few hours a week.

When Arlyn went to the dry cleaner or to the post office, when she went anywhere at all, she felt like standing up and shouting, *I'm in love with George Snow.* Everyone most likely would have cheered — George was well thought of. *Good for you!* they would have said. *Excellent fellow. Much better than that son of a bitch you're with. Now you can right what's wrong in your life!*

She couldn't stay away from George. When they made love in the back of his truck, or at his house on Pennyroyal Lane, Arlyn couldn't help wondering if he was one of those Connecticut people in her father's stories who had unexpected powers. But she knew that such people always waited until the last moment, until the ship was going down or the building was burning, before they revealed themselves and flew away. Whether or not they could bring anyone with them was impossible to know until that dire moment when there was no other choice but flight.

Although Arlie had never imagined herself to be the sort of woman who had an affair, lying was easier than she'd thought it would be. She would say she was going to the market, the post office, a neighbor's, the library. Simple, really. She brought along a clothes brush so none of George's collie's long hair would stick to her slacks or her skirts and give her away. Not that John was looking for evidence of her betrayals; most of the time, he wasn't looking at her at all. Whenever Arlyn thought about George, while she fixed eggs for Sam's breakfast or raked leaves, she did not smile, not unless she was certain she was alone. Then she laughed out loud. For the first time in a long time, she felt lucky.

The only one who knew about them was Steven Snow, George's older brother, and then only by accident. Steven had stumbled upon them in bed, as he shouted out, "Hey, Geo. You're supposed to be working at the Moodys', get your lazy ass out of bed." Steven had stopped in the doorway as they pulled apart from each other. He saw her red hair, her white shoulders, his younger brother moving the sheet to hide her.

They dressed and came into the kitchen, where Steven was having a cup of instant coffee. It had been three months since the day she'd first seen George on the roof. By now they were too much in love to be embarrassed.

"Big mistake," Steven said to his brother. And then, without meeting Arlyn's eyes, he added, "For both of you."

They didn't care. No one ever had to know, except for Steven, who didn't talk much to anyone and was a quiet, trustworthy man. They went on with their secret life, the life Arlie had once imagined as she had stood out on her porch. They did crazy things as time wore on. Did they think they were invisible? That no one would figure it out? They went swimming naked in the pond behind the dairy farm. They made love in the Moodys' house, in Arlyn and John's very own bed, with all that glass around so that anyone might see, the birds traveling overhead, the telephone repairman, anyone at all. After a while, Arlyn forgot to hide how happy she was. She sang as she raked; she whistled as she went down the aisles in the market looking for asparagus and pears.

And then one morning as she walked back from the school-bus stop, Arlyn happened to meet up with Cynthia, who was out for a run. Arlie had taken to avoiding her former friend. If she'd ever really been a friend. That was questionable now. All those glances between Cynthia and John. A woman with her own secrets had no business with an untrustworthy ally. Arlie hid in the bathroom if Cynthia dropped by. If Cynthia

phoned, Arlie made excuses, often ridiculous — she had a
splinter in her foot, she was dizzy from the heat, she had lost
her voice and had to squawk out her apologies. As for those
Friday get-togethers, there was no reason to sit through
those farces anymore. In fact, Arlyn arranged for Sam to
take recorder lessons on Fridays; hours in the waiting room
at the music school listening to the cacophony of student
musicians was preferable to seeing Cynthia.

"What do you know — you're still alive," Cynthia said
when they met up on the road.

"I've been so busy." Arlyn sounded false, even to herself.
She looked down the lane. She wished she could start running, past the Glass Slipper, all the way to George's, a place
where she could be herself, if only for a little while. She was
shivering, though it was a warm day. She didn't like Cynthia's expression.

"I'll bet you've been busy." Cynthia laughed. "Guess what
a little birdie told me about you? In fact, all the little birdies
are talking about it."

Arlie disliked Cynthia more than she would have thought
possible. Everything about Cynthia was repellent: her tan,
her white T-shirt, the blue running shorts, her dark hair
pulled back into a ponytail.

"I guess you're not the good girl you pretend to be," Cynthia went on. "Even if we're not friends anymore, I didn't
think I'd be the last to know."

"You're clearly mistaken." Arlie could feel something inside her quicken. A panic, a flutter, a lie.

"Am I? Everyone's seen George Snow's truck parked at
your house. You're lucky I haven't told John."

"Don't act as though you're so above it all," Arlie said. "You've been after John from the start. Do you think I'm stupid?"

"Actually, I do. All we've done is flirt. Unlike you and George. I heard you do him in his truck in a parking lot down at the beach."

Arlyn felt dizzy. Had this really been her best friend, the woman she'd confided in, invited to her home each and every Friday?

"If I got my windows washed as often as you did, the glass would be worn away," Cynthia said. "Sooner or later you're going to get caught, baby girl."

She wouldn't want to face off against John in divorce court. He might try to take away everything she cared about for spite. Even Sam. Then what would she do? Arlie must have turned even paler, her freckles standing out like a pox. She thought of the sort of war John might wage if he was angry enough, if Cynthia stoked his fury. Arlie began to imagine a custody battle, a lost little boy.

"Don't worry. I haven't told him." Cynthia seemed able to see right through her. "He's not home enough to notice anything, is he? But all of us gals on the road have been keeping track. We meet once a week to discuss your progress as a liar. Who would have thunk it? Little Arlie. Enjoy it while you can. I plan to be there for John when he needs me. Whenever that happens, I'll be right next door."

"I have to get home." Arlyn turned and started walking.

"Go right ahead," Cynthia called. "Fuck your window washer however much you'd like. But don't come crying to me when it all comes crashing down."

* * *

THE FIRST CRASH CAME WITH A CRACK IN THE WINDOW. One night rain came pouring into the upstairs hall. "Nobody noticed this!" John shouted. "What the hell are those window washers paying attention to?"

There were breaks in several of the roof panels, one in Sam's bedroom, as a matter of fact. It was a dangerous oversight. John fired the Snow brothers the next day, even though Steven Snow insisted they hadn't been hired for structural work. After threatening the Snows with legal action, John engaged a team to replace the broken windows, then found a new cleaning service, one that would be responsible for the yardwork as well. George's truck could no longer be seen near the house. Still, he continued to come around, even though Arlie told him to phone instead and she'd meet him at the beach. He couldn't stay away. Once he arrived on a bicycle borrowed from a neighbor's child, another time he was waiting behind the boxwoods, so that when Arlie went out to get the newspaper a hand reached for her, and pulled her into the hedges. There he was, George Snow.

Arlie began to worry. Fate had a funny way of getting back at you when you were selfish and thoughtless, and maybe that's what they'd been.

"Isn't that the window man?" Sam asked when they passed George's truck parked on their corner on the way home from the bus stop one day.

"He must be working for someone else," Arlie said brightly.

"He's looking at you funny," Sam said.

Cynthia had been completely wrong in her assessment of the boy; there was no child smarter than Sam.

"Maybe he's wondering why we're not waving," Arlie said. She and Sam turned and waved with both hands.

"Hello, window man!" Sam cried.

The truck pulled away from the curb and made a U-turn.

"He didn't wave back." Sam looked up at his mother.

"Let's have hot chocolate," Arlie said. She was crying, but it was windy and she didn't think Sam could see. She would have to make up her mind, she realized that now. It was stupid to think she could have it both ways. But if she left John did she risk the possibility of losing Sam?

"You don't like hot chocolate." Sam wondered if that was why she was crying.

"Sometimes I do," Arlie said.

How could she be someone's mother and be so selfish? After Cynthia, her eyes were opened. She saw the way people were staring at her at the market. She hurried through her shopping; then in the parking lot, Sue Hardy, who lived down the street, came up to her and said, "I'm just telling you as a neighbor — everybody is talking about that George Snow lurking around. I'm just warning you, Arlie. He's not the invisible man."

Arlyn called George that night, after John had gone off to bed. Sitting in the dark kitchen lit only by stars, she told him she thought they should take a break.

"Why would we ever do that, Arlie?"

"Don't come around," Arlie finally told him. "I can't risk this anymore."

In bed, watching John sleep, she became frightened of

who she'd become. She had never been the sort of person who lied and cheated; she felt such actions were poisonous and wrong.

"What is it?" John said when he woke to see her sitting up in bed. Arlie looked a hundred years old.

"Did you ever wonder if we were really meant to be together?"

"God, Arlie." John laughed. "Is that what's keeping you awake?" He had stopped wondering about that. He'd made a wrong turn and here they were, years later, in bed. "Go to sleep. Forget things like that. That kind of thinking doesn't do you any good."

For once, Arlyn thought John was right. She closed her eyes. She would do what she had to do, no matter the price.

She stopped answering the phone when she knew George was the one calling. She looked out at the sky and after a while the phone stopped ringing. She kept busy. She took up knitting. She made Sam a sweater with a border of bluebirds. One day she came home from the market with Sam to see George's truck in the driveway. George wasn't behind the wheel. He was right up by the house, sitting beside the boxwoods. Arlie felt her heart go crazy, but she calmly said to Sam, "Can you take one of these packages?"

She handed Sam the lightest grocery bag, and grabbed the other two from the backseat.

"There's the window washer," Sam said. He waved at George and George waved back.

Arlie took the bag of groceries and told Sam to go play ball. George Snow got up. There was grass on his clothes; he'd been sitting there a long time, waiting.

She told him she couldn't see him anymore. If she had to make a choice she would always choose Sam. Sam was throwing a ball against the garage door. She thought that his presence would keep the conversation with George on an even keel, but when she told George it was over, he got on his knees.

"Get up! Get up!" Arlyn cried. "You can't do something like this!"

Although Sam rarely paid attention to adults, he was certainly watching now. A tall man was on his knees. The ball Sam had been playing with rolled down the drive, then disappeared beneath a rhododendron.

"We can just take off and go away," George Snow said. "We'll leave right now."

He made it sound so easy, but of course Arlyn was the one who had something to lose. What about the child in the driveway whom she loved above all others? What about the man she had foolishly promised her future to?

"George," she said. "I mean it. Get up!"

He stood to face her. His coat billowed out behind him. It was too late. He saw it in her face. He wiped his eyes with his coat sleeves.

"I can't believe you're going to do this to us," he said.

He kissed her before she could tell him no. Not that she would have wanted him to stop. He kissed her for a long time, then he went to his truck. Sam waved to him and George Snow waved back.

"What was wrong with that man's eyes?" Sam asked later, when his mother was putting him to bed.

"Soot fell into them," Arlie said. "Now go to sleep."

That night when John came home he called her name in a loud voice. Arlyn's first thought was, *He knows! Someone has told him! Cynthia did it! Now I can run away!* But that wasn't it at all. She went into the kitchen and John was holding out his closed hands. It was Arlyn's birthday. She'd completely forgotten. She was twenty-five years old.

"Is this for me?" Arlyn said.

"I can't imagine who else it would be for," John said. "Let's take a look."

He opened his hands to reveal a strand of creamy pearls the color of camellias. The first beautiful thing John ever bought for her. He'd waited until now. Until she didn't give a damn.

"I should have a birthday more often," Arlie said.

It wasn't until they were in bed that John told her he'd found the pearls.

"Oh, don't be mad," John said. "You know I can never remember dates. At least you have good luck on your birthday! It's not every woman's husband who finds a treasure. They were under the boxwood. Maybe they've been there for a hundred years."

It was as though the pearls had grown outside their house, seeds planted in the earth, to arise milky as onionskin. Arlie looped them around her neck. Let that fool John think they'd appeared like magic, springing out of the earth or dropped from the sky by a red-winged hawk. She let John fasten the clasp even though they were most certainly a gift from another man, the one she'd loved. Not that it mattered anymore. She'd made her choice and if she herself lived to be a hundred she would never regret it.

Her choice would always be Sam.

SAM MOODY WASN'T LIKE OTHER PEOPLE. THE THINGS HE most often thought about were dishes, bones, vases, model planes, buildings made of blocks — things that could be broken. He secretly did things no one knew about. He broke things to hear how they sounded when they split apart. He put soot and glue into his father's good shoes. He collected dead things — beetles, mice, moths, a baby rabbit. He picked fallen sparrows off the lawn, ones that had crashed into the windows and dropped to their death. He watched them all change into their last element — dust or bone — and then he put them into a cardboard box in the back of his closet. He sprayed some of his mother's perfume around so that everything smelled like decay and jasmine. At night, to get himself to fall asleep without thinking scary thoughts, Sam stabbed his fingers with a straight pin. Having pain was easier than having bad thoughts.

He tried to dream about dogs — they were comforting; so was holding his mother's hand. He had the feeling that something terrible was about to happen. Did other people think that way, too? During the hours he spent in school it was with him: the terrible, unknown, encroaching thing. He searched for it in the playground while the other boys and girls were on the swings or playing ball. He kept looking for dead things. Moths, worms, the foot of a chipmunk so shriveled up it looked like a bow from a girl's ponytail. He

believed in signs. He was certain that if one good thing happened to him, everything else would be good, but if he found
one more dead thing, it would be the end of him in some
deep and unknown way.

The good thing happened unexpectedly. He and his
mother had often gone on adventures together when he was
younger; then his mother got too busy. Now she was available again. All of a sudden she asked him if he'd mind skip-
ping school and of course he said he wouldn't mind at all. In
no time they were driving to Bridgeport. He hoped they
were running away forever. Nothing he ever did was right
in his father's eyes. His father didn't even have to say anything anymore. The bad feelings had sifted from John
Moody's head into Sam's head. Once they were on the ferry
his mother let her hair down; it was so red and beautiful
people turned to stare. The water was wavy, and Sam's
mother went to the railing; she excused herself and vomited
into the Long Island Sound. A whoosh and a wrenching
noise. Sam felt bad for her. If his father were here he'd be
huffy and embarrassed because people were looking at her.
His father wouldn't understand that people weren't only
staring because she was sick; they were doing it because she
was beautiful.

"I just need a drink of water," Sam's mother said. She was
so pale the freckles stood out on her face the way they did
when she was upset or hadn't slept. He thought they might
be telling him something if he could only understand the
language of freckles.

When his mother felt better they went inside, to the snack
bar; Sam's mother had a glass of water and he ordered

French fries. His mother reminded him that they used to take train trips when he was a baby, and he said he remembered, though he didn't completely. A passing man asked his mother if she was feeling all right, and she said, *Yes, thank you for your kindness,* and for some reason Sam felt like crying when she said that. He was in kindergarten now. Too old for such things. Much too old to cry. He lay down on the bench seat with his head on his mother's lap. Halfway across the sound the ferry's foghorn echoed and they went out and stood on the deck.

"Lick your lips," his mother told him. When he did he tasted French fries, but he told her he tasted sea salt.

They got off at the ferry terminal, then walked down the street hand in hand. Sam's mother told him that his grandfather had been the captain of the ferryboat, and that he'd been brave and strong. The houses here seemed run-down. When they stopped and she said, *We used to come here all the time. Remember?,* he didn't. The house where Arlyn had grown up had been sold several times since her departure; each time it became a little more ramshackle. Arlyn had always kept her distance, but now she had an overwhelming desire to see inside. She went up the path and knocked on the door; she introduced herself as Arlyn Singer to the woman who lived there now, even though Sam knew his mother's name was Moody, just as his was.

"I used to live here," she told the woman, who was old and wearing her slippers, but who invited them to take a look around all the same.

They wiped their feet on a mat. It was a little house, with white woodwork halfway up the walls and wallpaper the rest of the way. There were peacocks on the wallpaper, blue and purple and green. Sam stared at them up close; when he blinked they looked as though they were shaking their feathers at him.

"That was my mother's dining-room table," Arlie said. The mahogany one they never used. "I left it behind. She died when I was very young."

Sam didn't like the sound of that one bit.

"We'd better go home," he told his mother.

"I suppose we should." But when Sam grabbed her hand and pulled she didn't move. "Gee," she said to the woman who now owned the house, "seeing my mother's table makes me feel like I'm seventeen again."

"Look, if you want that old table, take it," the homeowner said. "It's junk anyway. But don't expect me to pay you a cent for it if that's what you're after!"

"Oh, no! That's not why I came here!"

Arlie sat down and started to cry, right there in front of a stranger. The mahogany chairs were rickety and creaked under her slight weight. Arlie was making sobbing sounds that frightened Sam and he started to cry right along with her.

"Go outside and play," the woman who owned the house told him. "Stay in the backyard."

Sam went out, but he looked back through the window. The woman they didn't know might be a witch, after all. You never could tell. The inside of something was often so different from the outside. But through the glass Sam could see the woman bringing Arlie a cup of water; Sam thought it was probably all right. He could wander a bit and his mother would still be safe.

The yard bordered a large field of tall grass and butter-cups. It was pretty, prettier than the dirt-and-cement back-yard, so he went to have a look, deep into the grass that was as high as his head. He was looking for something, but he didn't know what it was. He thought the same was true for why his mother had come here. Searching for a message no one else could understand.

He saw it out of the corner of his eye. A little thing, curled up. If it was dead the message was clear: the terrible thing was about to happen. Alive, and he might have a chance. It was a baby squirrel, a tiny thing that had wandered away from its nest. Sam bent down and breathed in the smell of dirt and grass. He touched the squirrel and it made a mewl-ing noise. It was still alive.

"I found you," he said in a whispery voice. Maybe he'd be lucky, after all. Maybe terrible things wouldn't happen.

He heard his mother calling for him, first in a strong voice, then in a panicky one, as though she thought he'd floated into the air on the west wind, off to sea, back to Con-necticut. He didn't want to speak until he had finished up with his good luck. He carefully picked up the squirrel and put it in his jacket pocket, where there were cracker crumbs and an old grape.

"Sam!" Arlyn screamed, as though she were dying with-out him there.

She was standing in the yard behind the house, not so very far away, but the field was bigger than Sam had thought, the weeds and grass so high he couldn't see her. Just the roof and chimney of the house that used to be hers. He ran back through the grass, confused at first, but managing to follow her voice. He had a huge smile on his face, but when he reached his mother, she grabbed his shoulders, angry.

"Don't you ever do that to me again!" she cried. Her face was red and hot and streaked with tears. Her hair was tangled from the wind and Sam could tell she hadn't found what she was looking for inside that house. Not the way he had.

Arlie sank to her knees and held him tight. "You're everything to me."

Sam patted down the hair that looked all tangled. She always wore a strand of milky pearls around her throat. She always loved him no matter what.

They walked back to the ferry and found their seats. While they were going home, he showed her what he'd found. The little squirrel seemed dazed.

"I don't know if it will live," Arlyn said. "It needs its mother."

A man sitting nearby said to feed it bread softened with milk and keep it warm. They ordered a sandwich and some milk, mixed it up, and when they offered it to the baby squirrel, it ate a bit. After that, Arlie wrapped her scarf loosely around the squirrel. Their car was parked in the ferry lot, but instead of getting into it right away and heading home, Arlyn took Sam into the café for a treat. The squirrel was asleep in his pocket.

"You would be a good big brother," Arlyn said.

"I don't think so." Sam was serious. It wouldn't suit him.

"I know you would be," Arlyn insisted.

They were the only customers in the café. For once, Sam didn't have the feeling he had when he had to stick the pin into his finger to chase his bad thoughts away. He felt happy in the café, drinking hot chocolate while his mother had a cup of tea. When he got home, he would put the baby squirrel in a big box used for his blocks. He would listen all night long, willing it to stay alive.

"Maybe I would be good at it," he said to please his mother.

"But you'll always be everything to me," Arlyn said. "Even if I have twenty more children, you will always be first."

A man had come in and ordered some food and the cook was heating up the griddle. The cook broke three eggs, easy as that, crack, crack, crack. They weren't the only people there anymore.

"Are you going to have twenty children?" Sam asked.

He wondered where his father thought they were. If he'd called the school, or the police, or their neighbor Cynthia, whom Sam despised. Cynthia thought children couldn't hear conversations that weren't directly addressed to them, but Sam heard everything.

"Just one more," Arlyn said. "I think it will be a girl."

"What will we call her?" Sam had been thinking about names for the squirrel as well. Nuts, Baby, Good Boy, Sam Junior.

"Blanca," Arlyn said.

Sam looked up at his mother. She had already decided. He loved the sound of that name, how mysterious it was. "Why Blanca?"

"Because it means white as snow," Arlyn said. "She'll be a winter baby."

On the drive home, Sam thought about snow falling. By winter his squirrel would be healthy and all grown up and

Sam would take him back across the sound on the ferryboat, back to the field where the grass was so tall, and he would say, *Run away. Run as fast as you can. Go back home where you belong.*

SHE NEVER THANKED GEORGE FOR THE BIRTHDAY PRESENT he'd left behind, but she kept the pearls around her throat constantly, a testament to what they'd once had, and what, unbeknownst to George, they were about to have. As Arlie wore the pearls, their color changed to a pale oyster yellow in the first days of her pregnancy, when she was so anxious about being found out that she couldn't eat or sleep.

As for John Moody, he had no reason to doubt her; he believed the child they were about to have was his. When Arlie stopped worrying, the pearls then became a pure Egyptian white. All the same, it was a difficult pregnancy. Arlyn was often sick to her stomach, tired, on the brink of tears. But in her ninth month, she became less haggard, robust almost, and the pearls blushed faintly. Pink as the inside of an ear, pink as winter light. It was January, a harsh, frozen season, but Arlyn's presence was now so warm she seemed to heat whatever room she entered. Her hair turned darker, a deep blood red. The freckles she hated faded into nothingness. People in the shops in town stopped to tell her she looked radiant; she laughed and thanked them.

Shouldn't she be guilt-ridden over what she had done? Well, she wasn't. She surprised herself with the way she felt. At night when John was asleep, Arlyn sat beside the windows to watch snow drift down and she thought, *I am happy.*

It was a moment made of glass, this happiness; it was the easiest thing in the world to break. Every minute was a world, every hour a universe. Arlie tried to slow her breathing, thinking it might slow time, but she knew they were all hurtling forward no matter what. At night she read stories to Sam. She lay down beside him in his bed and felt his body next to her, the shape of his hipbone, his leg, his wiggly little feet. He smelled like glue and loyalty. By now Arlyn knew he wasn't like other children. There were more problems at school — he wouldn't listen, wouldn't behave; he often seemed to be in his own world, disconnected, missing homework assignments, ignoring party invitations. There were no friends who came to play. No after-school sports. No positive teacher's reports. All the same, at night when Arlie read to him, Sam was happy as well. They both were. The squirrel had indeed lived, and had been named William. He was now at home in the closet, nesting among a mess of torn-up newspapers and rags and peanut shells, tearing up the Sheetrock, chomping on the wooden floor, coming out to play in the afternoons after school.

William was their shared secret — John Moody had no idea the squirrel existed. That was how little he knew of their domestic life. Why, his wife and son could have had a tiger in a cage, a fox in the basement, a bald eagle nesting beside the washing machine and John would have been none the wiser. Arlyn could not remember the last time John had come into the child's bedroom to say good night, or the last time he had spoken to her other than to ask where his briefcase was or if she might fix him some breakfast. As for the pregnancy, it seemed to mean no more than that day's weather, a fact of their life, neither good nor bad, joyful nor regrettable.

John was busy, far too busy for the likes of them, fools who wasted their time on squirrels and books and happiness. He was at work on a huge project in Cleveland — a tower of glass, thirty stories, bigger and better than the Glass Slipper or any of his father's other buildings. John spent most of the week in Ohio, exhausted when he flew back for the weekend, wanting only peace and quiet.

"He'll come around," Arlyn's mother-in-law told her when she phoned. "The Moody men are better fathers to teenagers than they are to small children."

Arlyn laughed and said, "You always defend him."

"Wouldn't you do the same?" Diana asked.

"Absolutely."

Of course Arlyn would defend her own child no matter what. This was most likely the reason Diana had liked her daughter-in-law from the moment they met, when Arlie had knocked on the back door, an uninvited girl of seventeen. Arlyn might look placid, but there was a fierceness there, one Diana appreciated.

"How is my brilliant grandson?" Diana always asked when they spoke.

"Still brilliant," Arlie would inform her.

On this they always agreed. Arlyn was now reading the entire Edward Eager series to Sam, stories that had all taken place in Connecticut. They were up to *Half Magic,* in which the wishes made never worked out as planned. William the squirrel, which had been to the vet in town for all the proper shots, perched on the bedpost and listened, making occasional chattering noises, turning the bedpost to wood dust with his gnawing.

"Do you mind being fat?" Sam asked one night when he was being tucked into bed.

"Not at all," Arlyn said. So much the better; John Moody didn't come near her. She laughed to herself.

"I don't feel the way the children in those books do. They're hopeful. I feel that something bad is about to happen."

Sam had lovely big eyes. When he was tucked into bed, you wouldn't think he was the terror his teachers said he was, the one who locked himself in a coat closet or drew on the walls with crayons and ink.

"Well, you're a real-life child and they're fictional." Arlyn tested Sam's forehead for fever.

"I wish I was fictional," Sam said.

"Well, I want you just the way you are." Arlyn hugged him good night.

"What about William?" Sam said.

Arlyn laughed and patted the squirrel, then put him in his box for the night.

"Sweet dreams to you both," she called.

Arlyn wore the pearls to bed, enjoying the heat of them around her neck. Pearls were made of living matter, and so they continued to live. She had heard that George Snow was working in New Haven, that he and his brother had disbanded the business after the run-in with John Moody. As it happened, the new window washers weren't reliable; they were rather cowardly and refused to come and perch atop the Glass Slipper when there was inclement weather. The windows in the house were foggy on the outside, streaked with sleet. When Diana came up to help out as the time for the baby grew near, she complained about how dingy the house had become. The rooms were too big, the house too much for Arlyn to clean. As for Sam's room, it smelled of peanuts and dirt. Even worse, the toddler Diana had so adored was now a sullen six-year-old. Sam would not speak to his grandmother. He was withdrawn and shy.

"What's wrong with him? I hear him talking to himself when I pass by his room."

"He's perfectly fine," Arlie said. "He's just not like everyone else."

"Good lord," Diana said. "These are real behavior problems. That poor darling boy. Where is John in all this?"

"Cleveland."

"I see," Diana said.

The Moody men, Diana assured her daughter-in-law, could be detached, busy, in a world of their own. Well, maybe Sam was merely following that pattern, or maybe it was something more. Certainly, all was not well in this house. It was clear that the marriage was unhappy. Several times, Diana noticed a truck driving slowly by, late at night, headlights turned off. Once a man had gotten out to stand in the snow. Diana had watched from the kitchen window. The fellow disappeared soon enough, and there were no tire tracks when Diana went to look in the morning. Maybe he hadn't been there at all. Maybe she'd seen only the shadows the boxwoods cast along the road.

It was snowing on the night of the birth. John was in Cleveland and so Arlyn called a taxi service. "You don't mind, do you?" Arlie said when she woke her mother-in-law to watch over Sam. Arlyn was already wearing her coat; her packed overnight bag was by the door. "And don't be upset if Sam doesn't talk to you when you send him to school. He's not a morning person."

"Don't worry," Diana said. She was furious with her son, off working, leaving this poor girl to fend for herself. "I'll take care of everything here."

Blanca was born at eight minutes after midnight, a beautiful pale child who looked exactly like George Snow. She calmly let herself be held and cradled and nursed. She was cool to the touch and she smelled sweet. John Moody was called in Cleveland. Though the nurses were shocked that he was away working, leaving the new mother on her own, Arlie herself was grateful. She would have felt guilty if John had been standing by.

"My snow girl," she said to the baby in such a pure voice that the infant turned her head to hear more. "My darling, my daughter, my pearl."

When Arlie brought the baby home, Sam was waiting in the driveway. The taxi stopped and Arlie got out and there he was, waiting, no coat, no hat. Diana came running out.

"He refuses to come inside. He's been standing here all day. I was about to call the police. I thought he'd freeze to death!"

Arlyn smiled at her little boy. Snow was falling onto his shoulders. His lips were blue with cold.

"Is that her?" Sam asked.

Arlie nodded and brought the baby over.

"Blanca," Sam said. "She's beautiful."

Diana had had enough. She'd seen to it that John was taking the evening flight from Cleveland. *Mother, this is business,* he'd said when she'd phoned to tell him to get home. Diana had made a lot of excuses in her time; she was an expert, really, but she wasn't making excuses now. As a husband and a father, John was lacking. Diana looked at Arlyn and her children and she remembered how lonely she'd been as a young mother in this same house. She wanted to say, *Run away. Run as fast as you can.* Instead she reached for the baby. "I'll bring Blanca inside."

Arlyn and Sam stayed in the driveway a while longer.

"Now we're all here," Arlyn said. "My dreams came true. I wanted a son just like you and a daughter just like Blanca."

It was getting even colder and they needed to go inside. They walked along the driveway toward the door, but at the last moment Arlyn pulled on Sam's sleeve, holding him back. Arlyn lay down in the drive; she flapped her arms, making a snow angel. He watched her for a moment, then followed suit. They were so cold and wet, it no longer mattered how much snow they got into.

They stood up and studied their angels. "There," Arlie said, sounding satisfied. "That's for good luck."

Sam was shivering now. He went up to his room. He was supposed to take off his wet clothes, but he let the damp sink into his bones. The angels they'd made in the driveway were beautiful, but they were sad, too. They made Sam think of heaven and of the end of the world. He couldn't bear to think of anything bad happening to his mother or to Blanca. He had a bad feeling, as though he were sinking. The truth was, Sam had a secret, one he hadn't told. His mother had been so excited about the baby; she was too happy for him to tell her why he'd been standing outside in the driveway in the snow, refusing to come inside.

It wasn't because Blanca was coming home. He'd been out there all day because William had died. That morning Sam had opened the closet to give the squirrel his favorite meal — an apple with peanut butter — and there William had been, curled up in his nest, unmoving. Sam closed the door and went out to the driveway. He kept a pin in his pocket and stabbed at his fingertips, but that sort of pain wasn't enough to get rid of what he felt. When he went to bed that night, instead of crying, he counted to a hundred. *One, nothing could touch him. Two, he was miles away. Three, he was flying high above houses and treetops,* one of those rare Connecticut people his mother told him about, people who belonged to a strange and little-known race. He might be one of them; a boy who could fly away from danger and heartbreak and never feel a thing.

ARLIE FELT THE LUMP WHEN BLANCA WAS THREE MONTHS old, while she was breast-feeding. Her breasts had been bumpy and engorged with milk, but this was something else entirely. Just what she'd always feared. Something in the shape of a stone.

John Moody had finished his building in Cleveland — it had been dubbed the Glass Mountain and people in that city were highly critical of its height. Now John was back. The baby had softened him a bit; maybe it was all right to coo and fuss over a daughter if not over a son, or maybe he'd actually heard his mother when she told him how disappointed she was.

John was in the kitchen having coffee on the day Arlie found the lump. He'd actually poured Arlyn a cup. He was trying to be considerate. When he looked up to see Arlie standing there in her nightgown, her hair uncombed, he forgot about the coffee.

"I think something's wrong," Arlie said.

John Moody knew his was not the happiest of marriages. He felt he'd been trapped; his youth had been taken from him. He had still never been to Italy, although he'd taken several courses and could now converse in halting Italian, a Venetian dialect, with his teacher, a lovely young woman he'd made love to twice. Three times would be an affair, he told himself. Once was only an experiment, since he'd been so young when he'd married. Twice was simply to be polite so as not to hurt the poor woman's feelings. When he started working on the building in Cleveland he'd stopped the classes; he had received several messages at his office from his Italian teacher, but he hadn't returned them. Frankly, he was settled into his marriage; his wife no longer expected him to be anything he wasn't. She knew him.

"Look, everyone has problems," he said to Arlie. He'd thought she was a free spirit, but she was a worrier, really. "You can't let difficulties stop you. You can't just give up, can you?"

Arlie came to the table. She stood in front of him and took his hand. His true impulse was to pull it away, but he didn't. He wanted to read the paper, but he forced himself to be there for her. On the evening before his mother had left, she pulled him aside to say, *Be kinder*. So that was what he was trying to do. Arlie had just had a baby, after all, and couldn't be held responsible for her actions or her moods. Or so Jack Gallagher next door had told him when John complained about how erratic Arlyn was. But then Jack had no children, and in a matter of weeks he'd have no wife. Cynthia had made it clear to John Moody that she was available; she had filed for divorce and Jack would soon be moving out. So much for his neighbor's advice. As a matter of fact, John had known about the divorce before Jack himself had. One night soon after Arlie came home with the baby, Cynthia had been waiting for John in the driveway, desperate for someone to talk to, someone who would understand.

He could deal with his own wife, surely. The newspaper could wait. But instead of wanting to talk, Arlie did something that completely surprised John. She placed his hand on her breast. He felt the lump right away; all at once he realized how long it had been since he'd touched her. And now this, a stone.

"Maybe this is normal. Maybe you should stop breast-feeding and it will go away."

That was the way he thought about life. He believed in logic and denial in equal parts, but Arlie knew better. She thought about the instants in time she'd had. Standing on the porch waiting for John, giving birth to her babies, racing along the beach with George Snow while he threw stones at the sea, the snow angels in the driveway, the way Sam reached for her hand. This moment was the dividing line

between the *before* and the *after*. No more hanging globes of
time. No more forevers. Sitting in the doctor's office, dozens
of mammograms, making dinner for Sam and John, rock-
ing Blanca to sleep, calling Diana to ask if she would come
back up from Florida to help out with the children after Arlie had her surgery. It all happened so fast; the past hung
above Arlyn as though imprinted on air. She thought of it as
a ceiling she walked beneath. She tried her best to remember
her own mother. Arlie had been three years old when her
mother became ill, with what, Arlie had never been told. If
she'd known it was the same cancer she herself now had, she
would have known to check herself and be checked, but
people didn't talk about such things. Cancer was a spell with
evil effects; said aloud, the very word was capable of putting
a curse on the speaker.

The worst was how little she remembered of her mother,
only bits and pieces — red hair, like her own, but with a
darker sheen; a song she sang, "Stormy Weather"; a single
story she told, "Red Riding Hood." Three years with her
mother and that was all Arlyn could recall. Her own little
girl was three months old, not three years. What would she
possibly remember? A red shadow, a voice, a strand of
pearls she played with as she nursed.

Arlie thought carefully about what she wanted to do before her surgery. She treated it as though it were her last day
on earth. She kept Sam home from school. He had been
more withdrawn since his pet squirrel died, though Arlyn
had tried to explain why the loss had happened. She'd told
him there was a natural order to all of life, and that he had

done his best to care for the creature. No one, not the president, not the man in the moon, could say who would live and who would die.

Arlie read to Sam all morning on the day before her surgery. They were up to *Magic or Not?* — almost done with the Edward Eager series of Connecticut marvels. Arlie brought the baby into bed with them so she could feel how alive both her children were. Blanca's gurgles; Sam's warm body stretched out beside her. Sam was tall for a six-year-old; he'd be like his father, rangy, needing to duck under doorways. Arlie wanted Sam to have everything; she wanted the world for him. With so little time, she did the best she could; at lunchtime, she took the children to the ice-cream parlor on Main Street and let Sam order a Bonanza, the sundae of his dreams — four flavors of ice cream, chocolate and butterscotch sauce, lots and lots of whipped cream, red and green maraschino cherries. He ate about a third of it, then held his stomach and groaned.

As for John, he was at work. Not as heartless as one would think: Arlyn had told him to go, said she wanted the day to be normal, otherwise she wouldn't get through it. Or maybe he simply wasn't a part of her perfect day. Maybe she wanted John gone for reasons she could barely admit to herself. Maybe she had to see George Snow one last time.

Late in the afternoon, she brought the children to Cynthia's.

"Arlie," Cynthia said. Her eyes filled with tears at the sight of her neighbor.

"Can you watch them for me?" Arlie had her car keys still in her hand. It was April and everything outside was greening.

"No," Sam said. "Don't leave us. We hate her."

"You see," Cynthia said helplessly.

Arlie led Sam into Cynthia's hallway, then handed the baby to her neighbor. They might not be friends anymore, but sometimes friendship was the least of it. "I need you," Arlie said.

"I won't stay in a witch's house," Sam told his mother.

"He won't." Cynthia looked down at the baby in her arms. Blanca gazed back at her.

"Okay, then take them home, the back door's open. They'll be happier over there. Let Sam watch TV and give Blanca a bottle. Heat it under hot water, then test it to make sure it's not too hot."

"I'm not an idiot." Cynthia sounded as though she might cry. "Just because I don't have children doesn't mean I would burn her mouth."

"Of course you won't. I know that, Cynthia. I trust you." Arlie turned to Sam. "Do what Cynthia says for the rest of the day unless it's utterly stupid. I'm asking as a favor. I need you to."

Sam nodded. He had an awful breathless feeling, but he knew when his mother meant something.

Arlie got into her car and drove to New Haven. She knew where George was living. She had looked him up in the phone book months ago. She'd called once, then had hung up before he answered. If he'd known Blanca was his, he would have come after them. It would have been a mess. Now, everything was a mess anyway. Arlie drove too fast. She felt hot all over. Around her neck, the pearls George had left for her were feverish, colored with a rusty tinge.

She parked across from the three-story house where he rented an apartment. She guessed it was the top floor. She wished she could see the mailboxes and find his name printed there, but she stayed in the car. Good thing; just then his truck pulled into the driveway. He was working in a pet store. George and his brother no longer spoke; they'd had a terrible argument after they'd been fired by the Moodys. Frankly, George avoided most people, preferring the quiet camaraderie of parakeets and goldfish. He got out of his truck, then went around the back for a backpack and a lunchbox. His collie, Ricky, jumped out. The dog looked older, but George looked the same, just far away. It had been only a year since Arlyn had seen him, so how could it feel like forever? He was whistling as he walked from the driveway, up to the steps to the porch. Then he was gone, the collie at his heels, the door slamming.

She didn't get out and tell him. She almost did, but she had always been afraid of stones, and the path to his house was made of them, small round bits of gravel. It was too late. It was too awful and unfair to come to him now. Arlyn was holding on to the steering wheel so tightly her fingers turned white. Lights went on in the third-floor apartment. If she'd gone with him when he asked her to leave John, they would have had this year together. Now there was only pain and sorrow to share. She didn't want Blanca fought over, pulled apart, even at this cost. At least she'd seen him. Another perfect moment in her perfect day.

Arlie drove home slowly, trying not to think of anything but the road and her children at home. She'd been granted more than most people. Real love, after all, was worth the price you paid, however briefly it might last. There was one glitch in the day, a horrible one: a pre-op consultation at the hospital, scheduled late so that John might accompany her. The sky was turning dark blue. April blue. Inside the hospital it was terribly bright. Arlie was the last patient of the day. Did they save the best or the worst for last? That's what Arlyn wanted to know. The doctor was young. He told her to call him Harry, but she couldn't do that; she called him Dr. Lewis. If he wanted her to call him by his first name the prognosis must be bad. John was there with her and she was grateful; his presence stopped her from breaking down. She knew John didn't like bad news, difficult women, tragedy. Could it be that she had never cried in front of him? Not even on that day in New Haven when she came to his dorm so convinced of the future; she'd only wept after he was gone. She wasn't about to start now.

Dr. Lewis would see the extent of the cancer when he operated; there would be two other doctors, residents, assisting in the surgery, and the thought of a team of people inside her made Arlie shudder. It took a while before she actually understood they planned to cut off her breast. She stopped thinking after that, didn't even consider further complications. She cleared her mind. Time had stopped. She had insisted that it do so and it had. The drive home was silent and lasted a decade. She thanked Cynthia, who had made dinner for the family. After dinner, John walked Cynthia home. She put her arms around him and he fell into her. Cynthia was there for him, the way she'd promised to be. She took him home, then upstairs to her bedroom; her love wasn't a crime, it was a gift, that's the way Cynthia saw it, and that was the way John Moody received it.

Alone in the Glass Slipper, Arlie put the baby to sleep, then washed up. Every dish was an eternity, but that was fine. She wanted it all to last. She didn't mind John's absence; she liked the stillness. That night in Sam's room, the story Arlie whispered took a hundred years to tell. It was Sam's favorite story, her father's story about the flying people in Connecticut. "If I'm gone," she told him afterward, "that's where I'll be. Right above you, flying. I'll never really leave you."

Sam had the bones of his squirrel in a cardboard shoebox in the back of his closet. He knew what happened after death.

"There's no such people," he said.

"Yes, there are."

"Prove it," Sam said.

So Arlyn did something crazy. She took Sam up to the roof. She led him through the attic to the door that opened onto a flat glass space. This was the place where George Snow had been standing when she first spied him. Clouds were rushing by the moon. The trees moved with the wind. Arlyn could feel those people her father had told her about all around her. They were the ones who never left you, no matter what.

"See them?" Arlyn's voice sounded strange, small and lost.

All Sam saw was the huge universe and the darkening sky. Blue, black, indigo; the horizon was a line so shimmery it made him blink. He realized that his mother's eyes were closed. He knew they were in a dangerous place. Something rustled in the trees. Something beautiful.

"Yes, I do," Sam said.

Arlyn laughed and sounded like herself again. She'd opened her eyes. She had already added this to her instants in time as the very best moment of all. A breathless, gorgeous, dark night. She felt so oddly free, untethered to earth. But even if she could have flown away, she would never have left her son. One more second was worth everything. They went down the steps into the attic, back to Sam's bedroom. Arlie tucked in his blankets and wished him a good night's sleep. She waited there beside him until he was dreaming, until his breath was even and deep; then she stayed a while longer, right there in the chair, until he opened his eyes in the morning. "I knew you'd still be here," Sam said, and for once in his life he had some small hope that not everything in the world was a lie.

JOHN MOODY WAS A FIXER, AND A BUILDER, AND A PLANNER; in times of sorrow he did what he knew best. He designed a project in order to have something on which he could concentrate. A ridiculous endeavor, people in town said, a huge pool set behind the Glass Slipper, a beautiful thing as John conceived it, rimmed by slate with an infinity edge that led the water into a smaller pool below on the hillside. The hole had already been dug by the backhoes by the time Arlyn came home from the hospital. It was twelve feet in the deep end and the digging seemed endless, through rock and through clay. Clods of red mud and shards of shale littered the lawn.

The noise could be deafening at times, and Arlie kept her windows closed and the shades drawn. It was June and she was dying while she listened to the bulldozers and the cement mixers. It had been the rainiest spring on record and now everything was so green the leaves of the lilacs and the rows of boxwoods looked black.

The tumor reached under her chest wall and was entwined through her ribs. Her surgeon could not get it all. Her bones had turned to lace. She called her doctor Harry now; it was that bad. The oncologists put her on a schedule of radiation and chemo, but after a month she was so desperately ill they took her off. She was not an experiment, only a dying woman, one who soon enough had lost her red hair. She had braided it before the chemo began, then cut it off, ten inches long. The rest fell out on her pillow and in the shower and as she walked along the lane, slowly, with Cynthia supporting her when she grew tired. "Hold me up," she told Cynthia. "I'm depending on you."

"I'm not that strong," Cynthia said once.

"Oh, yes you are," Arlyn said. "That's what made me want to be friends with you in the first place."

Arlyn kept the braid of hair in a memory box she was making for her children, stored alongside photographs of the family, pictures Sam had drawn for her, Blanca's plastic name bracelet from the hospital. When the time came, Arlie would add her pearls. After she'd gone through radiation, the poison from inside her skin had soaked into the pearls; they'd turned black, like pearls from Tahiti, exact opposites of what they should be.

Twice she had seen John Moody walk through the hedges

at dusk, headed toward Cynthia's house. He thought she wouldn't know because he was now sleeping in the den, but she knew. She rarely left her room now so John must have felt safe to seek comfort next door. The last walk Arlie had taken was the one when she collapsed; Cynthia had stood in the street screaming for help and an oil truck pulled over. The driver was a heavyset man who had carried Arlie home.

"You must be one of those flying men from Connecticut," Arlie had told him.

His wings were probably huge.

"In my truck I surely do fly." The oil man's own mother had recently died. Although he was a tough, no-bullshit guy, he didn't seem that way now. "Just don't tell the police and get me arrested."

"I won't," Arlie assured him.

After that, John had hired a nurse whose name was Jasmine Carter. Jasmine gave Arlie her medicines and helped her bathe and dress. Jasmine took care of Arlie, and Diana Moody came up to take care of the children. Arlie still made sure to hold her daughter close at least once a day; every night she read to Sam, and when she couldn't see the words anymore, he read to her.

"Do you hate me without my hair?" she asked Sam one night. It used to be that they would read in his room and he'd be the one in bed. Now it was reversed, but they never mentioned that.

"I like you better this way," Sam said. "You're like a baby bird."

"Chirp chirp," Arlyn said.

Sometimes, when her hands were shaking, Arlie needed

help in order to eat. She felt like a bird. She tried to hide her decline from Sam, but it wasn't easy. Arlyn didn't care what anyone said about Sam. He knew things other children did not. Certainly, he knew what was happening now. He held a glass of water so she could sip from a straw. When she was done, he put the glass on a woven coaster so it wouldn't leave a ring on the night table.

"Sometime soon you're going to take my pearls and put them in a special treasure box that I have," Arlie said. "They're for your sister."

"What do I get?" Sam wanted to know.

"You had me all to yourself for six years," Arlie said. "Maybe we'll get to seven."

"Or eight or nine or ten or a thousand."

It felt like a thousand years already. It was as though she had used up all her time, but was still hanging on. She could not stand the noise outside, the men shouting as they poured cement, the clicking as the tiles were put in, aquamarine-colored tiles from Italy; John had ordered them straight from the factory outside Florence, that's how good his Italian was now. He had sat beside Arlie's bed and showed her the catalogs of tiles. Sky blue, azure, turquoise, midnight. *Turchese. Cobalto. Azzurro di cielo. Azzurro di mezzanotte.* She'd fallen asleep in the middle of the conversation, and in the end John chose the tiles he liked best.

George Snow didn't know about Arlie until one afternoon when he happened to meet up with his brother at a bar in New Haven. George was having a late lunch, a cheeseburger and a beer. He wanted to be left alone, but Steven came to sit beside him. Right away, as though they hadn't stopped talking to each other months ago, Steve spoke of the man who was responsible for their failed business and their nonexistent relationship, though he'd sworn he'd never say the name aloud.

"That bastard Moody is putting in the swimming pool to end all swimming pools. And with her in the middle of dying."

George Snow would forever after remember that he had just put down his glass when he heard the news. His brother went on speaking, but George didn't hear a word. He heard only about her.

"Are you talking about Arlyn?"

Steve realized what he'd blundered into. "She's sick, man. I thought you knew. I just wanted to tell you how sorry I was."

George threw some money on the bar and went for the door. His brother called, and when George kept on going, Steven followed him into the parking lot.

"Seriously, George, she's not your wife and it's not your business. They went ahead and had another kid, didn't they?"

"When was that?" George said, stunned.

"This past winter. I thought you knew."

George got in his truck and took off. He had a panicky feeling inside his chest. He could be angry at his brother all he wanted, but George knew he had only himself to blame for not knowing. He'd moved to New Haven so he wouldn't run into Arlie; he'd been a coward in the face of her rejection. He'd figured if she had changed her mind, she would have contacted him. He'd figured she made the choice to stay with John. Now everything he'd been so sure of was evaporating.

George Snow was driving so fast little stones flew up and

hit against his windshield. When he got to the street where she lived his panic worsened. There were four trucks parked in the driveway, so he pulled onto the grass. The lawn was soft from all the rain in the spring and his tires sank in deeply, but George didn't give a damn. As an ex–window washer he noticed that the windows were in bad shape, streaky and matted with leaves and pollen.

As he sat in his parked truck, not knowing what to do next, a woman came out of the house. George recognized her as the mother-in-law. She had Sam in tow — it was Friday, music lessons — and in the mother-in-law's arms, the baby. A real, live baby. George Snow watched them get into a car and pull away. He was dizzy and overheated; he felt as though he'd just woken from a dream in which he lived in a third-floor apartment with an old collie and worked in a pet shop. But now he was awake. He left his truck and went up the drive to knock on the door. When no one answered, he rang the bell; he just kept his hand on it until it sounded like church bells. A woman George didn't recognize opened the door. "Stop that," she said. "Have you no consideration?"

George Snow walked past the strange woman, into the hallway. It was so dim inside, as though he'd wandered into a dark wood.

"Stop right there." The woman was a nurse. Jasmine Carter. "You'd better do what I say or I'm calling the police."

"I'm going to see Arlyn."

The house used to seem perfect to George; he knew it so well from looking through the windows. But it wasn't the way he remembered it. Standing in the hall, he couldn't see outside through the glass.

"Oh, no you're not," Jasmine said. "I'm in charge of Arlyn and I'll tell you what you'll do. Do you have any idea of what's going on here?"

"She'd want to see me."

Jasmine and George stared at each other and George knew he was being assessed. Who exactly was he to think he had any right to anything? He thought about the children in the driveway. He thought about all he didn't know.

"I'm going to see her no matter what you say," George told the nurse after he introduced himself.

One thing he clearly was was a man who would cause a ruckus if Jasmine tried to get rid of him. And he was more; when he said his name, Jasmine recognized it. It was the name Arlyn said in her sleep.

"Well, if you want to see her, you'd better be prepared. I won't have you upsetting her with your reaction. Get all of the bullshit out right now. What you're about to see isn't pretty."

"I'm okay," George said.

"You won't be," Jasmine said. "Trust me."

"You don't know anything about me."

"I know she talks about you when she doesn't intend to. Most probably, she wouldn't want you to see her this way."

George hadn't thought about how terrible it would be to love someone and see her in pain. He had not had a glimpse of Arlie in more than a year. He had begun to heal, if anyone could call a life spent alone and cut off healing.

"I'm okay," he said. "No matter how she looks."

He followed Jasmine upstairs.

"She's sleeping a lot. She wishes she could go outside,

but it's just too hard for me to carry her. Fifty pounds is my limit."

As they walked along, the glass ceiling above them was streaked with pine needles, pollen, leaves, raindrops, a mourning cloak. They walked past the children's rooms.

"Does the baby have red hair?" George asked.

"Blond." Jasmine had been a nurse for fifteen years. She could sense certain truths in an instant. "Like you."

Jasmine knocked when they reached Arlyn's room; she opened the door and peeked in. "Someone here to see you."

No response. Jasmine nodded to George to follow her inside. They could hear the tile men finishing up the pool and the dreadful cranking of the water trucks unfolding their hoses.

Jasmine went over to the lump in the bed. "Lucky girl, you've got a visitor."

"Send them away." Arlie's mouth was dry and cottony from the high dosages of Demerol the doctor had prescribed. She didn't sound like herself. It was as though the words hurt.

Arlyn's back was to them, but George could see her head. No red hair, no hair at all. He could feel a stone in his throat. He hated himself and he hated the world and he hated this instant in time.

"Arlie," he said. "It's me."

He could tell that she recognized his voice because she responded; her back curled more rigidly, like a turtle in its shell. For an instant, she seemed to stop breathing.

"He can't see me," Arlyn said. She'd been snapped back into the world from her dreaming place and it didn't feel good. It felt as though her heart would break.

"Blindfold me," George said to Jasmine. "I don't have to see her to be with her. I promise I won't look at you," he told Arlie.

"You're crazy," Jasmine said, but she took a scarf from the top dresser drawer, wrapped it over his eyes and tied it tight. "He won't see a thing," she assured Arlyn. "He just wants to sit beside you, honey."

"I'm vain. I want him to remember me as I was." Arlyn was whispering but George heard her perfectly well. Jasmine had sat him down in a chair beside the bed. He could feel Arlie's breath. He could feel the blankets against his knees and the wooden bedframe. He'd made love to her there once. Quickly, guiltily, with great pleasure.

"He doesn't even know about the baby," Arlie said.

"I'm going downstairs for a few minutes." Jasmine understood what this man wanted — the same thing everyone wanted: time. "Call if you need me."

"I should have come back," George said. "If I had come here over and over again, you would have said yes and left with me."

Arlie took his hand. For a moment he was shocked by how cold she was. She brought his hand up to the pearls.

"Oh," George said. "I threw them under the hedge when you told me to go."

The pearls had never been off her throat, except during medical procedures, and even then she'd had one of the nurses slip the pearls into her uniform pocket beneath her surgical robe. During radiation she'd had them in her locker with her belongings, there at all times. For luck, for love, for no reason at all. They'd been his mother's pearls, he'd never gotten to tell Arlyn that, and his grandmother's pearls before that.

They sat there for a while, hand in hand, in an instant of time neither wanted to end. Her vision was going, but she could see him, the way people see clouds — beautiful, racing by, casting shadows.

"I was never going to leave Sam. Anyway, you're lucky I didn't come with you. Then you'd be stuck with me."

But he was stuck anyway, even though she hadn't come away with him. George lowered his head and cried. He made a sound that was low down inside him, all hurt, nothing else. He could see through the haze of the scarf Jasmine had tied over his eyes. He saw it all.

"Now I'm the one who's stuck," Arlie said. "I hate being trapped in this room. I've considered leaving my body before I die. I keep thinking about grass and the boxwood hedge. The way the sky looks when you're lying on the ground staring up."

This was the most she had spoken in a week and the words had exhausted her. She waved her hand. She couldn't say more. She felt like the luckiest person in the universe to have George Snow sitting beside her. *Put us in a jar,* she thought. *Put us in eternity.*

Through the scarf George could study her pale face without a single freckle; they had all disappeared. There were her beautiful cloudy eyes. Oh, it was her. Arlie. So tiny. Wasting away. Sixty-five pounds, but still here.

"If you let me take the blindfold off, I can carry you outside. Otherwise I might fall down the stairs and kill both of us."

Her laugh was like water.

He took the blindfold off. Jasmine was right. Seeing Arlie fully was harder than he'd thought it would be. He saw how blotchy and swollen her face had become. He saw the veins in her scalp. Around her neck there was a string of black pearls that looked nothing like the necklace he'd left under the hedge.

"They're the same ones," Arlie told him. "They turn colors."

"Really? Magic?"

"Radiation. I think they soak up whatever is inside me."

George lifted her out of bed. She weighed nothing. She smelled like illness and soap. The pearls looked like strange black marbles.

"Will we fly?" Arlyn asked.

"Possibly," George answered.

He grabbed a blanket and folded it around her, then carried her down the stairs. Jasmine was in the kitchen, fixing herself some tea.

"Diana will be back with the children in half an hour," Jasmine warned. "Who told you you could take her outside?"

"She wants me to." George opened the back door.

Jasmine came over. "I don't know about this," she said. "She gets chilled so easily."

"It's what she wants," George said.

The nurse didn't stop George from taking Arlie into the bright light of the backyard. The water pumps were chugging; the tile men finishing up the rim of the pool were shouting to each other. George went up to the pool man in charge.

"Shut off the water and get out of here," he said.

The pool man looked at Arlie, then shouted to his men. The pool was nearly full. No problem. They could come back another day.

"Get out of here," George told the tile men. Tiles from Italy sat in a pile. A few were chipped, most were perfect. The tile men didn't speak English. George kicked an empty box in their direction.

"Go!" he shouted. He stomped his feet like a bull. "Leave!"

George Snow looked like a crazy man carrying a ghost. The tile men were afraid of blackbirds and ghosts at the workplace. Bad luck and accidents, that's what such things meant. Crazy men were even worse. Bad luck all around.

While the workmen were packing up, George took Arlyn out to the lawn.

"Faster," she said. "Fly me there."

He ran, then spun in a circle.

Arlyn laughed. "Not that fast."

She was out of breath. George stopped. He dropped the blanket on the grass, then set Arlie down and rolled the blanket back to cover her, like a cocoon. He heard shouting, but he ignored everything except Arlie's face. It was John Moody doing the yelling, home early, chastising the work-men, who were supposed to be finishing the pool that week. When John heard they'd been ordered to stop by the fellow on the lawn, he approached George Snow. John figured George must be one of the pool men. How dare he hold up the work?

"I want you off this property," John told him.

"Do you?" George said.

"Don't come back looking for a paycheck."

George got up from the grass. The clouds were flying overhead. When John Moody was close enough, George punched him straight in the face.

"What the hell is wrong with you?" John was bleeding heavily from his nose. The grass under his feet had turned red. "Don't think I won't call the police. I'll have you arrested right now. The cops will be here before you have time to get away, you son of a bitch."

George walked over to John and grabbed him. "You had a fucking pool put in while she's dying. All she can hear all day long are the bulldozers. Every noise goes right through her. Is that how you take care of her?"

John Moody saw the blanket on the grass then. Something small was wrapped inside. It was Arlie. His wife. John looked at George carefully. Now he recognized him. The window washer.

"I'm going to be here every day," George Snow said. "And you're not going to call the police or anyone else."

George Snow looked dangerous, insane. John understood why he'd never noticed him working on the pool before. He was someone who didn't belong.

"George," Arlyn said faintly. "Make him go away."

"There's nothing you can do to me," George told John Moody. "I have nothing to lose."

"Okay," John agreed. He did not wish to be punched in the face again.

"I mean it!" George said.

"Look, if she wants you here, you'll be here."

George went back to Arlie. He lay down beside her, feeling the prickly grass through his shirt.

"Did you kill him?" Arlie said. A whisper.

George laughed. "Nope."

Arlie closed her eyes.

"Closer," she said.

George moved as close to her as he dared, afraid he might hurt her.

"Did you see the baby?" Arlie's voice was so weak it seemed to be coming from another planet.

"You don't have to talk."

"I named her for you. You understand, George, why I didn't tell you."

"It doesn't matter." George felt as though he'd never understood anything in his life, least of all what was happening to Arlie. He felt like jumping off a building, stopping time. Instead, he looked at a blade of grass. He looked into Arlie's cloudy eyes.

"Don't fight for her, George. I want her raised with her brother. I want her to be happy. I'm sorry if I hurt you by not telling you. I wanted everything to be simple, but it's not."

"It's all right, Arlie. Stop worrying."

"Do you think she'll remember me? She won't have either of us now."

"Maybe it's more important for us to remember her."

Arlyn laughed. "You're a funny man."

"Hilarious," George Snow said.

The sun had shifted and shadows were pooling, so George lifted Arlyn and carried her back into the house. There was the mother-in-law at the table, looking at him with frightened eyes. And the baby in the stroller. Seven months old. Blond. His little girl. She would grow up here and have everything. Except her mother.

George carried Arlyn upstairs and put her into the bed, then backed out so Jasmine could bathe her and dole out her medicine. The mother-in-law had come up behind him. She looked worried.

"You don't work on the pool," she said.

George felt as though he could tear someone apart. "I'm Blanca's father," he said.

"What are you going to do?" Diana Moody asked.

"I'm going to come here every day," George Snow said. "I won't be in your way."

"I mean after that. When Arlie is gone."

George Snow looked at Diana.

"John doesn't have to know anything," Diana said.

"He's not my concern."

"No." Diana understood. "He doesn't have to be."

Diana had known there was someone else. One night when Arlyn was in horrible pain, Diana had sat on the bed rubbing her back. It was then Arlie had told her mother-in-law she'd done something wrong; she admitted that Blanca wasn't John's child. She didn't even regret it; inside her marriage, she'd been dying of loneliness.

"I understand," Diana had said to her daughter-in-law. She herself had been lonely in her own marriage. "What's done is done. Now you have a beautiful daughter, so it's all for the best."

Afterward Diana couldn't help studying the baby, her blond hair, her dark eyes, her singular features, so unlike

John or Arlie. She had known Blanca's father as soon as she saw him. So now she asked the hard question.

"What are you going to do about Blanca?"

"After Arlie's gone I'm going to drink myself to death. So you don't have to worry about me stealing the baby."

Diana Moody put a hand on his arm, which was a terrible mistake. He started to cry. How embarrassing to be embraced by a woman you didn't know, a woman old enough to be your mother; even worse to be grateful that someone was telling you everything would be all right, that time would heal, even if every word she said was a lie.

ONE AFTERNOON, WHEN THE SKY WAS CLEAR AND THE weather was hot, Arlie called her mother-in-law into her room and asked her to buy a cemetery plot.

"Oh, I couldn't," Diana said. "That's for your husband to do."

"I can't ask John."

John Moody had become somewhat unwound. He couldn't be around sickness, he said. He was no good with it, no good to anyone. Several times Diana had gone downstairs for a drink of water or a Tylenol in the middle of the night and had caught him out on the lawn, walking home in the wet grass. When she'd switched on the porch light, John had blinked in the glare, stunned and guilty, but not guilty enough to stop sneaking to his neighbor's house in the evenings. Sometimes he spent all night. Diana gave her son the benefit of the doubt. Surely, this nonsense with the neighbor started after Arlie took ill. Marriage was complicated, after all; Diana Moody understood that. Maybe John was reacting to that George Snow fellow coming by every day. Anyway, John was not adept at grief or at showing compassion. The truth was, he was not someone you'd ask to buy a cemetery plot.

"I trust you to do this for me. Find me someplace where there's a big tree," Arlie told Diana. "So I can fly away from the top branches."

Diana asked Jasmine to watch the children. She put on her good black suit and her gold necklace and earrings and she wore a hat that she saved for special occasions. She drove out to the cemetery, stopping to ask directions at the gas station. The life she'd led here once seemed like a dream. The lanes here in Connecticut were winding, green, shadowy. There were fields with stone walls she'd never noticed when she lived here; she'd been so busy with her life, although, frankly, the meaning of that life escaped her now. Dinner parties, tennis, her son, her husband. Not even the time to look at the stone walls, built a century earlier when cows roamed the pastures.

When Diana reached the cemetery she parked and went in. It was the oldest cemetery in town, Archangel. Diana had scheduled an appointment and a Mr. Hansen was waiting for her in the chapel. He was very compassionate, and he offered to drive to the site, but Diana said she would follow along in her own car.

"Single or family?" Mr. Hansen asked.

Diana could not bear to think of Arlie out there all by herself. "Family."

As she drove behind Mr. Hansen's van to the far side of

the cemetery, she heard rustling in the back of the car. She hoped a bird hadn't flown in through the open window. She looked in the rearview mirror. Someone was under the blanket she kept in the car for the baby. If a carjacker had suddenly leapt up, insisting she drive to the Mojave, Diana would have been grateful. *I will,* she would have said. *You bet. I'll drive forever if I can just get out of this mess.*

"Who's there?" Diana said in her sternest voice. Probably not the best tone to take with a carjacker, but clearly the right way to get her grandson to sit up and reveal himself.

"Sam Moody," Diana said. "What on earth are you doing here?"

"I wanted to see where you were going," the child said.

The funeral director's van was slowing down. Diana was pleased to see lots of big trees. Oak, cedar, ash.

"The boneyard," Sam said.

He really was an odd little boy. Was it possible not to like your own grandchild?

"The cemetery," Diana corrected.

"I know what happens to things when they die," Sam said. "Dust and bones."

"There's more. There's a spirit." Diana felt sick to her stomach. The heat, perhaps, and all this bad luck.

"Yeah, right," Sam said. "That's a load of crap." They had come to a stop. "Nice trees," he noted. "Can I climb one?"

"Absolutely not." The funeral director was motioning to Diana. She did have to keep the child in line. "Maybe if you're good."

Diana and the boy got out of the car and walked over the

grass. They reached a cool, green spot with six plots. "Fine," Diana said to Hansen. "I'll take it."

Sam went to the center of the empty circle beneath a huge sycamore tree. He lay down and gazed through the leaves. There wasn't a cloud in the sky.

"Good choice," he said. "It's peaceful."

His voice was childish and reedy and Diana hated herself for not liking him all these years.

"Climb the tree," she said. "But not too high."

Sam leapt from the grass, whooping with joy.

"That might be dangerous," Mr. Hansen advised. Sam was throwing himself onto the lowest branch, not a particularly strong branch from the looks of it. Not a particularly agile child, either.

"I'm buying burial plots," Diana said. "His mother's dying. Let him enjoy himself."

"I suppose," Mr. Hansen said.

"In your line of work, you must value life enormously," Diana said.

"No more than anyone else," Mr. Hansen said.

They stopped at the ice-cream shop on the way home. Diana had a vanilla cone. Sam had a Jumbalina — it was even bigger than the sundae his mother sometimes allowed him. Six kinds of ice cream, butterscotch, hot fudge, and strawberry sauce. All that ice cream made Sam sick; he threw up in the washroom, then was ready to go. He used to think his grandmother was a witch. She was old and she didn't seem to like him and she had spindly fingers with big knuckles. Whenever she spent the night in the guest room, he would check under her bed after she'd left, looking for bones and poison. Now he was so tired he let her hold his hand on the way to the car, even though he didn't like to be touched by people who weren't his mother. He supposed a witch's touch was all right, it probably washed right off in the bathtub. Or maybe she was a good witch who could reverse time and make his mother well again.

"Can you fix my mother?" he asked on the way home.

"Unfortunately, I can't," Diana said.

She was honest. Sam had to give her that. When they pulled into the drive, that man's truck was there. There was a collie sitting in the passenger seat, sticking his head out the window and woofing.

"Who owns that dog?" Sam asked. He knew a big man sat by his mother's bedside every day but he didn't know that man's name or what he was doing there. He looked a lot like the man who used to wash the windows.

"A friend of the family," Diana said.

Sam didn't understand; he was a part of the family and he wasn't friends with the man with the truck. They went inside. Jasmine was in the kitchen with Blanca, feeding the baby some cereal. When she saw Sam, Blanca let out a chortle.

"Baby baby stick your head in gravy," Sam said cheerfully.

Blanca laughed so hard cereal came out her nose.

"Is that a nice thing to say?" Jasmine asked.

"She looks like a volcano," Sam noted.

"You look like a dirty boy, honey. Go upstairs and wash up for dinner."

Jasmine's voice was usually strong and pretty; now it sounded shaky. Sam knew about these things, the underside of the world, the part you couldn't see. Something was more wrong than usual. Out on the patio, Sam's father was having a drink and looking at the pool. He looked smaller than usual. He didn't turn around.

"What are we having for dinner?" Sam asked. It was a test. He watched Jasmine carefully.

"We're having whatever you'd like," Jasmine said, when ordinarily she just said *chili* or *hamburgers* or *macaroni*. She was too busy to give you many choices.

Sam went through the hall and up the stairs. His mother's door was open. He had started to feel his mother wasn't there anymore. When he talked to her, sometimes she didn't hear him. Sometimes she spoke to somebody who wasn't in the room. She was like those people she'd told him about, flying above the rooftops. She weighed so little that now when Sam got into bed beside her he felt bigger, stronger. She was made up of bones, but of something more. Maybe it wasn't all a made-up story when people talked about a spirit. Maybe something else was there.

Sam's mother liked to look right into his eyes, and Sam let her do it even though her breath wasn't so good anymore and her eyes were milky. Every time she breathed out there was a little less of her. Every time she spoke there was less as well.

"Tell me a secret," she'd said to him last night. She was like a bird, hollow bones, little beak, shivery bald head.

The sky had been dark and the lawn looked black. He had thought about the ferryboat ride on the day he found William the squirrel and the angels they'd made in the snow. He'd thought about her long red hair and the fact that even when he was horrible and out of sorts she loved him anyway.

"Just one?" Sam had said.

He'd felt her knees against him, knobby, like pieces of stone.

"One."

Her eyes were big. You could fall into them. *Mother, Mother, are you there?*

"I'm six years old," Sam said.

Arlyn had laughed a bit. Her laughter sounded like her. It was her. "I know that."

"But I'm going to stay that way," Sam confided.

"No, you won't," she told him. "You'll be a big man. You'll be so tall your head will hit the sky."

But that conversation had taken place last night, and last night was over. Now Sam stood in the hallway outside his mother's room and listened to the man who was supposed to be a friend of the family crying. He had no idea grown-ups could sound like that. Sam knew what had happened; he stayed in the hall a moment longer in order to have one more instant of still having her just as she'd always been, safe inside his mind. Then he walked into her bedroom. There was still the smell of her, the shadow of her, the bare skull. The man had his head in his hands.

"I'm sorry," the man said, as though he'd been caught doing something bad. He had her pearls in his hands. They were big hands and the pearls looked like small black seeds. "She said to give them to you."

Sam looked at the person in the bed; it wasn't his mother. It was just a shell, the way his squirrel had been on that other bad day. Sam took the pearls and brought them to his room. In the back of the closet was the box with everything that mattered. The photos, the pictures, the cards, the braid of her hair, his squirrel's pelt and bones. He wrapped the pearls in a tissue, then put them in the box. He did it carefully. Sam was not like other boys, who would not have taken such good care of a necklace. He was different. He planned on keeping his word. The secret he'd told his mother was true: he was never going to grow up. He refused to go past this day when his mother left him. No one could force him because he'd already decided. He was never going to say good-bye.

A House Made of Stars

IT WAS A WEDDING SHOWER, ALL IN GOOD FUN, held at a psychic tearoom on Twenty-third Street. Meredith Weiss knew she should have claimed to have a migraine or a previous appointment, but Ellen Dooley was her old college roommate, and privy to the tricks Meredith often used to avoid social contact. Clearly, there was no gracious way out. Meredith dragged herself downtown from the Upper West Side, where she was house-sitting a huge apartment for a family that was traveling in Italy. Meredith had gotten a temporary job at the gift shop in the Metropolitan Museum of Art. Everyone who worked there was overqualified and undermotivated. Meredith herself had a degree in art history from Brown, not that she cared about art anymore. In high school she had been a champion swimmer; now she could barely bring herself to get out of bed in the morning. She couldn't sleep, but she couldn't quite wake up, either. She was twenty-eight, six years out of college and a million miles away from knowing what she might possibly do with her life.

Her ex-roommate Ellen was the only one she knew at the party, so it was possible for Meredith to drift into the background as the psychic told good fortunes all around, with an especially brilliant future foreseen for the bride-to-be, including four children and a fabulous sex life. The psychic was an Irish woman with a lovely lilting voice; her cheerful predictions all but put Meredith to sleep. It was hot outside; heat waves rose from the asphalt into the still, gray air. Meredith collapsed into a chair that overlooked the street. At least the tearoom was air-conditioned. The others were all talking about where they'd go to dinner later in the evening. No one included Meredith. It was clear she didn't belong, despite the silk nightgown she'd given Ellen, which everyone declared was the best present of all. She'd picked lingerie she herself would never have worn, a flimsy, silly thing. Naturally the others all loved what she hated. It was always the same for Meredith: she was the outsider who never seemed to speak the commonly shared language.

Meredith had brown hair and dark, ebony eyes; she was long and coltish, with a swimmer's body, but out of the water she was awkward. Poor gasping fish. Although she had spent most of her childhood and adolescence in one pool or another in suburban Maryland, she had come to dread water. Sometimes she called in sick to work when there was a heavy rain, then went back to bed so she could hide under the covers. People who met her sometimes had the impression she was mute. Because she was a loner, she was a listener as well. She noticed things, strange odds and ends, facts no one else cared about: how many stairs led up to the museum, how many cracks there were in the ceiling of the borrowed bedroom where she was staying, how many museum employees she had caught smoking in the restroom. Useless bits and pieces. Now, for instance, while the other women had cake, some gooey blue and white concoction, Meredith looked out the window to see a tall man leaving his black sedan in the parking lot across the street.

The man on the far side of Twenty-third Street left his keys with the attendant and ran his hand through his hair. He was wearing a gray jacket and he loped through traffic, followed by a red-haired woman. Meredith assumed they were husband and wife from the way the man made his way without bothering to see to the woman's safety. A typical married pair. Meredith's parents had been the same before they divorced; bickering whenever they spent more than a few hours together, living separate lives long before the papers were signed.

Meredith hoped that this couple, now headed toward the

psychic's door, were the next clients. Then the party would at last come to a close and she could beg off dinner and grab a cab back to her borrowed apartment. At last, Ellen was gathering her gifts together. The dreadful nightgown, the jokey sex manuals, the satin sheets. The psychic approached the corner of the room where Meredith was in hiding. Exactly what Meredith dreaded most. Someone interested in her future.

"How about your fortune?" The psychic's name was Rita Morrisey and she had a knack for telling people what they wanted to hear. From a distance she had figured the best bets for this shy woman would be a boyfriend and a trip over water to a new horizon. Now the psychic wasn't so sure.

"No thanks," Meredith demurred.

The bell over the outer door jingled and the tall man came inside. He slammed the door, once again not bothering to wait for his wife. He was near forty, a worried, good-looking man. He situated himself in the waiting room and gazed around uncomfortably.

"Poor fella," Rita said.

"Where's his wife?"

Rita Morrisey glared at Meredith. The psychic had a foxy face, quick and distrustful. "What wife?"

"The red-haired woman who was following him in the street."

"Don't screw around with me," Rita said. "He's a regular customer. He's being haunted by his first wife."

Meredith peered into the waiting room. The tall man was alone; he'd grabbed a *National Geographic* and was leafing through it. "He doesn't seem like someone who'd come here."

"Well, you never know, do you? For your information, he's got all sorts of things going on at his house in Connecticut. Soot, voices, dishes. It's classic. Those are the signs."

Meredith was confused. "Signs?"

"Of a specter. Dishes breaking, voices in the middle of the night, soot on everyone's clothes, shoes lined up in the hallway, cabinets open. I figure it's the wife. Pissed-off creatures usually are at the root of such things. The betrayed, the lost, the confused. They linger."

The rest of the party was ready to go. They traipsed into the waiting room, obscuring Meredith's view of the couch. Now Meredith was the one who was lagging behind. "Come on!" Ellen called. "We're starving."

While Meredith hesitated the others went out the door; she could hear their laughter as they trooped down the flight of stairs that led to the street.

"Walk by and forget him," Rita Morrisey told Meredith. "A tormented soul is nothing to mess with."

"I don't believe in specters," Meredith said primly.

"So much the better for you."

"I don't believe in anything," Meredith admitted.

But the psychic was no longer listening. She peered into the waiting room. "Mr. Moody. Please come right in."

The tall man bumped against Meredith in the doorway as he came forward for his reading and she headed into the waiting room.

"Sorry," Meredith said.

He paid no attention. Didn't even nod.

Meredith went on into the waiting room. The red-haired woman was there now, on the couch. She was young, in her midtwenties, wearing a white dress and soft leather shoes; her hair reached her waist and she had so many freckles they all ran together over her forehead and cheeks.

"Hello," Meredith said.

The woman looked past Meredith.

"Ready, you slowpoke?" Ellen had raced back in. She grabbed Meredith's arm and led her out. They took the flight of stairs two at a time; out into the sweltering heat. "We've decided to walk to Union Square and have dinner. There's a fabulous place Jessie says she can get us into. She knows the chef's brother. Or cousin."

Meredith blinked in the white light of summer. Lies did not come easily to her.

"I wish I could," she said. Right.

"But you can't. You never can."

"I'm antisocial. You know that about me."

Ellen kissed Meredith on both cheeks. "I love the nightgown."

As soon as Ellen and her friends had gone off, Meredith crossed the street and went into a market. It was so hot and humid that her skin was already slick with sweat. This New York City heat made summer anywhere else seem like kid stuff. Still, for Meredith it was a relief to be somewhere made of concrete; no pools, no grass, just the melting asphalt and the blur of traffic. Meredith bought a guava juice, making certain to stay in front of the rotating fan beside the register as she paid, then uncapped the bottle. She glanced at the street; through the storefront she could see into the tearoom window. The red-haired woman was standing there. She opened the window. Soot fell down from the ledge.

Meredith put her juice on the counter.

The red-haired woman's dress moved in the breeze like a cloud.

"Don't do it," Meredith said.

"Hey, lady, don't tell me what to do," the fellow behind the cash register said.

Across the street the woman was now standing on the window ledge. She put her arms straight out and the white dress billowed around her.

Meredith ran for the market door and pushed it open. Smack, that heat again. Bricks and stones. Soot and ashes. Meredith looked up in a panic; all she could hear was the crashing noise of Twenty-third Street, the buses, the trucks, the sirens. It took an instant to focus.

There was no one on the ledge.

It was hot, too hot to think straight; summer was always bad for Meredith. Swimming-pool season. She would have liked to crawl under the bed until fall, until the air was crisp, the leaves yellowing. A far better time of the year.

She headed toward the subway stop on Eighth Avenue, but then she noticed the parking lot where she'd first seen the tall man. In the first row there was a black Mercedes with Connecticut plates. Meredith went over to the parking attendant's kiosk. "I think I'm supposed to meet my husband here. Tall, wearing a gray suit."

"The Mercedes," the attendant said. "He said he'd be at least an hour."

The attendant handed Meredith the key. The name and home address had been marked down in a scrawl she squinted to decipher. *Moody. Madison, Ct.*

She quickly handed back the key. "My mistake. I think I was supposed to meet him somewhere else. This isn't our car."

Meredith took off running, hailing a cab on Eighth Avenue. She threw herself inside, legs sticky against the vinyl seat. She usually didn't splurge on taxis; she didn't think she was worth it. Now she leaned forward and said, "Hurry up. Let's go!"

"Hey, relax," the taxi driver told her. "You'll get where you're going."

But where exactly that might be and how she might get there, Meredith couldn't say.

You could hear water in the Moodys' yard. It was the first thing anyone noticed when approaching the house, one pool running into another over the infinity edge. The first smell? Cut grass and chlorine. Summer. Country. Something you could sink into the way day sinks into dusk. First sight? The boxwood hedge, twelve feet tall, and then, like a mirage, the Glass Slipper. All that glass and steel. The trees reflected back to Meredith as though she were doubly lost in the woods.

Atop the glass was the one flat place on the roof, a precipice that could be reached only from the attic. That was where Sam Moody was, arms akimbo. He could feel the breeze that carried the swallows. Sweat poured down his face and his back. He was sixteen years old and tall, just as his mother had predicted. He hit his head everywhere he went, but not here where there was only the sky.

Sam had been to some pretty bad places in the past two years. Darkened doorways and basement apartments where he'd had to crouch. Underpasses, where the concrete was inches above his scalp. Dead-end streets, where he had to fold up on himself and walk small so no one noticed him and beat the crap out of him.

Up on the roof he didn't have to bend or bow; the world was endless, seamless. He took deep gulps of air.

His stepmother was the first to spy him, when she came out to the front path for the Saturday newspaper. She shielded her eyes, squinting; she realized it was not an enormous stork, only him, Sam, the bane of her existence. Cynthia started yelling. He couldn't quite make out the words, but frankly, he never listened to her. She was always ordering him around. Cynthia raced into the house and brought his father out. The big gun, the authority figure, the man in the moon. His poor, stupid father who threatened to call the police.

"This time I'll have you taken away," John warned his son.

Actually, *away* was where Sam Moody wanted to go. Some distant and blue and unreachable place. It was hotter on the roof than he'd thought it would be at this hour in the morning. Usually he was still in bed at this time, late to summer school to make up the math class he'd failed; he could sleep right through Cynthia yammering at him to get up and out on time. This morning he had set his alarm, but he was awake before it rang, up with the birds.

He was done with math and summer school and a life of bullshit. He could smell the spicy odor of the boxwoods and the bitter scent of chlorine. His little sister had pool parties on the weekends and every kid on the block came to swim and piss in their pool. When such festivities occurred, Sam stayed locked in his room until Blanca knocked on his door and said, *It's okay. They're all gone. You can come out now.*

The old man and Cynthia went back into the house. It was air-conditioned. Why should they sweat out here with him when he refused to listen to a word they said, let alone climb down? Sam was idly waiting for the police, wondering if his father would have the balls to really call and report him or if John Moody was merely sitting in the kitchen, steamed and silent as usual. Sam's father blamed him for everything. Not just his failing grades, and the car accidents he'd had, and of course the drugs — not that the old man knew the extent of that, either. Aside from all of his own misdeeds, Sam also took the rap for weird happenings that had nothing to do with him. Broken dishes in the kitchen, soot falling out of the chimney, murmured voices in the hall late at night.

It was most likely Cynthia who was sneaking around, then placing blame. Cynthia trying to mindfuck them all. Yet again. She had a mean streak, a pissed-off streak, a black and white streak, acting as though she was so smart when she was an emotional idiot about most things. For instance, she thought Sam was attempting to kill himself this morning. She thought that was why he was out on the roof, when he never intended that at all. If that's what he had wanted to do, it would have been easy. He wouldn't have had to call attention to himself. No, if Cynthia could admit what a bitch she was, she would know why Sam had to escape. And if she ever had the guts to acknowledge what a bastard the old man was, she would be scrambling to get free herself.

It was interesting to have a bird's-eye view. Everything was so much smaller. Sam had smoked some weed before he climbed onto the roof, just for a buzz. No major drugs at this hour of the day. One time he'd taken a tab of LSD and come up here and it had been a mistake. He was so disoriented he couldn't tell which direction led to the stars and which to earth.

A car was pulling up and parking. Not a police car or an ambulance, just a crappy VW Bug. A young woman got out. Tall. In her twenties. She was wearing jeans and a tank top and sunglasses; her dark hair was pulled into a ponytail and she looked confused. Maybe she was a police cadet in training. Sam was so intent on watching her that his feet slipped. He was wearing basketball sneakers and they squeaked on the glass. Quickly, he caught himself from falling, his arms flailing, as though he were trying to catch the air.

The woman, Meredith Weiss, looked up.

A mirage, she thought. *Like the window ledge. A stork that looked like a teenaged boy.*

But no, he was real enough, and smoking a cigarette.

"Is your name Moody?" she called up to the roof.

"Sam," he called down.

"I'm Meredith."

"Good for you." Sam's voice hurt from the raised decibel level. He was not a shouter. He was more the silent type. He had once lasted an entire month without saying a single word to his father or Cynthia. He thought his muteness would drive them crazy, but the plan had backfired: they'd seemed relieved.

"I've never been to Connecticut before," Meredith told the boy.

"It's green and boring. So you might as well turn around and go back to where you came from."

Meredith laughed. "It's hot here. Almost as hot as New York. Want some limeade? I've got two containers."

Sam was sweating so hard his shirt was drenched. The sun was intense up here. The air wasn't moving. Sam's legs were wet with sweat and his feet inside his sneakers were slippery. "Okay," he said.

Sam slowly crawled down toward the attic door, then hoisted himself through; once inside he shut the trapdoor and locked it. He went down to the second floor, then to the first, through the kitchen, where his father and Cynthia were fighting.

"I am not doing this," Cynthia was saying. "It's the same thing over and over again, and we put up with it."

Sam's father had his back to everyone, as usual; immobilized, as usual.

"I see you're calling the police," Sam said.

They looked up at him as though he were a ghost.

Before they could stop him, Sam went through the house, then out the front door. The woman with the VW was standing in the driveway, leaning on her car. She had produced two small cartons of limeade. Well, at least there was somebody who didn't lie about something.

"Much better than lemonade," she said.

Sam accepted one of the cartons of juice and opened it. It was rare for him to find anyone amusing. "And so green."

Meredith nodded to the roof where Sam had been. "How do things look from up there?"

Sam sneaked a look at her. She was serious. She wanted to know. Who was she anyway?

"Distant," he said. "Especially if you're stoned."

"Umm." Meredith gulped some of her drink. She knew he wanted a reaction and she wasn't about to give him one. Who was she to judge? A dysfunctional museum cashier who had nothing better to do than drive around chasing specters.

"And you're here because?" Sam was actually interested, which didn't happen very often.

There didn't seem to be any reason to lie. Not completely.

"I'm lost," Meredith said.

The parents were watching from the living-room window. They looked like fools.

"Father, stepmother," Sam said when he saw Meredith looking at them. "Sister's at ballet lessons. She's the good one."

He'd timed it that way, so Blanca wouldn't be scared with him being on the roof. She was just a kid.

"Fuck," Sam said when Cynthia and his father came out. "Heads up. Morons approaching."

"Can we help you?" Cynthia called to Meredith.

"I don't know. I was lost. I happened to see your beautiful house, so I pulled in the driveway and we got to talking."

In point of fact she had driven to Madison center, gone

into the pharmacy, and looked up Moody in the local phone book. Mockingbird Lane. Not so difficult to find.

"Get in your room," the father, John Moody, said to Sam. "I'll deal with you later."

"Maybe you should call Social Services," Sam said to Meredith before he sauntered away. "Report parental abuse. Thanks for the drink."

"Do you mind telling me how you did that?" John Moody asked Meredith once Sam had gone inside.

"I just got off Ninety-five and I got all turned around . . ." Meredith began.

"I don't mean getting lost. How did you talk him down?"

"I don't know. He's just a kid," Meredith said.

She looked at John closely; he had that same worried look he'd had at the tearoom on Twenty-third Street. The red-haired woman was nowhere around. Meredith looked up. There were no window ledges. Just sheets of glass joined by flat steel beams.

"Maybe you can get him to go to summer school," Cynthia said. "God knows I can't."

"Because you screech at him like a damned banshee," John told her, right in front of a stranger.

"If my authority wasn't continually undermined, maybe I wouldn't have to."

Cynthia was wearing shorts and a white cotton shirt. She had taken up tennis. Her knees were bothering her, so she'd given up running, still she needed something that took her out of the house. She wasn't looking to play at Wimbledon, only to have a few hours to herself, away from this mess of a family. She'd asked that nurse who took care of Arlyn, Jas-

mine Carter, to stay on as a nanny, but the nurse had informed Cynthia that her job was to take care of sick people
and that it was Cynthia's job to take care of her stepchildren.
Arlyn had probably turned the nurse against her. Well, who
these days was on her side?

Cynthia had become the nervous type. Now, for instance,
she was jangling her car keys. "Look, I have to get Blanca
from ballet and drop her back here before I go to meet
Jackie at the club. Thank you," she said to Meredith. "Seriously. You're good with kids." Cynthia got into a white Jeep
parked at the far end of the boxwood hedge. "I want you to
hire her," she told John. "I don't care if her name is Lizzie
Borden."

"It's Meredith Weiss," Meredith told John as Cynthia
drove away.

"We haven't been able to keep any help for more than a
month," John Moody said. "Sam is so difficult. And it's all
fallen onto Cynthia."

"I hear running water," Meredith said. "Is something
flooding?"

John Moody nodded for her to follow around to the rear of
the house. There was the pool, with its waterfall streaming
over the infinity edge into the second, lower pool. Meredith
saw past the first edge when she stood on tiptoes. Swimmers
feel the pull of water, and Meredith could still feel it. Her
skin started to itch.

"I was a swimmer in high school." Right away Meredith
felt stupid for saying anything about herself. Why would
this strange man care?

"I don't think Sam's ever been in the pool. Not once."

"And you have a little girl?" There were gnats in the air and Meredith waved them away. She hadn't been swimming for years. People said swimmers had muscle memory; throw such a person into water and she'd start swimming laps. Meredith felt thirsty as she gazed at the pool; utterly parched.

"Blanca. She's ten." John Moody looked out at the lawn. "She's not the problem."

John had been having stomach troubles lately, out of the blue. Maybe it was an ulcer, or something worse. He wasn't about to go to a doctor and find out. Ever since Arlie, he'd had a fear of doctors. He was on his own regimen; he stayed away from salt and caffeine. Soon after Cynthia stopped running, he'd taken it up. Ten miles a day. Anything to get away. Every day he saw signs of something he didn't want to see: all he'd done wrong in his life. Standing there with him, Meredith could feel a wave of sadness, so strong it almost knocked her down. She thought she saw something on the roof of the house. Just a cloud. A fluttering of white.

"And the children's mother?" Meredith wanted to say, *Did she have red hair? Does she follow you everywhere? Does she appear and disappear before your eyes?*

"Gone," John said. "Cancer."

"Maybe I'll go check on Sam before I get back in the car. Make sure he's okay."

"Of course. That's very thoughtful. But let me show you the house before you go. It's actually quite famous. The most famous house in Madison."

The Glass Slipper was as impressive on the inside as it was

from without; there was light everywhere, green all around. Sam's room was upstairs. Meredith felt dizzy on the staircase. So much glass. A spaceship hurtling through the infinite universe. A specimen jar in which moths and beetles were kept.

John pointed Meredith toward Sam's room, and she thanked him and went to knock on the door. "Just saying good-bye," she called when it became clear Sam wasn't about to open the door for his father or stepmother.

When he heard that it was Meredith, the lock slid back. There was the smell of smoke in his room. Acrid and woody.

"Enter," Sam said.

The place was a mess. Clothes strewn everywhere. The walls painted black under a ceiling of glass.

"Amazing," Meredith said of the ceiling.

"All the bedrooms are like this."

"Wow. You're lucky."

"You don't know the first thing about me, so that is one fucking stupid assessment," Sam said. Menacing. Pulled back.

Was that supposed to scare her?

"I meant about the ceiling," Meredith said. "It's a great room. I couldn't pretend to know whether you were lucky or not in life since I don't know you."

But she could guess, couldn't she? Not so lucky. The mother gone, the stepmother furious, the father so distant, looking for something that might or might not be there.

Sam laughed. "Yeah, everyone in town envies me for my ceiling."

They listened to music for a while; he had an old turntable and records that Meredith had listened to as a girl.

She could have stayed a while longer, she really had nothing to go back to. That's when she thought she'd better leave.

"I've got to go," Meredith said. "I'll probably get lost on the way back to the city."

"I wasn't going to kill myself up there, you know," Sam said.

"I know."

Meredith was well aware that if you were serious about it, you didn't try to pull in an audience. Maybe she did know Sam in some deep way.

"At least, not this time," Sam said. "I see the point of it, though. Exit stage right. You pull your own strings."

Meredith noticed the collection of knives on his desk.

"Your father lets you have these?"

"My father is an ass. Plus they're antiques. Japanese ceremonial knives. They aren't sharp enough to do any damage."

"Well, good," Meredith said.

"And that's not my style. Blood and gore."

"Mine either," Meredith said.

"You really are lost. Am I right?"

Sam held his breath. He wanted someone to be honest with him. Anyone. Even a stranger.

"Lost as in I don't know my way around Connecticut?"

"Okay." Sam grinned. No one told the truth. "Sure. If you say so. Stop by if you're ever lost around here again."

Meredith went downstairs and found John Moody waiting for her.

"Look, I don't know how you got him down from the roof, but if you'd ever be interested, I would hire you in a minute. Wherever you're working, I'd pay you more to help

Cynthia out. And room and board, of course. And medical. Look, I'd pay your car insurance if you stay. Bottom line — you can handle Sam — it will be a first."

"Are you asking me to leave my glamorous job at the gift shop at the Metropolitan Museum of Art?"

Meredith was joking, stalling, but John stared at her, confused. Maybe he thought it was a shakedown of some sort. Maybe he didn't care what it was as long as she stayed.

"I could double what the museum pays you," he said.

"Sam's that bad?"

"Not when you're dealing with him. That's the point."

"I'll think it over."

John walked out with her. From where she stood on the porch, Meredith looked down the driveway. Someone was waiting out there. A young woman in the shadow of the boxwoods.

"Do you see that?" Meredith asked.

Before John could respond, Cynthia's Jeep pulled in and parked.

"Would you consider it?" John asked.

"I might," Meredith said.

Cynthia got out, as did a blond girl of ten wearing a leotard and ballet slippers. The girl ran across the gravel driveway. She was skinny, all elbows and legs, and her hair was in one long braid to her waist.

"I'm going to be one of the mice in the end-of-summer dance festival!" the child declared. "I'm a mouse! It's the second-best part."

The girl stopped when she saw Meredith standing beside her father.

"Oh, hi."

"Blanca, this is Meredith," John Moody said. John looked at Meredith and she looked back at him. "She may move in for a while. Help around the house."

"Well, thank the lord." Cynthia dropped Blanca's dance-gear bag on the floor. "Honey, I don't know where you came from or where you're going," she said to Meredith. "But you just saved my life."

AT THE BEGINNING OF THE SCHOOL TERM, CYNTHIA handed over Blanca's schedule, neatly typed out. School hours, ballet lessons, art class, soccer team, doctor's checkups, dentist appointments, friends' birthday parties, tickets to the Dance Umbrella season. Whenever Blanca did have free time, she usually had her nose in a book or wanted to be driven to the library. But what of Sam? For him there was nothing. No schedule whatsoever. There had been appointments with psychiatrists, social workers, mediators, and an enforced sports program run by a former marine. Sam had refused to go. He had the dreadful habit of stabbing himself with pins, and there were scars all over his arms, but they couldn't do anything about that, either. Nor could they stop him from performing a trick he had taught himself: he hung like a bat, upside down, from a large crab-apple tree. He could do it for hours. Once he had fainted after half a day spent in this contorted pose in the heat, and had suffered a concussion when he fell headfirst to the ground.

His after-school activities? They couldn't seem to control

those, either. Drugs and alcohol, with a continuing escalation of the amount and the potency. The powdery stuff Cynthia had found in his room wasn't cocaine, as she'd thought, but heroin. For those who didn't want to know, it was possible to misunderstand just about everything. Some days Sam slept twenty hours at a time. You could pour a pail of water over him, as Cynthia in a fit once had, and he still wouldn't budge. Some nights they could hear him scurrying around until dawn. There was a night when he'd walked and hitchhiked to Providence and back. He said he'd wanted to try johnnycakes, a Rhode Island delicacy, crumbly pancakes served with butter, but really there was someone he knew selling Ecstasy who could be found outside a RISD dorm. They knew he was haunting the bleakest neighborhoods of Bridgeport and taking the bus to lower Manhattan; they didn't want to think about the reason why. It was a very small leap from pins to needles. It was simple really: you stabbed yourself, and instead of feeling pain, you felt nothing at all.

Even when Sam took up normal habits, things went wrong. For a while he lifted weights obsessively, more and more rings added on; he couldn't seem to stop until Cynthia got so sick of hearing the barbells clanking all night long she had someone come and take everything away, donating the equipment to the homeless shelter downtown. She geared herself up for a huge explosion. But Sam didn't say a word when he saw the weights were gone. In the morning, however, all the good china from Cynthia's first marriage was broken into shards.

Sam denied having anything to do with it.

"Fucking fingerprint me!" he'd shouted. "Take me to the police station. I fucking dare you!"

"Actually, it was my fault." Blanca had heard the ruckus and was watching from a doorway. "I was reaching for a pitcher to make lemonade and everything fell down. I was too scared to say anything."

Sam turned to Blanca. He laughed out loud. He knew his sister. "No, you didn't. It's completely out of character for you, Peapod."

"Next time I promise I'll tell when I do something bad," Blanca said prettily. "I thought I could sweep up the dishes and make everything right."

"Liar, liar," Sam chided, but no one paid the least bit of attention. Except for Blanca; for her brother's benefit, she waggled her crossed fingers behind her back.

"It's fine," Cynthia assured her stepdaughter. "Don't worry about it. Everything from my first marriage was bad, even the china. I never used it."

Blanca had grinned and stuck her tongue out at her brother. She could get away with things, too, especially when it meant protecting him.

"I really didn't do it," Sam said to Blanca and Meredith later on.

"Who cares? She said they were horrible dishes," Blanca said.

When she had some time alone, Meredith went out to the garage to look through the trash. There was the broken china in a barrel. The shards felt like pieces of ice. On the very edges of the plates was a black line. Soot. One of the signs of a specter. Meredith had heard a voice outside her room the first night she'd slept there. It was the room where Jasmine Carter, the nurse, had lived during the worst of Arlyn Moody's illness. Meredith had been lying in bed looking up through the glass ceiling at the wash of stars above her. There was the Milky Way swirling through the night. Someone said, *Water.* Well, it was probably herself, thinking aloud. She was thirsty, so she went downstairs and got a drink. She was wearing a T-shirt and running shorts, what she always slept in. Her feet were bare. She stepped in something and looked down. A neat pile of bird bones had been heaped on the floor. There must be a cat, and this his dinner, all that was left of a poor wren or a mockingbird. Meredith went outside. She liked the country at night, the darkness of everything. It was odd for her to live in such close proximity to a pool. Still, she was drawn to the sound of water. She walked through the damp grass and sat at the edge, dipping her feet in. John Moody didn't overheat the pool. It was a perfect temperature.

"Not going to drown yourself, are you?" Sam was outside in a chaise, there in the dark, smoking hashish. The scent was perfumed and rich.

"Aren't you afraid you'll get caught?" Meredith said.

"I just did," Sam said. "Water, fire, air. Which do you pick?"

"Water," Meredith said. "I meant caught by your dad or Cynthia. What you're doing is illegal, you know. If I find it in your room I'll throw it out. Fair warning."

"My room's double locked. Plus, there's an endless supply of drugs available if you know the right people." Then Sam announced, "I choose air."

"What is that pile of bones in the kitchen?" Meredith asked.

"Found them on the lawn. I thought I'd leave them as a present for Cynthia."

"You are the perfect son." Meredith laughed. "Put out the pipe."

"Stepson." Sam took another hit, then tapped the ashes onto the patio.

"I heard a voice outside my room." Meredith swiped the pipe when Sam placed it on a glass table. She planned to toss it in the trash basket.

"First sign of insanity," Sam said. "What did the voice say to you?"

"Water."

"Hmm," Sam said. "Interesting. To me the voice always says that life is a pointless mess of dust and bones and shit."

"Sam," Meredith said.

"I'm warning you," he said to her. "Don't even try to get through to me or whatever it is you're doing. I'm a lost cause."

But she did try. It was her job, after all. But it was something more, her mission, perhaps. Maybe that's why John Moody had so wanted to hire her in the first place; he could tell she was a fixer. She desperately wanted to succeed where others before her had failed. Still, there seemed to be no way to get Sam up in the mornings. She tried multiple alarm clocks, loud radios, banging pots and pans together outside his door. No response. Blanca was the opposite, prompt as could be. She came down to the kitchen ready for the day, her hair braided, her homework packed neatly away, a book open before her as she ate toast and jam.

"We better not wait for him," she usually advised Meredith. "If you drop me off and then come back for him you can still get him to the high school in time for homeroom, but I wouldn't count on him being awake."

They were still trying. Sam hadn't officially dropped out of high school; he just never went.

"Maybe we should get him a tutor," Meredith suggested to John Moody. "Or I could do it. Then he could pass his GED and have a high-school diploma."

"He wouldn't agree to do it," John told her. "If something might possibly make me happy, he's constitutionally unfit to accomplish the task."

"I don't think it's about you."

They looked at each other. They were in the kitchen and John was fixing himself a drink. There was the sound of ice.

"I think it's about her," Meredith said.

"Cynthia has tried her damnedest with that boy. She's gone way beyond the call of duty, so let's not blame Cynthia."

John Moody was already done with the conversation. But he had to get past Meredith, who blocked his way.

"I meant his mother," Meredith said.

For all Meredith knew the red-haired woman might be out behind the boxwoods right now. There were always shadows where there shouldn't be. In the driveway, on the lawn, beneath the lilacs. All anyone had to do was look.

"His mother is gone," John Moody said. "End of conversation."

"Is she?"

"Isn't she?" John said.

"You don't feel haunted? You don't feel her presence?"

Cynthia was out in the hall. She'd been listening in, not liking the intimacy between Meredith and John. Now she stepped into the kitchen and looped her arm around her husband's waist.

"You don't mind if I take him away, do you?" Cynthia asked.

Ever since Meredith had come to Connecticut, she'd felt Cynthia watching her. This wasn't the first time Cynthia had lurked, eavesdropping. Narrowed eyes and a smile each and every time, as though trying to figure out a puzzle. She'd sit on a chaise and watch as Meredith stretched out on a blanket spread over the lawn, reading, making the most of the time when Blanca was off at school. Sam still isolated himself in his room, which he was coating with fluorescent paint that would glow when he turned on a black light. Blanca and Meredith, on the other hand, spent huge amounts of time together. Meredith had had no idea that children could be so interesting and smart. Frankly, she felt more comfortable with Blanca than she did with most adults. Connecticut felt safe, a bubble floating above the real world.

"I still don't get it," Cynthia said one September afternoon. Everything green was turning to gold. Meredith was out in the driveway waiting for Blanca. The school bus stopped at the end of the lane, and it took Blanca seven minutes to get to the house if she ran, eleven if she dawdled. Cynthia had come outside to wait with Meredith, something she'd never done before. She was usually too busy. She was probably missing a tennis lesson at this very moment.

"Get what?" Meredith asked.

"Your presence."

"Excuse me?"

"You seem so happy here. Could it be that you're fucking my husband and this is all a big joke on me?"

Birds seemed to be attracted to the Glass Slipper. Now, for instance, a flock of blackbirds alighted in the hedges all at once, filtering down from above.

"What happened? Really. You can tell me," Cynthia said. "How did it start? Did you meet in the city? Did you start off at hotels, fucking him all night long? Then I suppose you thought, what the hell — you might as well move into his house, do it just a few doors down from the wife. She's only a second wife. She has no authority."

"I think you'd better stop this." Meredith was deeply embarrassed for them both.

"Do you? Am I supposed to believe that you were desperate to become a full-time nanny for a delinquent teenager? That you just happened to show up at this house?"

"You're imagining this." Meredith felt like pouring a bucket of water over her employer. *Why would you ever think I'd want him in the first place? I want nothingness, that's why I'm here. The bubble. The green lawn. The blackbirds. The quiet.* "And you obviously don't trust your husband."

Cynthia let out a laugh. "He's doing to me what he did to her. Screwing someone new while I'm sleeping in our bed."

The school bus approached. Meredith always made certain to be out in the driveway at the right time, waiting. Today was Monday, Blanca's free day, no dance lessons, no soccer; all Meredith had to do was fix her a snack and help with her homework.

"Blanca's on her way."

"And you still haven't told me." Cynthia wasn't letting this go. She was ready to make a scene, whether or not Blanca might overhear. "Are you and my husband involved?"

"I haven't had sex with anyone for twelve years," Meredith said. "Not that it's any of your business."

"What royal bullshit," Cynthia said.

"Whether you believe it or not, it's true. I'm here because I have nowhere else to go at the moment. I have no career. I thought I could take this time and think things through."

"You really haven't had any sex? As in nothing?" Cynthia was sounding a little less hysterical.

"Nothing. Not even anonymous sex. Not even virtual sex. I had a boyfriend who died in high school, and that was the end of things."

"I'm sorry. I really am. I had no idea. I just couldn't figure out why on earth a well-educated, attractive woman would take a job here."

"I like the kids."

Simple, really, though it was a conclusion Cynthia would never have reached. Sam was like a dog who could tell who was afraid of his bark and his bite; he scared his stepmother. He always had. "As in both of them?"

"I get Sam. I understand him."

"Good lord," Cynthia said. "I don't know whether to revere you or pity you."

"Both will be fine."

Cynthia grinned. "I just won't attack you. How about that?"

"Do you see anything over there?" Meredith pointed to the hedge. The shape of a woman's foot, a leg, green leaves, a knee. There were bits and pieces mostly, except when John was around and it was possible to see the entire person.

"I see that the lawn needs to be mowed," Cynthia said. "The landscaper is horrible."

"Just so we're clear — I have absolutely no interest in your husband. I mean none."

"Well, neither do I, but I'm still fucking him."

Both women laughed. They looked at each other, not sure what they were if they weren't adversaries.

"Well, I'm not," Meredith assured Cynthia. "And I don't intend to be."

Here came Blanca whistling and hopping along the driveway. Meredith waved.

"Hey, Bee," Meredith called.

"Tons and tons of math homework," Blanca called back.

"She likes you better than she likes me," Cynthia said sadly as Blanca approached.

"I'm not a threat, Cynthia. I'm just here to help out. That's all."

Meredith had a picnic set up on the patio, a place where math might not be so distasteful. "You made limeade!" Blanca's favorite. Blanca ordered the universe in terms of a list of favorites: Favorite food — pasta. Favorite family member — Sam. Favorite grandparent, well, only grandparent, really — Granny Diana. Favorite subject at school —

anything but math. Favorite novel — whatever she was reading that week.

Meredith met Blanca halfway to the patio and together
they headed across the lawn. Meredith was barefoot and the
grass was prickly on her feet.

"I'm so glad you're here," Blanca said. "You're so good at
math. You're good at everything."

"I wish." Meredith laughed.

"You are," Blanca said.

Maybe that was why Meredith was in Connecticut; just to
be near someone who thought she was worthwhile. Twelve
years ago Meredith had been sixteen. Sam's age. Those years
had passed in a blur, pointless instants melding together into
a single shadow. They said time healed all wounds, but
Meredith hadn't gotten over what had happened. The past
continued to feel current, every moment before a thousand
times more important and truer than the life she had led
since. She hadn't felt anything for twelve years. She hadn't
even tried.

She had seen the needle marks on Sam Moody's arm and
the cuts on his arms. Those Japanese knives in his room that
he swore were dull-edged antiques were sharp enough to do
damage. Meredith had been there herself. She understood
exactly what Sam was doing. Trying to feel something, anything at all. She would be a far superior tutor in such matters
than she was in algebra. She knew all the angles. The one
thing she knew for certain was that when you were in pain
you knew you were alive, if being alive was what you
wanted. If, when you came right down to it, it was of any
worth at all.

* * *

SAM WENT MISSING IN OCTOBER. HE'D DONE IT BEFORE, but for only a night or two, giving them a good scare before dragging himself home from Bridgeport, hungover, sick from drugs, ready with some cock-and-bull story not even he expected his father and Cynthia to believe. But this time was different. Four nights passed, and then five. There was something sorrowful in the air, a shock wave of regret. John Moody sat in the living room every night, but Sam didn't appear. It got so that John would have been happy to see a sheriff's car pull up, lights flashing. Yet John believed that a call to the police could easily create more trouble, so a private investigator was hired. Sam had been seen in Bridgeport, running with a crowd of drugged-out friends, but he was difficult to pin down, and his snarky little circle didn't tend to be helpful; even when they were paid off, they gave false information. Sam was elusive; he knew how to get lost.

On the sixth night of his disappearance, Meredith went to look for him herself. She rattled down the trash-strewn streets of the projects where Sam was quite well-known. People said, *Sure, Sam, that crazy dude,* but offered nothing more. Meredith noticed very few women hanging out on stoops and in doorways; only young men. Men in trouble, men worn out, men who had nothing more to lose. Meredith drove past the bus station, looking for teenagers, and parked her car outside a seedy liquor store. She showed a photograph of Sam to everyone who went in the store, but no one could help. "Give it up," some nice older woman told her. "He'll come home when he's good and ready."

When Meredith got back to the house, John Moody was in the living room, still waiting.

"I think it's hopeless," he said.

"Not quite yet. Maybe he's staying with a friend."

"I don't mean Sam. I mean me as a parent."

Meredith sat on the couch. She was wearing her navy blue coat because there'd been a chill in the air. She didn't take it off.

"I must have done something wrong in a previous life," John Moody said.

Meredith laughed. "This isn't about you being punished. It's not about you at all. It's about Sam."

"But I am being punished. That's become clear to me. That's what I believe."

Meredith wished she had come in through the kitchen and had managed to avoid John. She felt guilty that she'd never let on how she'd come here in the first place, that she'd known who John Moody was before she ever arrived at this house. She knew exactly what type he was: a desperate man willing to ask a psychic for help.

"I don't think I believe in anything," Meredith said.

"How nice for you," John said. "If you don't believe in anything, nothing can let you down. Unfortunately, I believe we all pay for our mistakes. We burn for our sins."

John Moody excused himself and went upstairs. It was unseemly for him to be talking to a babysitter about such things. Bone close, blood close, close as sorrow moved you. Anyway, Sam clearly wasn't coming home; it wasn't even night anymore. The sky was brightening, and in the Glass Slipper light spilled down from above.

Meredith had almost told John Moody the truth: *I see her, too. I followed her here. I think if I believe in anything, I believe in ghosts.* Instead, she said nothing; as always, she simply did her job. When she found ashes, she swept them into the dustpan. Birds in the house were caught and set free. Broken china was tossed in with the trash. Shadows were overlooked. But Sam — how did they overlook his absence?

"I'm sure he'll be back by tonight," Blanca had vowed for six, and then seven, and then eight days in a row.

They had to go on about their lives, didn't they? The world didn't stop because one person was missing, whether or not they wanted it to. Real life continued more or less unchanged. Newspapers were delivered, dinners served, chores done. One afternoon Meredith drove Blanca to the library to take out books for a report on religions of the world. While there, Meredith noticed a sign announcing a lecture at the end of the month: "The Physics of Ghosts." A Yale professor and a graduate student would be debating the "reality" of the next dimension.

Blanca came up behind Meredith. "My father says that sort of thing is crap."

"Does he?"

Meredith carried half the books once they were checked out and Blanca the other half. Blanca seemed to be favoring Buddhism. She was a believer, although she didn't quite know in what. Her bookaholism was growing. She was always ducking into the bookstore, spending too much time at the library. Beneath her bed she had a cache of books Cynthia would never have approved of, all sorts of things a girl her age was not supposed to read, from Salinger to Erica Jong.

"My father says psychic phenomena is nonsense," Blanca amended. "I added the *crap*."

"Lovely vocabulary, Bee."

"Thank you ever so much."

On the drive home, as they were rounding a corner, chatting about what their favorite section of the library was — fiction for Blanca, history and biography for Meredith — and listening to a country-and-western station, they saw Sam. They had, for a few brief moments, actually forgotten he was missing. Libraries and an armful of books could do that to a person. And even when they spotted him, Sam seemed like a ghost himself, pale, wavery, an image they might have conjured. But no, it was truly Sam. He was outside the market drawing on the sidewalk. A small crowd had gathered around to watch. There was color everywhere. It looked like blood and blue feathers and white bones. But it was only chalk and concrete.

"Why are all those people around him?" Blanca asked.

Meredith pulled the car over and opened her door. "Stay here."

Meredith walked toward the crowd. People were laughing as though they were watching a circus act. Maybe it was amusing if you didn't know him: a stoned-out kid in filthy clothes scribbling madly, drenched in colors.

Sam had covered nearly an entire block with his chalk drawings. He'd done this in his room, illustrating every wall with glow-in-the-dark paint; now he seemed intent on covering the rest of the world, or at least this part of it. Saturating everything in a vision of his own. It was not a world anyone would choose to enter of his own free will. These were nightmares, dead bodies, dead birds, skeleton men carrying two-bladed axes, winged figures without faces flying above burning buildings. Sam's arms and face were turquoise and scarlet and black.

Meredith made her way to the front of the crowd. Sam was so busy he didn't even notice her. She crouched down beside him. He glanced up and didn't seem surprised in the least to see her.

"Hey," he said without stopping work. Sam's eyes were all pupil; he was seeing what others could not, would not, want to see. He'd been taking psychedelic drugs for several days. He would never remember how he'd gotten back to town. Maybe he flew. Maybe that was it. He was in a tunnel in Bridgeport and he simply willed himself back to his hometown.

"How long have you been doing this?" Meredith asked.

An entire block's worth. His hands, she saw now, were bleeding. Halfway between the dry cleaner and the market there was a chalk drawing of a woman in a white dress. Her hair was red.

"I started around midnight. I was on my way home, and it just came to me. All in one piece. I didn't even have to think."

He'd been at it for fifteen hours, all through the night and morning, into the afternoon.

The market manager came out and tried to disperse the crowd. "The police are on their way," he shouted to Sam. "I'm not kidding. This is private property."

"Actually, the sidewalk belongs to everyone, asshole." Sam didn't stop drawing for an instant.

"Why don't we go home now?" Meredith suggested.

She glanced toward the parked VW. There was Blanca, opening the door so she could watch. The red-haired woman seemed to rise from the concrete. She was translucent; Meredith could look right through her to a parked minivan.

"Come on." Meredith reached for Sam.

"Fuck it, Merrie! I'm busy!" Sam snapped his arm back. His eyes were bright. "Don't you see I'm doing something! For once! Really look at me!"

No one had called her Merrie for years. She felt as though everything she'd ever done was a mistake; she'd never been able to save anyone and she couldn't seem to do it now. All at once she knew that was why she was here. The true answer to Cynthia's question. How could an educated, attractive young woman such as herself accept this thankless task? Because she couldn't let Sam sink.

There was a siren somewhere. People in the crowd were jeering. Someone said something about Satan at work. Those nightmare figures. The skeletons with the double-bladed axes. The woman with blood instead of hair.

"Here's my plan," Meredith said. "We'll leave this here for people to enjoy and we'll get some supper and talk things over. Blanca's in the car waiting. She's missed you, Sam."

"There is no fucking *we*." Sam continued to work. His knuckles were bleeding, but blood meant nothing to him. *"We'll leave this here and go back home to prison,"* he said in a singsong, mocking Meredith. Instantly his fury returned. "This is *me*. Only me!"

"I want to hear about it. I want to talk about it." The

damned sirens were almost on top of them. "Come on, Sam." The one thing Meredith didn't want was for them to have to deal with the police. Was she an enabler? Then so be it. She truly believed no good would come of a drug test or a jail term. Not for Sam. He would drown in the authorities' good intentions. "We have to go now."

"You might think I'm crazy, but I can see what a person thinks in his eyes." Sam swept his hands out over the sidewalk. The mass of color, the crimson, the ghosts. "I can put the inside outside. This is me on the sidewalk. Nobody ever sees me."

Blanca had left the parked car and was close by. She'd overheard her brother; her face looked so solemn she didn't seem like a child anymore.

"Go back and wait for us, Bee," Meredith told her. "Call your father at work."

Blanca didn't listen. She was a good girl who never disobeyed, but she disobeyed now. She went to Sam and knelt beside him. A film of blue chalk dusted the cuffs of her coat. "I know it's you."

Sam stopped coloring. He was breathing hard.

"I see you," Blanca said.

Sam started to cry. He couldn't remember the last time he'd wept. It hurt, like little daggers inside his eyes. He was exhausted; he'd been there on the sidewalk since the middle of the night, thinking and thinking, making his world appear, and now his hands were scraped raw.

"Come home with me," Blanca said.

"I don't think I can," Sam said.

"We're begging you," Meredith said.

"Never beg anyone, Merrie. It's beneath you. You have more character than that."

Two police cars and an ambulance had pulled into the parking lot of the market. The manager was waving his arms around, signaling the authorities. Sam remembered the feeling he was having now. He'd had it before, a long time ago. The knives against his legs, the pins in his fingers, the bones of his squirrel, the way his heart had broken. Everything was in pieces. He'd put the pearls his mother had given him in the cardboard box, and he hadn't looked at them since.

Two officers approached and tried to speak to Sam.

"Don't fucking talk to me, man. I'm busy. Can't anyone see that? Why don't you open your eyes? That's all it would take."

When the officers reached for him, Sam scooted out of their grasp. When they grabbed him, he hit anything he could connect with. They got him down on the sidewalk then. Chalk dust flew everywhere. Blanca covered her ears. The way Sam screamed was too terrible to hear, as though he would die if he didn't finish his drawings. His world would not be complete and then he would fade away into nothingness. Ashes. Soot. Broken china. Hollow bird bones. Ghostlight.

Meredith held Blanca when the police dragged Sam through the parking lot. Blanca was calling for her brother, but no one heard her. The crowd was still there, and some people applauded. Someone must have pointed Meredith and Blanca out to the police, because an officer from the second car came over and asked for Sam's full name and address and telephone number.

"Don't tell them anything!" Blanca said. She tried to get away and run to the ambulance, but Meredith held her back.

"Can we go with him?" Meredith asked the officer. "This is his sister."

"Let me just take down all the information we need for the files," the officer said. "Everyone calm down."

So they did. They had no choice. Blanca cried quietly and hid her face in Meredith's coat. The ambulance pulled away while Meredith was reciting their address. *Glass House. Last House. Lost House.* They could see him soon enough at the hospital, the officer assured Meredith, where he would be held for observation and drug testing. There were official procedures. Weren't there always? They had to give the situation some time. Already, the manager of the market was hosing off the sidewalk.

"Look what they're doing!" Blanca cried. "He's disappearing."

It was amazing how many colors there were, all running into the gutter in a stream: a dozen shades of blue, twenty different reds, and all that black soot, like a nightmare given form, the insides of a heart, destroyed so easily, done away with before anyone could stop the damage, or salvage what was lost, or even try to save him.

THE COURT ORDERED THAT SAM UNDERGO REHAB IN THE hospital for three weeks if the drug charges against him were to be dropped. Luckily, he'd had only a small amount of hashish in tinfoil stuck in his pocket. During this time he refused all visitors, requesting only that his sister come to see him. John Moody forbade this. There was no reason for a ten-year-old girl to be subjected to drug rehab. But the children's father could construct whatever rules he wanted; Blanca still managed to get over to the hospital every day. It was Meredith who discovered this; she'd come to retrieve Blanca from dance school and noticed that while all the other girls were piling out of the front door, Blanca was approaching from the road. The next day, after dropping Blanca at the library, Meredith waited in her car, parked behind a hedge of pines. Blanca left the library after fifteen minutes and Meredith drove after her, following at a distance as Blanca walked to the hospital. When she came out a while later, Meredith honked the horn. Blanca got into the VW. No excuses. Nothing. She looked straight ahead.

"Did you get to see him?" Meredith said.

"I write notes and he answers. One of the nurses takes mine in and then brings me his."

"What does he write?"

"I write. He makes pictures."

Meredith thought this over.

"I can just drive you here and then we don't have to pretend you're at lessons or at the library."

"Really?" Blanca was such a good girl that all the lying she'd been doing had taken a toll. Her hair seemed dull and stringy and her face had broken out.

"Really."

On the day Sam came home, they made a chocolate cake

to celebrate. He had to still like chocolate; he couldn't be that changed. Cynthia went and got ice cream and when Blanca and Meredith seemed surprised, she said, "I don't wish bad things for Sam, you know. I wish him well."

During this time, whenever the children's grandmother called and Cynthia answered, Diana Moody hung up. Diana wanted to speak with Meredith.

"Cynthia knows you're hanging up on her," Meredith told Diana. Diana had recently had a stroke, and she was upset that she couldn't come to help out. She thought of Meredith as her alter ego, the one person who would tell her the truth.

"I didn't like Sam when he was a little child," Diana admitted one day when she phoned. "I thought he was rude, but he was simply honest. He didn't keep anything inside."

"He's still the same," Meredith said.

"That's why he hurts," Diana Moody said. "There's no barrier to stop the pain."

John Moody was the one to go and get him. Sam glared as his father signed him out and he was given his wallet and packet of chalk. "Thank you and fuck you all," Sam said to the nurses.

"That's enough," John Moody told him.

"I'll bet this was for my own good," Sam said.

"I don't want to play games with you." John felt so old he couldn't believe he'd ever been a young man out for a good time, looking for a party, thinking his whole life was ahead of him.

"Actually, I can't remember you ever playing a single game with me. No wonder I can't play baseball. Or basketball. Or tennis. Or fucking horseshoes for that matter. Thanks, Dad."

"You want to blame me for your lack of athletic ability?"

They hadn't even left the ward and here they were, already.

"What's the point?" Sam said. "You don't understand me any more than you ever understood my mother."

"Don't you dare mention her," John said.

"Fuck you. She's my mother. She was nothing to you. I'll mention her all I want. If I want to say one word for the rest of my life and it's her name, I will. So don't push me."

They didn't speak again on the ride home. In the driveway, they got out, slammed the doors shut, then tried their best to avoid each other on the way inside. Sam didn't bother going into the kitchen, though they called to him, and Blanca chased after him.

"Thanks but no thanks, Peapod," he said to his sister when she told him about the cake. "You have it."

Things turned really bad two days after he'd come home. Forty-eight hours and he was up on the roof again, high as could be. He'd only been to the corner store and for a long walk, and somehow he'd managed to score. It was early morning, and John Moody was headed out to work when he realized what was going on. He was in the driveway and he felt a chill. He stopped and put one hand up to shade his eyes. He felt as though he were watching a film: a man's son climbs onto the glass roof and stands there, waiting for the next gust of wind. Does the man run and rescue him? Does he stand there, so incapacitated he cannot move? Or does he climb up alongside the boy and make the leap himself?

Going to the tearoom on Twenty-third Street had done no good. That was just a foolish last-gasp attempt to be free of Arlie. It wasn't just soot and voices and dishes and ashes. He truly saw her. In the morning, walking down the hall; at dusk, beside the boxwoods. Other men might have convinced themselves all they were seeing were shadows, only a grid of light, but John knew better. It was her. She was young, the way she'd been when they first met, when he'd gotten so lost he couldn't find his way. He saw her now, as a matter of fact, up on the roof, in the reflection of a cloud, in the movement of the wind. The white dress, the long red hair. He spied her from the corner of his eye, just the shape of her, and every time he saw her he knew: he hadn't done right by her.

And now. Once again. What was the right thing in this situation? Call the police to rescue his son? Or would that make matters worse? He wished he could ask Arlyn's advice. There on his perch on the roof, Sam seemed to be nodding off; his eyes were closed. The drugs must bring him peace, John thought. For an instant that poor boy could stop thinking, stop being himself. He could float there, above them all.

Meredith ran outside in her nightgown. She'd spied Sam through the glass ceiling of the second-floor hallway. She couldn't remember having run so fast before, down the stairs, onto the grass.

"Go after him," she said to John Moody, who seemed to be paralyzed, as always. "Go up to the roof and talk him down."

John wished he had a net, or another lifetime, or a different pair of eyes. More than anything, he wished he could find a way to go back in time. *One, he had been lost since the day he made a wrong turn. Two, he had married the wrong woman, although which one had been more of a mistake he couldn't say. Three, he was a man of reason who never expected to have to deal with such things.* John Moody was overwhelmed. He wished he could stretch out beneath the boxwoods and breathe in their spicy scent and never have to think or talk or do anything again.

"Are you just going to stand here and watch him fall?"

Wasn't it John who was falling? When he dreamed, he was in a tree or on the top of one of his own buildings; he dreamed he was tumbling down and yet there were stars rushing at him. At night, when he opened his eyes, he knew Arlie was close by. Behind the curtains, on the window ledge, beside him in bed, her head on the pillow. What had once felt like a curse had become a comfort. He'd wanted to get rid of her, yet now he found himself searching her out. *Arlie?* he whispered late at night, while he sat in the kitchen, while Cynthia was asleep in their bed. *Are you there?*

"Good lord!" Meredith said, disgusted. "Why can't you ever do anything to help him!" Meredith raced back into the house, then took the flights of stairs to the attic door. She climbed through so fast she was dizzy. Her heart hurt. She pushed the door slowly so she wouldn't accidentally knock Sam off the roof. "Knock knock," she said. She saw his sneaker a fair distance off, so she popped the door open the rest of the way.

"It's not a suicide attempt," Sam said. "So don't start with that crap, Merrie. I'm not an idiot."

Meredith crept out onto the glass roof. Her nightgown made it difficult. She hoped she wouldn't fall. God, it would be a horrible obituary if she did. *Unmarried, overeducated nanny slips to death and breaks every bone in her body. Lost woman found in pieces. She could never save anyone, least of all herself.*

"There are reasons to live, you know."

"Jesus, the next thing I know you'll be getting me a fucking puppy. You'll tell me everything will be fine if we just clap our hands and believe."

Sam looked shaky. He was wearing jeans and a jacket and he was sweating. He'd been more unstable than ever since he got home; he moved like a sleepwalker, unsteady on his feet. He was done ingesting any kind of garbage he could get his hands on. Psychedelics took him to a place he didn't want to be. He had his own nightmares; he didn't need any assistance with expanding his mind. He wanted to close his mind down, give it a rest. It was heroin only from now on. The sleep without dreams. Everything he needed, wanted, had to have. He kept his works in his night-table drawer; the needle and strap and spoon neatly rolled up in a piece of worn suede. It was what gave him a reason to live, actually. Wake, live, move — all of it revolved around getting high.

"Actually, that's not a bad idea. I think you should have a pet."

"Don't even think about it."

"Unconditional love," Meredith suggested.

"Doesn't exist. And why are we even having this conversation? I wanted fresh air. Not the air that bastard breathes and exhales."

They looked down on John Moody.

"He means well," Meredith said.

Sam spat out a laugh. It was an unremarkable day for most people in their town, and here he was, deciding whether or not he should attempt to fly.

"I come from another race of people entirely," Sam said.

He glanced at Meredith, gauging her reaction.

"Me too."

Sam rolled his eyes. "No, you don't."

"Living is better than the alternative, Sam. I swear on my life."

"In all honesty, what's that worth? A nanny's salary and a used VW?"

"Someone with a terminal disease would want to shake you. They'd trade with you in a second, for just another day, a week, a year. You're wasting what you've got."

"Maybe I could fly," Sam said more to himself than to Meredith. "It's a possibility. You can't know if you don't try."

"Maybe *I* could."

"Will you stop that? Don't repeat every damn thing I say. Don't think you're like me. Why don't you just call the police and leave me alone?"

"I happen to love you. I didn't want to or think I could, but I do."

"Well, if you do, there's something seriously wrong with you," Sam said.

They both laughed and the laughter drifted down to

John. When he heard them, John Moody didn't know if he was relieved or angry. Laughing on the roof while he was sweating down here, late for a meeting, trapped in a big mess of a life that he could have avoided if he'd never stopped to ask for directions. He never did that now. He wouldn't even think of slowing down. He'd circle around for hours in his car rather than pull into a gas station and ask for help. It wasn't pride that stopped him, it was fear. Look where a wrong turn had led him. He simply couldn't risk it again.

Often, the life he might have had came to him, the life he was supposed to have before he made a wrong turn. There were two well-behaved children who waited for him at the door when he arrived home from work and a perfectly trained German shepherd dog who went running with him in the evenings. Or it was Paris, and he lived alone in a vast apartment. Or it was Florida, somewhere on a golf course, someplace quiet, not even the sound of birds. But in all these places, there was always a woman in a white dress. She was so young, little more than a girl. She must have put a spell on him; that's how the whole thing began. He wasn't the sort of person who would walk into a stranger's house, sleep on her couch, find her naked in the kitchen, be willing to do anything in order to have her. He'd been with only three other girls before Arlie, one in high school, two in college; they'd been furtive encounters, less sexually exciting than anxiety provoking, with the girl saying no while John begged until she finally relented and they did the deed.

It was the way Arlie had given herself to him that stayed with him. A perfect instant in time. His footsteps in the kitchen. Arlie turning to him from the sink. Lost and then found. Discovered in some deep way. He was stuck there, he realized that now; that young girl with red hair sifted through his reality forevermore. Now, for instance, he'd been so intent in his thoughts that when he looked up he was surprised to find that Meredith and Sam were no longer on the roof. It was as though they had flown away when he wasn't looking.

"My father never cared about me," Sam said.

They had gone downstairs to the kitchen, where Meredith was fixing tea, hoping to sneak some food into Sam. She made toast, but Sam waved it away. He was watching out the window. John Moody was staring at the lawn.

"Maybe I jumped and he just doesn't know it," Sam said. "Maybe he'll stumble over my body."

"Eat this toast," Meredith said.

"Without peanut butter?"

Merrie got the peanut butter from the cabinet.

"You can't see love," she said.

"Bullshit." Sam opened the peanut-butter jar. He went through a period when he was younger when he would eat only peanut butter and jelly. "You definitely can."

"Really?" Meredith said. "Show me."

Sam grinned and tore his toast apart, offering her half. Merrie sat down beside him at the counter and ate toast and drank tea. They decided to leave the dishes for Cynthia to wash.

"Thanks," Meredith said even though she hated peanut butter. "You were right."

Sam grinned. "Finally right about something."

*　　*　　*

BLANCA AND MEREDITH WERE WALKING ALONG MAIN
Street on the way to the bookstore, when they came upon
the pet store. Snow's Pets. Meredith had never noticed the
shop before. Behind the glass were basset-hound puppies.

"I can't believe how cute they are." Blanca tapped on the
glass and one of the baby basset hounds came over and
licked the glass. "Oooh," Blanca crooned. "This one. Sam
would love it."

"Sam doesn't want a puppy," Meredith informed her
charge.

"Look at its ears! They're so long it's tripping over them."

They decided to go in, just to look. The bell rang over the
door, and the man cleaning out fish tanks looked up. George
Snow. He'd opened the shop three years ago, knowing that
sooner or later this would happen. He had promised Arlie
he'd never search the child out, although he'd gone to several dance recitals, seated in the back row; he'd gone to
many of her soccer games. He wondered sometimes if he'd
been wrong to make a promise like that, but Arlie had held
on to his hand until he'd sworn it.

"Shout if you need help."

"I don't think we will," Meredith called back.

"We need help!" Blanca called at the very same time.

George Snow laughed and came over to look at the puppies with them. He couldn't believe how tall Blanca was; she
had a dancer's posture and she wasn't shy.

"I'm taking the little one in the corner," George told

them. "The runt of the litter. I used to have a collie, but he died of old age. So I'm ready for a pup."

"I love your puppy," Blanca said seriously. "But I love this one more." The silly one that had licked the plate-glass window.

"Which one don't you love?" Meredith wanted to know.

"I'll give you a discount," George Snow said. "Actually, you can just take him. I'll never be able to sell all these puppies."

Meredith noticed the resemblance between Blanca and the pet-shop owner. Brown-eyed blonds with narrow faces and long eyelashes.

"Are you related to the Moodys?" she asked. "We really couldn't take something like this without paying."

"Just trying to find this pup the best home possible." George lifted up the puppy and placed it in Blanca's arms.

"His name is Dusty," Blanca said, and then, embarrassed to have claimed the puppy as though it were her own, she added, "But Sam should pick his name."

"No. Dusty's a great name," George Snow said. "I think I'll call mine Rusty." Mr. Snow put together a package of dog food and bowls along with a collar and a leash. "If you want some obedience lessons, you can bring him back and I'll help you train him."

"Your mom is going to have a fit," Meredith told Blanca.

"Stepmom," George Snow said. "I knew the family way back when," he added when Meredith gave him a look.

"I can't believe I let you do this," Meredith said on the way home.

"You didn't let me. I'm old enough to make some decisions."

"Uh-huh. Don't blame me if they won't let you keep him."

"You're kidding, right?" Cynthia said when they walked through the back door.

"He's for Sam," Blanca said, kissing the basset hound on the nose.

"Unconditional love," Meredith added.

"Is that the kind of love that will make the poop in the yard disappear?" Cynthia asked. "Because I won't have anything to do with this creature. You can quote me on that."

Blanca and Meredith carried Dusty up to Sam's room. They knocked on his door. Blanca hid behind Meredith, holding on to the puppy. Sam opened the door a crack. The smell from inside was dreadful, the stink of old laundry and cigarettes and rotting food.

"Whatever you're selling, I'm not buying." Sam's words were slurred. He'd recently gotten off, and his mouth was caked with dried saliva. It was getting worse. They all knew that. All he wanted was that dreamless sleep.

"Ta-da," Blanca said as she jumped before her brother with Dusty in her arms.

"You actually got a puppy? I told you explicitly — no fucking puppies. I can't be responsible for that thing. You know me. I'd leave it somewhere and it would die of starvation or something."

"His name is Dusty," Blanca said. "I thought you'd love him."

"You go on and love him," Sam told her. "I'm not genetically inclined."

Meredith and Blanca took the puppy back down to the

kitchen. "We can get him something else," Blanca said. "We'll find the right pet."

The puppy raced over to Cynthia, who was cooking dinner at the stove. He stepped on his ears and tripped.

"Oh, you poor thing." Cynthia bent down and picked up Dusty; she fed him a bit of hamburger meat from her fingers.

"Sam doesn't want him." Blanca was gathering together the puppy food and the dog dishes. "We have to take him back to the store."

"You can't take him back!" And then, as though startled by her own response, Cynthia added, "It's not humane! He's used to us now."

"I thought you didn't want him," Meredith said.

"I don't," Cynthia said firmly. "But he's not going back to some wretched pet shop where he's treated miserably."

"It wasn't wretched," Blanca insisted. "Mr. Snow is nice. He said he would train Dusty for free if we wanted him to."

"Really? Mr. Snow said that? Well, I had Newfoundlands when I was growing up," Cynthia said. "I'm perfectly capable of training one little basset hound all by my lonesome."

"What about the poop in the yard and on the rugs?" Meredith reminded her.

"Here's your water, Dusty," Cynthia said, setting down a dish in the corner, and that was that. No more discussion.

"We have to get Sam something else," Blanca kept saying all through the week. "Something that suits him." Blanca took this quest seriously. "Something he'll love."

Meredith went back to the pet shop one afternoon while Blanca was at school and Sam was up in his room, sleeping.

She was there to look around; maybe pick up a chew toy for the puppy, who was gnawing on the legs of the kitchen table.

"Hey there," George Snow said when she came into the shop. "How's Dusty?"

He'd sold all the other puppies except for the one he'd kept; that pup was sleeping in a box behind the dog-food display.

"Dusty's fine when he's not pooping or chewing on something," Meredith said. "Looks like Rusty is, too."

"Blanca's not with you?"

Meredith noticed that Mr. Snow's brow furrowed exactly the way Blanca's did when she was worried, an occurrence that happened far too often for a ten-year-old girl.

"Do you have some connection to Blanca?" Meredith asked. "Is that why you gave her the puppy?"

"I was a friend of her mother. Friend of the family. Did you need more dog food?"

"I need a pet for Blanca's brother. He's not a fan of puppies."

"Sam."

"Yes. Sam."

"He's not your average boy," George said. "His mother used to tell a story about people in Connecticut who could fly when need be. Maybe he's one of them. They grew wings when they had to escape. When the ship was going down or the house was on fire."

"We're pretty much at that stage," Meredith said.

George led her into the back room, where there was a makeshift kitchen and a lunch table. On a perch in the corner there was a small parrot. The bird was green with ultramarine and red and orange streaks.

"Get out," the parrot said to them.

Meredith laughed. He sounded exactly like Sam.

"I swear I didn't teach him that. He's a foundling. Someone left him on the doorstep in a box. I guess they couldn't keep him anymore. I call him Connie, short for Connecticut."

"Cynthia would kill me."

"The stepmother. I knew her. A runner. Lived next door."

"She switched to tennis. But I think she's giving that up, too."

"She won't even notice the parrot. You don't have to walk it or throw a ball for it." George gave the bird a peanut. "Connie's only a baby. Winston Churchill's parrot lived for a hundred years. This is a pet that won't up and die on Sam and disappoint him, like everything else has." George Snow cleared his throat; he wasn't comfortable having a serious conversation with a stranger. "I heard about what happened outside the market."

"Well, that." Meredith wasn't about to discuss Sam with this man. "I can't afford a parrot. And if you know the family then you know John Moody would never pay for one, let alone approve of it."

"Well, Connie's free."

Meredith studied the angles of Mr. Snow's face. He seemed so familiar, so kind. "Are you the kind of friend of her mother's that Blanca should know about?"

"Well, she does know about me. I'm the pet-store man."

Meredith packed the parrot and all of its belongings into her VW. The foul-tempered creature muttered and squawked all the way home. She felt like turning around and bringing the bird back to the shop, but she headed home. She thought about how easygoing Blanca was, how different from Sam and John Moody. A kindhearted girl who thought about others and worried too much.

"You cannot bring this thing into the house," Cynthia said when Meredith carried in the perch and the nighttime cage and the sacks of food and the cuttlebones and the bells. "This time I mean it. Birds are filthy."

"Get out," the parrot said.

"Oh, nice. Why not a vulture?" Cynthia was fixing chicken for dinner, and the naked uncooked bird sat in a glass dish atop the stove. The little basset hound was at Cynthia's feet. He trotted over to sniff the birdcage. "Stay away from that thing, Dusty!"

"Maybe a pet will snap Sam out of his own world and back into ours."

"Was he ever in ours?"

"Let's try. Let's just fucking try something before we lose him completely."

The women stared at each other. Dusty was wagging not just his tail but his whole body.

Cynthia nodded. "I'm sure in no time Sam will teach it to call me a murderess, but maybe that will give him some pleasure." She was stunned by what had just happened between herself and Meredith. "I cannot believe you said 'fucking' to me. Like it's all my fault."

Cynthia was worn down by everything. She wasn't much like the woman George Snow remembered. She'd completely given up tennis. The most she could manage was a long walk in the morning with Dusty. Sometimes she started crying for reasons she wasn't clear on.

"It is not your fault," Meredith said.

"Fine," Cynthia said. "One week. If that thing is flying around my house and pooping, he's gone." She went back to adding onions and mushrooms to her chicken dish. "I do have a heart, you know."

"No one ever said you didn't," Meredith said.

"I know you don't like me. You take their side. But I wasn't so horrible. I didn't know she was dying when John and I got involved. He didn't tell me until two months after she'd gotten the diagnosis. And then he cried and I felt sorry for him. So I deserve to have to deal with parrots and drugs, I guess. It's payback. And by the way, Sam disappeared this morning and I have no idea where he is. I can damn well guess, unfortunately."

When Blanca got home, she was thrilled with the parrot.

"It's perfect!" she said, even though the bird had tried to bite her as soon as she reached out her hand. "Sam will love him."

They could all guess that if Sam was out of his room, he'd gone to New York. He owed people money in Bridgeport, and the last time he'd gone there he'd come back bloodied. He stole from purses, piggy banks, and coat pockets and went to New York. This time he took the silver serving spoons from Cynthia's first marriage.

By the time Sam arrived home via taxi, Blanca was already in bed. It was long after midnight. Meredith was sitting on the stairs in her nightgown. Sam's eyes were half closed as he stumbled in. He was deep in the land of no dreaming. Right in the center of the deep, dark nothingness.

"Hey," he said as though Meredith sitting on the stairs at two in the morning was perfectly natural. "What's up?"

"Blanca and I got you something. She tried to wait up for you."

Sam stank of sweat and his coloring was bad. He went around Meredith and continued up the stairs.

"Did you want to tell me where you were?" Meredith said, following him.

"Do you think I'd tell you the truth?" Sam said.

They had reached Sam's door.

"If you don't love your gift, I can take it back."

"I'll hate it whatever it is. We both know that."

"I'm not so sure."

Sam opened the door to his room and there was the parrot on its perch.

"Holy shit," Sam said.

"The pet-store owner told me to tell you he's from an old Connecticut race that can fly."

"Did he?"

"George Snow," Meredith said.

"A man with feelings, the poor idiot. I remember him. Cried his eyes out. Do you think he was in love with my mother?"

"I don't know." Actually, she was sure of it.

Sam approached the parrot and offered his arm. The parrot eyed him, then moved sideways along the perch onto Sam's arm.

"He's heavy," Sam said in wonder. "Say something to Meredith," he told the parrot.

"Get out," the parrot said.

Sam threw his head back and laughed.

"I love him," Sam said. "I truly do."

Meredith could feel something inside her breaking apart.

"Does he say more? Can I teach him to say whatever I want him to?"

"You can try. I have no idea what his vocabulary might be. He was a foundling. George named him Connie."

"Does the murderess know about this?"

"Cynthia has a heart," Meredith said. "Somewhere in there."

"What about the old bastard?"

"Sam," Meredith warned. "Cynthia will talk your dad into it. If you want to keep it."

Sam sat on the bed and stared at the parrot.

"What you're doing is too dangerous, Sam. If you keep on with all these drugs I'm going to switch to the other side. I'll tell them to send you back to rehab."

"It's done. I swear it." Sam meant it at that moment. But he'd meant it many times before. This much was the truth: "I can't afford it anyway. I'm broke and it's such a waste of money."

"Just so we both understand: the parrot is a bribe."

Sam turned to her and grinned. "The best bribe ever." The usual whirring inside Sam's head had slowed down and he could feel something straight on. It was almost like happiness, if only it wasn't so slurred. It was damn close. Close enough.

Sam allowed Meredith to hug him. "Enough," he told her, pushing her away when she made some sappy comment about what a great kid he was. "Let's not go overboard."

Meredith went downstairs to make herself a cup of tea. She stopped when she saw John Moody stationed in the living room. At first she thought Cynthia had told him about the parrot, and that he was waiting up to give Meredith a piece of his mind, maybe even fire her, but his attentions were elsewhere. There was the woman in the white dress sitting across from him. Meredith had to concentrate and block out everything else in order to see her, but she was there. A faint haze, fine as soot.

Meredith sank down on the last stair and peered under the banister. John Moody was crying, no noise, just his hands over his crumpled face. It was the hour when the grass outside looked silver and time moved so slowly it seemed to stop. A second lasted forever, and then, just as quickly, was gone. John Moody's first wife was fading into the chair, like the edges of a cloud. Even her red hair was evaporating into nothingness. The entire room was washed out by darkness, shadow upon shadow, so that a person had to squint to see anything. There was only one bit of color, a dark blue feather on the floor, the color of the sky when it's broken in half and the core of the universe can be seen.

IF LOVE COULD TIE YOU TO A PLACE FROM WHICH YOU never wished to roam, then wouldn't it be sensible to suppose that after death it might also tie the atoms that made you to that very same place?

The younger physicist, Daniel Finch, a graduate student at Yale, posed this question to his audience of twelve semi-interested people in the reading room at the library. The brain itself functions because of electrical impulses. Who was to say such impulses ceased to exist at the time of death? And if they did not dissipate, wouldn't they remain in place at the time of death rather than travel with a lifeless body, nothing but a shell now that it was not animated by whatever one cared to call the force within us — the soul, the anima, or, more rationally, the web of neutrons and protons at the core of life.

The older physicist, Ellery Rosen, sighed heavily. He had seen excited young men believe in things before; the older one was, the more unattainable faith became.

"Actual proof that electrical impulses remain intact outside the body is nonexistent," Rosen said.

The two men were writing papers for the same journal. Their differences were so extreme one might think they were enemies, but in fact, Daniel had been Ellery Rosen's student; they had lunch together at least twice a week.

Professor Rosen began to cite studies that refuted Daniel's theory. It was rather dry material, statistics and the like, and right away they lost one of the twelve in the audience — Myra Broderick, who had to pick up her son at soccer practice.

"See you next week," Myra called to the librarians. The upcoming speaker was an astrologist who had published a book called *Stars in Your Eyes.* Everyone was looking forward to that event.

"Is there proof of God?" Finch asked. "Most of the tenets

of our culture and education are theoretical. Why do we need proof that a force animates the human being just because we have not yet correctly named it? And why do we assume this force doesn't endure after death?"

They lost another member of their audience, Henry Bellingham, whose wife signaled to him now that she'd found all the books and tapes she needed for that week. Good thing, because Henry didn't like the mention of God in what seemed to be a negative way.

"Well, tell me this," Rosen said as the hour ended. The two speakers each seemed far more interested in what the other had to say than their audience did. There was a good bit of rustling in seats. "Have you yourself ever directly experienced the sighting of a ghost — or energy beyond the confines of the human body?"

"Actually, no," Daniel Finch said. And then cheerfully: "At least not yet!"

There was a smattering of polite applause at the end of the lecture. The physicists packed up their briefcases; they were riding back together in Ellery Rosen's old Land Cruiser.

"I've experienced it." Meredith Weiss had come up to the podium and was standing beside Daniel Finch. Startled, he turned to her so quickly he nearly tripped off the raised platform. He hadn't even heard her approach.

"Be forewarned," Rosen whispered to his ex-student. "Kook alert."

"Why would a spirit be attached to a place?" Meredith asked. "If you even want to call it a spirit, but let's just use the term for convenience' sake. The place has changed. It's no longer the same place as when the person's energy impulses were there. Here's my theory: wouldn't it be more likely that time was the element a spirit would be attached to? That would mean a ghost is an entity that can't let go of what was and isn't anymore."

Daniel Finch was staring at Meredith as she spoke. She had extremely dark eyes, that was what he noticed first. She was about his age, give or take a year or two, but she seemed younger somehow. Her ponytail, that was probably it. Or the fact that she wore no makeup. She was nearly thirty, but she looked like the students he taught. Only much more serious. More beautiful. And that wasn't all; she was a woman with a theory. He couldn't believe his luck.

"Yes, yes, and next you'll insist that ghosts want ice cream and chocolate sauce I suppose," Ellery Rosen said. "Can we go?" he asked Daniel. "New Haven awaits."

"I could drive you back to New Haven, if you wanted to discuss this." Meredith was suddenly aware of how bold she might sound. She added, "Or not."

"Don't be bamboozled by her looks," Rosen said, thinking he was whispering again. "She could be hopping mad."

"I certainly am not." Meredith was wearing a plain wool coat and had a sensible striped scarf around her neck. She had recently taken up knitting and had found it soothed her nerves. "I was an art history major at Brown."

"I think I'll stay," Daniel Finch told Ellery Rosen.

Rosen clapped him on the back. "Idiot," he said warmly. He turned to Meredith. "He was my favorite student. Promise me you're not a lunatic."

She crossed her heart. "I swear."

"Well, I suppose, given the evening, any statement can be considered empirical evidence. Enjoy each other's electrical impulses."

When Ellery left, Daniel and Meredith found seats at the nearest table.

"So is this interest of yours personal?" Daniel asked.

Meredith's legs were so long their knees knocked against each other; they both had to make a conscious effort to sit back in their chairs so it wouldn't happen again.

"I think I'm living in a haunted house," Meredith said. Definitely a whisper. Daniel leaned in close.

"Any mental illness involved?"

"I beg your pardon?" Meredith's cheeks flushed red.

"I didn't mean you, necessarily. There are theories that upset, stressed-out people can create the same effects as a true haunting. Most poltergeist incidents are said to take place where there are angry or upset teenagers."

"Well, we have that, but the teenager in the household seems to have nothing to do with what's happening. I'm a nanny. I'm overqualified."

Daniel went on to explain the correlation between the living and the dead in a true haunting. The qualities most often noted in the living who experienced such contact were innocence, sorrow, or guilt. Meredith was nodding, listening to every word. She had the darkest eyes Daniel had ever seen.

"Is there someplace we can have coffee?" he asked.

"No. Everything closes at nine. Small town," Meredith explained.

The librarians, Daniel noticed, were staring.

"The library, too," Meredith said apologetically. "Nine p.m. is closing time. And this is the late evening. Usually it's six. I think we're wearing out our welcome."

They went out, saying good-bye to the librarians, pushing open the glass doors. There were only three cars in the parking lot, one of them Meredith's VW.

"I've experienced physical manifestations. Voice, dishes, and soot," Meredith confided.

"The signs of a specter." Daniel Finch nodded. "Some people say birds often accompany a spirit. I've just been reading about it. Swallows in the chimney. A starling suddenly caught in a room. The birds seem to be startled by the surge in electrical impulses."

"There are so many birds on the lawn in the morning I can't even see the grass some days."

"How did you come up with your time/specter theory?"

"Time/specter theory. I like that. Well, it's because every time I've seen her she's in a different place. I feel that she's stuck in time. She follows different people in the family around."

"Does she follow you?"

"Oh, no. Although I can see her. Mostly she seems to follow her husband."

"Love," Daniel said.

"Or the opposite of love." They had crossed the parking lot. Meredith unlocked the VW's door. "Shall I drive you to New Haven?"

"Actually, I'd like to see the house. If I could."

Driving there, they were quiet. Their breath fogged up

the windshield and they laughed about that, then fell silent. Daniel wished the ride would last forever. Meredith cut the headlights at the start of the drive so as not to disturb anyone in the family. They approached in the dark; the Glass Slipper appeared above the hedge of boxwoods like an iceberg. It was always such a shock to see, even to those who lived there.

"Wow," Daniel said. "Modern. Not what I expected."

He hadn't expected Meredith, either. Neither one wanted to leave the car. They were in a bubble. Yellow leaves fell through the dark night. The last few cabbage moths wandered from lamppost to lamppost.

"You expected some haunted gloomy hall? It's the Glass Slipper. It's famous. The owner is an architect, and his father was the architect who designed it. The birds I mentioned are always trying to fly right through it."

They got out and walked in the shadows of the boxwoods.

"How old was your ghost when she died?" Daniel said.

"Twenty-four or -five."

"Young."

They followed the slate path in the dark.

Meredith held on to Daniel Finch's coat sleeve so she wouldn't stumble, or so she murmured. Perhaps it was for another reason entirely. She felt drawn to Daniel in some weird, deep way. He was tall, with dark hair; he had a generous mouth and an easy way of carrying himself. When he listened, he truly listened. Meredith felt like a moth. Fluttering. Confused. It was a chilly night, with the possibility of frost. Daniel huddled close to Meredith, his heart racing.

"We should be quiet," Meredith whispered.

Daniel was having second thoughts. He was a theoretical

physicist, not a ghostbuster. What if his mentor had been right? If so, Daniel was here with a crazy woman and he didn't even have transportation of his own.

"Look down at the path," Meredith said.

On the slate was a ribbon of black soot, leading them on. They followed around to the patio. They had the urge to hold hands, but neither reached for the other. All the same, they were stepping into something together and they knew it; something more than pools of darkness in the crisp night. Anything could happen. Spirits summoned; spirits sent away. There was the faint echo of voices. Daniel felt his skin go cold at the sound. But it was nothing fantastic waiting for them, only the children of the family sitting at the patio table — a tall, skinny boy of seventeen who had a parrot perched on his shoulder, and a blond girl of eleven who had a copy of Edward Eager's *Magic by the Lake* in front of her. Actually, from a distance they looked quite charming. Until you noticed the boy's surly expression.

As soon as Meredith and Daniel stepped from the shadows, the girl went to Meredith and threw her arms around her.

"Sam said we had to get out of the house," Blanca said.

Lately, Sam was sleeping nearly all day. There were purple circles under his eyes. The more he slept, the darker they were. The family and Meredith no longer discussed his condition. Sam tried to keep his word about staying clean, but he never did. He was back at it. Meredith knew he was going through her purse, stealing more bits and pieces from the house. Candlesticks. A silver tea set. Whatever he could get his hands on. His one interest outside of procuring drugs was the parrot. He cut up oranges for the bird, bought fresh lettuce, made certain there was plenty of seed and biscuits; he spent hours trying to teach the bird a few choice curse words. *Fuck a duck* was the one Connie had recently learned to repeat.

"You have a date," Sam said as Meredith and Daniel approached. "Where'd you find him, on the side of the road?"

"At the library," Meredith said.

"Get out," the parrot said. "Fuck a duck."

"I was trying to teach him to say *Fuck you, Cynthia,* make it really personal and meaningful, but he simply won't do it."

"He just says *You,*" Blanca said.

Sam was studying Daniel. Six feet tall, shaggy hair, wearing an old overcoat, his briefcase in hand. A teacher type for certain.

"Dump this guy, Meredith. He's a nerd. Just look at him. Who the hell carries a briefcase around?"

"I'm a physicist." Daniel Finch sat down across the table from Sam. He could see how dilated the kid's eyes were. He noticed the scabs on Sam's face. Opiates were itchy.

"Yeah, well, why don't you tell me what our purpose on earth is if you're so fucking smart?"

"That's for the philosophers to figure out. I don't deal with the meaning of life, just the essence."

"Touché," Sam said. "Good one. Who needs meaning, right? Fuck meaning."

"Sam," Blanca said.

"Ef meaning. Is that better? We all know what it effing means, we just don't say it. That's the proper way to live in the world. Avoid truth at all costs."

Sam had lost a good deal of weight since the incident with

the chalk. He didn't seem like anyone's little boy anymore. He looked worn, and when he got ornery like this, bitter. Sometimes Meredith felt she could see the old man he would become in the way his face was settling. His hands shook when he was high and Meredith noticed they were shaking now.

"So are you going to fuck him now or later?" Sam asked her.

Blanca put her hands over her ears. "Stop saying that word!"

"Sorry, Peabee." Sometimes Sam forgot Blanca was only a kid. She seemed so old. He probably said too much in front of her. Showed her too much of what was inside him. "I'm on a talking jag," he apologized to one and all. "Don't listen to me."

"He said Cynthia might kill us," Blanca told Meredith. "That's why we had to get out of the house. That's why we're out here. She was a murderess who would kill us in our sleep."

"I meant she would kill us emotionally," Sam said. "Spiritually. She's already murdered me."

"That's not what you said," Blanca insisted. "You said she would come after me with a carving knife. That we might have to fly away."

"Well, she might!" Sam said. "You know we can't trust her."

"Sam!" Meredith said. No wonder poor Blanca always looked worried.

"I don't know what I said," Sam told his sister. "I was

rambling. It was just a what-if situation. Do you think I'd ever let someone get to you with a carving knife? I'd cut them in two first."

Blanca looked cheered. "Really?"

"Maybe in three parts."

"I'll get them to bed," Meredith told Daniel. "Don't disappear."

"Yes, my sister is an infant and I'm six," Sam said. "Put us to bed, nanny dear."

"It's chilly out here for Connie, did you ever think of that?" Meredith asked him.

Sam slipped the parrot into his coat pocket. "I thought you were used to the cold climate of Connecticut," he said to his pet.

While Meredith guided the kids inside, Daniel was considering her theory — that the deepest attachment of all was not to a person or a situation, but to a time. He was thinking about the way he couldn't stop looking at her.

"God, I'm sorry," Meredith said when she returned. She'd brought out a bottle of whiskey. She hadn't bothered with glasses. "I figure we need this. Sam's not what you think," she said after she took a swig. "He's a good boy, really. He's talented. He just got sidetracked by drugs."

"You sound like his mother," Daniel said.

"Well, I'm not."

"He needs rehab."

"He needs a lot of things," Meredith said tiredly. "He's been in rehab."

"Look." Daniel pointed above them. Ashes were falling

from above in a thin, fine line. They looked like snowflakes, only they were black. Maybe it was chimney soot or debris from a passing plane; maybe it was an odd weather disturbance, black sand picked up from some foreign shore now deposited on the lawn.

"What happened when he was six?" Daniel asked. "Sam mentioned something about that age."

Meredith took a drink and passed the bottle over. "His mother died."

"So that's how you came up with your theory. People get trapped in time, so spirits must get trapped, too?"

"No," Meredith said. "I came up with it when I realized I couldn't get past being sixteen."

At that moment Daniel didn't care if he ever went back to New Haven or if he ever finished his dissertation. This was the purest instant he had ever experienced; the way he felt inside right then. If he had to be trapped in a *forever* he would choose this very moment. The black night, the few yellow leaves still clinging to the bare trees, the beautiful dark-eyed woman drinking whiskey, the way she gazed at him, the way she made him feel.

"And that's a bad thing?"

"It is for me. I ruined someone's life."

"I don't believe that."

"You don't know me. I used to be a swimmer, now I'm terrified of pools. I can't get past the bad thing that happened."

"So you're stuck in time. Like your ghost."

"She's not mine." Meredith took the bottle of whiskey and drank deeply. "But we're alike. Unable to move on."

Daniel Finch thought it over. He felt pierced by desire. He was utterly lost and he simply didn't care.

"Break down the time you're stuck in." Matter destroyed re-forms in a different guise. Her terrible past could re-form into the present, for instance; it could become this moment with him.

"How?" Meredith's face was tilted toward him. She was utterly concentrated, her brow furrowed.

"Do the thing you're most afraid of."

"Just like that?"

"Don't think. Thinking is overrated."

"How can an academic say that? Anyway, I always assumed it was feeling that was overrated."

"That's where you're wrong."

Meredith looked at him.

"Just like that?" she said.

He nodded. "Don't think."

Meredith got up and went over to the pool. She felt breathless and stupid and terrified. She stood on the edge. There were a few yellow leaves floating in the dark water. Daniel could barely make out her form in the dark. Meredith took off her coat first, then her shoes. She slipped out of her jeans and her underpants, her sweater and her bra. She refused to think. Her mind was static, electric, filled with the present, filled with yellow leaves, this moment, this water, this time.

Daniel watched her move toward the pool, stunned and thrilled. He would never be free of this, not that he'd ever want to be. He could see the outlines of Meredith's body now. Her long, creamy back. She was gone before he could look as carefully as he would have liked to; he would have liked to gaze at her forever, but one splash and she had disappeared into the black water. He had no idea whether he was supposed to follow her or, like some specter himself, merely slink away through the soot and the boxwoods to another time and place.

It was cold enough for Daniel to see his breath in the air. He wasn't much of a swimmer, but he didn't think about that. He took off his clothes. He crossed the patio, slacks and shirt and underwear left behind in a pile along with his briefcase and coat. He stepped onto the edge of the pool. Meredith was already treading water. She watched him lower himself into the deep end like a large, shy fish. He was clumsy and he made her laugh. He paddled over.

"You're a terrible swimmer," Meredith said.

"I am. But I play Ping-Pong. And I can ice-skate." He was shaking. How embarrassing. The cold, the whiskey, the strangeness of the night.

"Someone killed himself because of me once," Meredith said.

"People kill themselves because of what's inside them, not because of other people."

Daniel felt absolutely hypnotized. He wasn't treading water, only floating.

"Is that a principle of physics? Suicide can only be caused by one person?" Meredith asked.

"*Sui* means oneself," Daniel said.

"You think you're so smart."

Daniel floated closer. He put his hands on her waist. He

felt charged. His mentor Dr. Rosen would have a good laugh; human beings could indeed be reduced to currents and impulses. Wasn't that what desire was made of?

"I haven't done this for so many years," Meredith said. The wet ends of her hair streamed over her shoulders.

"Gone swimming?"

Meredith laughed, a little.

He moved closer, arms around her, so that their faces touched. The black water swished around them. A few leaves fell from the maples without a splash.

"I haven't made love to anyone. Loved anyone."

Daniel kissed her and didn't stop. Not until she pulled away.

"We'll drown like this," Meredith said.

"Good. Let's."

Daniel kissed her again and the rest was easy. Easier than it had been all those years ago when she'd been too afraid and too young, when everything that shouldn't have happened did, and she couldn't stop it or even understand it.

SHE WAS A LIFEGUARD THAT SUMMER, FORCED TO WEAR THE official red bathing suit of the town pool when she would have preferred a black two-piece. She was the captain of the high-school swim team, her event the two-hundred-meter butterfly; she felt strong, invincible, ready to jump in and rescue someone. All day she sat on the high, white wooden chair, a whistle around her neck; she smelled like coconut oil. She had no idea how many little boys dreamed about her in her red bathing suit. All through the year she'd been involved with Josh Prentiss, the captain of the boys' swim team, but now this summer she wanted to be free. She was only sixteen, not ready to be tied down.

"Be honest," her friends told her. "Tell him you just want to be friends."

She told him, but he wouldn't listen. Late at night the phone would ring and Merrie would lie in bed, frozen. She vowed to her parents it was someone making crank calls, but they all knew who it was. Josh had begun to lurk around the house, peering in the windows, scaring the hell out of her mother when Mrs. Weiss found him in the backyard. How had love come to this? This twisted dark place. The phone calls, the fear, the look on his face when he drove by the house.

Her friends told her he'd get over it, but they didn't know Josh; they had no idea he watched Meredith at the pool from his parked car every day. They didn't know she couldn't sleep at night, that her dreams were filled with dark water, ringing phones, brutal fear. He left strange things for her by the girls' locker room at the pool: a photo with her face cut out, a black sock torn to pieces, a dead field mouse completely wound in tape.

And then the bad, unstoppable thing happened, one day in August, a hot, clear, perfect morning. When Merrie arrived at the pool there were several squad cars parked outside and an ambulance was up on the sidewalk. She heard the EMTs talking: Josh had climbed the fence in the middle of the night, and Meredith knew why. He'd wanted to somehow hurt her the way she'd hurt him. He'd watched her, knew her schedule. He did it in the pool for Meredith's benefit; standing outside the gate, she could see something immersed in the deep end. It looked like a bag of laundry or a sack of rocks until she realized it was a body. Before the officers forced Meredith back, insisting she had no clearance to be there, she saw a line of red in the water, a twisted, dark thread.

Meredith dropped to her knees so hard and fast the concrete tore at her skin and left scars. She put her head on the ground. People all around her thought she was praying, but really she was begging for time to rewind. One day, that's all. A few hours. Time enough for her to talk him out of it, or go back with him if that's what it took.

Everything smelled bitter, a mix of chlorine and blood. One of the officers helped her to her feet and took her into the snack bar. He found her ID in her gym bag and phoned her mother. The officer on the phone told Mrs. Weiss there had been an accident; the pool was closing for the rest of the season and she needed to pick Meredith up right away.

Mrs. Weiss parked by the gate while the officer brought Meredith to the car. Meredith seemed in shock; silent and shaking under her skin.

"Don't think this is your fault," Meredith's mother said. "I won't have that, Merrie."

But Meredith didn't have to think it over. She knew the truth. She never went back to the pool. She saw his body every time she closed her eyes. She wanted to go to the funeral, but she was afraid of his family. On that night, after everyone else had grieved and gone home, Meredith took her mother's car even though she didn't yet have her license. She knew enough; she had taken driver's ed. She drove to the cemetery and climbed over the wall. In the dark the headstones were either black or white; she didn't stop searching until she spied the freshly dug grave. The air smelled like pine and earth. Children in town swore that if you entered this cemetery after dark and called out a dead person's name, his ghost would come to you. Meredith called out Josh's name. She sounded like the wind; she called for a long time, but no one came to her. No one answered. This wasn't what was supposed to have happened. They were both supposed to go on with their lives.

Meredith felt herself click off. A key into a lock. A body sinking. He had wanted to teach her a lesson, and he did. The rest of high school was a dream; she didn't even bother to go to graduation. Meredith applied for early decision to Brown; she did her work, got good grades, and never once went on a date. She barely spoke to anyone at college, except for her freshman-year roommate, Ellen Dooley, who was an extrovert and wouldn't let Meredith sleep all day on the weekends.

Things happened in her family: her parents stopped talking to each other, then separated, each moving out of state. There was no reason for Meredith to ever go home again, except that she did. She'd been going back every year. It was her secret; one she held close. She visited the cemetery, not on the anniversary of Josh's death or on his birthday — she might have run into his family on those dates — but on the anniversary of the day they met. Every time she went, she called out his name. They said a ghost couldn't refuse your call, but this one did. All she wanted was forgiveness; all she got was silence. She stayed so long that on several occasions she'd found the cemetery gates locked when she went to leave, and she'd had to climb over the wall.

This year she asked the Moodys if she could have time off in April. By now she had been seeing Daniel Finch every weekend for several months. She had started to swim regularly at the Yale pool, and swimming made her feel again. She was almost done with the past, but not quite.

Daniel called one Friday night only to have Cynthia inform him that Meredith had gone home. "She never mentioned a trip to me," he said. "She never even said where she grew up."

"Annapolis, Maryland. She's staying at a hotel at the Baltimore airport. She'll be back tomorrow."

Usually Meredith headed straight to the cemetery after checking in to the hotel, but this trip was different. Meredith turned off the highway one exit earlier than usual. She was thinking about Daniel as she drove, imagining the way he looked when he slept. He slept deeply; in the morning when he woke and she asked what he'd been dreaming about, he always said, *You.*

She went to the police station in town. It took a while before they understood what she wanted — someone who could talk to her about the incident at the town pool all those years ago. Someone who'd been there. They directed her to the sergeant, who'd been at the scene; he was the senior officer now, but back then he'd been one of the young policemen who had watched her sink to her knees on the concrete and pray.

"I wasn't really praying. I just wanted time to go backward."

"That's a prayer." The sergeant got out the file; it was all public information now. "You want to tell me what you're looking for in all this? Because there's nothing in the files that will help you. Just the bare facts. He didn't even leave a note. But off the record, it wasn't the first time the police were involved."

"No, I never phoned the police."

"I mean the first time he tried. We'd been called to the house twice the year before." Before he and Meredith were a couple.

"You're making this up," Meredith said.

"Why would I?"

She looked at the sergeant. He was a perfectly ordinary man. "Because you've seen too many people in pain. Because you're a nice man."

"Because it's true."

She'd been too distraught to notice this officer all those years ago when he helped her into her mother's car, but she looked at him carefully now.

"I wouldn't lie to you," he told her.

"No, I don't think you would."

Meredith didn't go to the cemetery. Daniel had been right. Josh had been alone in his decision; his pain had been his alone, a burden she couldn't share.

Meredith drove around, and when it was getting dark, she went back to the hotel. Her phone was blinking when she got to her room. Daniel had left a message. He'd be waiting for her at Bradley Airport when she flew back in the morning, unless she phoned and told him not to come. She took a long shower and got into bed, and for once she slept well. It wasn't a wasted trip, it was just over. She woke be-

fore the alarm began to ring, and the truth was she was
ready to leave before dawn.

I T WAS J OHN AND C YNTHIA ' S TENTH ANNIVERSARY AND IT
was time to celebrate. They were celebrating not just the
marriage itself, but, more important, the fact that against all
odds, after ten years of trying, Cynthia was pregnant. Cynthia herself was blissed out; she looked like another person,
the angles and anger gone. She had been planning the party
for months. Tents on the lawn, a jazz band, dinner catered
by the Eagle Inn, buckets of iced champagne set out at every
table, although Cynthia herself had stopped drinking. She
had read everything she could get her hands on regarding
prenatal nutrition and had surprised herself with the passion she had for her pregnancy. She took walks twice a day
with Dusty and did prenatal yoga every afternoon. Even
John, usually so dour, seemed overjoyed about the baby. A
second chance to do something right.

Cynthia and John asked Meredith to stay on, but she had
already moved to New Haven and was living with Daniel
Finch. She continued to help out part-time. She hated leaving Sam and Blanca behind, but Sam was nearing his eigh-
teenth birthday, and Blanca was twelve, very grown-up and
capable, perfectly able to get to and from ballet lessons and
art class all by herself on her bike.

Meredith was handling the place cards for the party, writing each name in calligraphy while sitting at the table over-
looking the pool. She would miss swimming here. Daniel
vowed that when they moved to Virginia, where he'd gotten

an appointment at UVA, he would make sure that wherever they lived had a pool. It didn't matter how much it cost. Rent or buy. Condo or house. He didn't care if he had to pay off the pool for the rest of his life.

Daniel had asked Meredith to marry him, but she'd told him she needed time.

"Our relationship began because of time," Daniel said. "You believed a person could be tied to a time so strongly that even death couldn't sever the connection. Do you sincerely think more time will give you your answer if you don't know now?"

"It might. And it might not."

Daniel gave her a diamond ring that had belonged to his mother. It was antique, set in platinum.

"I'll wear it," Meredith told him. "But I'm not committing to anything."

All the same, as she helped with the Moodys' party, Meredith wondered how she would feel if it were her own wedding she was organizing rather than Cynthia and John's anniversary party. For starters, she would want it small. No people she didn't really care about. No crowds of drunken partygoers dancing all night.

"Do you realize you've invited everyone in town?" Meredith said when Cynthia came out to join her.

It had been a gorgeous spring. Not too much rain. Not too many mosquitoes. The basset hound followed at Cynthia's heels, stepping on its own ears. The dog was devoted to Cynthia. He howled whenever she went out without him and nothing John Moody did could dissuade the dog from sleeping in their bedroom, although thankfully Dusty's legs were too short for him to leap onto the bed.

"Dear Dusty." Cynthia scooped him up. "I promise I won't neglect you when the baby arrives. I'll still feed you hamburger." She checked through the responses. "Actually, I haven't invited everyone. George Snow, for instance."

Meredith looked up from her place cards.

"John may be blind. I'm not. George was here night and day when Arlyn was dying. You and I both know the truth. Just look at Blanca. She has nothing of John in her."

"She's smart and talented. She resembles him in that way. Did you invite Helen and Art Jeffries?" The owners of the Eagle Inn, who expected to be invited to every event they catered.

"Thank you for remembering. I'll phone them this afternoon. What will I do when you're gone?" They had never really liked each other, but they'd worked well together.

"You'll hire someone else. You'll be fine."

"I want you here early on D-day in case I need you," Cynthia said. "Especially if Sam acts up."

Sam had been even more withdrawn lately. He was leading a parallel existence while living in the same house as the rest of his family. They didn't bother him; he didn't bother them. Worked out just fine. Fewer fights, fewer scenes. Live and let live. But there was always that worry that something would snap. Something he did would break their calm life apart and leave them whirling through the dark.

"We don't want him upsetting John's mother," Cynthia said.

Diana Moody had managed to come up from Florida for the party, though she was ailing. Her stroke had slowed her down, and she'd recently been diagnosed with diabetes.

"We were thinking of committing Sam to a drug rehab center before the event, it just made sense timewise, but Diana got wind of it and got all upset. She thinks of him as a child."

"I don't know what will happen to him if he doesn't get help soon," Meredith said. "Once he turns eighteen, you won't have the legal right to make those decisions."

"I just want to have this party without incident, then we'll think of what to do next."

"I thought I could save him," Meredith said.

"No one could," Cynthia said. "But at least you tried."

It was Blanca who called when it happened, the sudden snap, the crack in their lives that broke the quiet in two. It was the day of the party, naturally; a Saturday. Meredith and Daniel were in bed. They had planned to sleep as late as they could, until Meredith was due at the Moodys' to help with the party. The phone rang at 6:30 a.m.

"Don't answer," Daniel told Meredith.

She did it anyway. "What if someone's died?"

"Then we'll find out later. Or tomorrow."

Meredith said hello into the mouthpiece. She could hear breathing. She knew Daniel was probably right.

It was Blanca. A very quiet Blanca. "He's disappeared."

Meredith was looking at sunlight coming in through the shutters. The air was filled with swirling dust motes.

"He does that, Bee. You know he does," Meredith assured Blanca. "He'll be back."

"This is different. Cynthia found drugs and she flushed

them down the toilet. Sam went crazy. He was so mad it was scary. He said she had no right to throw out something that belonged to him. It was a violation of his personal rights. He pushed her down. Not on purpose or anything. He was just trying to get past her. She was standing in the doorway refusing to move, blocking his way. He told me he was going to New York. He's never coming back. He said he had to fly away. It was in his bloodline."

"Shit," Meredith said.

"My grandmother got so upset, they had to call a doctor. She told Cynthia she'd never even tried to understand Sam. Now they're not speaking, either. He left Connie. I don't know what to feed him."

"Give the parrot a cut-up apple and some of the seed in the bag in the kitchen," Meredith told her.

Daniel was wide-awake now: *Sam?* he mouthed. When Meredith nodded, he said, "Tell Blanca to press redial on the phone in his room to see what his last call out was."

Blanca did so and called back with the number her brother had last dialed.

"Is your dad out looking for him?" Meredith said.

"Are you kidding? When Sam pushed Cynthia down he hit Sam."

Blanca had begun to cry. She was hiding it, but Meredith could hear her snuffling.

"Blanca, calm down. I'll take care of it."

"I don't think you can."

"I'll come by the house to talk to your dad before I go searching. I promise."

Meredith hung up and went for her clothes.

"Maybe it's time to call the police," Daniel suggested. "For his sake."

"He hasn't committed a crime. Anyway, you don't know him — the harder you chase after Sam the farther he'll run."

"Then try the number Blanca gave you."

No one answered the first call. But it was not yet 7:00 a.m. Meredith tried again.

At last a young woman picked up. A sleepy hello.

"Can I talk to Sam?"

A pause. Something muttered. Then, "Sam who?"

"Sam who belongs to a race of people who live in Connecticut and can fly."

"Sure. If you say so."

There was some background noise, then Sam got on the phone. "I'm not going back," he said. No hello, of course. No *Who is it?* And most assuredly, no apologies for all the worry caused.

"Okay, but can I bring you your clothes? And you're not leaving Connie, are you?" He did love that parrot; she had to get to him however she could.

"You're tricky." Sam sounded very far away. Wasted.

"Who's the girl who answered the phone?"

"And nosy. Nosy Merrie who wants to change the world. Okay, you can bring everything here if you promise to stop asking stupid questions. And you can't tell the old man where I am."

Meredith wrote down the address. Manhattan. Nineteenth Street. Apartment 4C. She quietly got dressed.

"You don't think I'm letting you go alone, do you?"

Daniel was already out of bed and pulling on his pants. "I don't even know why we're so involved in these people's lives."

"Because I know what happens when you're not involved."

"I'm sorry." Daniel went to her and pulled her close. She hadn't even bothered to brush her hair. She just wanted to go. "Everything bad that happens in this world isn't necessarily your fault, you know."

"How can you be sure?"

"Because I am," Daniel said.

They went to the Moodys' house. The tents were already set up on the grass, yellow and white, floating like clouds. But the very tops of the tents were coated with soot and the caterer was having a fit — every dish that had been brought over the night before was now broken. Plus, half a dozen birds had been caught in the tents and no one could manage to chase them out.

"Birds, ashes, dishes," Daniel said. "This party appears to be doomed."

Cynthia came out to the drive. Her face was chalky. The dog followed at her heels.

"I won't have him coming back here and John agrees," she said. "He pushed a pregnant woman. What will he do next?"

"Fine," Meredith said. "I can understand."

Daniel waited in the driveway while Meredith went into the house. Blanca and her grandmother were sitting on Sam's bed. Blanca was already wearing her ice blue party dress and her hair was in a long braid. Just recently her legs had gotten longer. Diana Moody was still in her bathrobe. She hadn't been looking forward to this event, and now she thought she might beg off and stay in bed even though she'd traveled all this way.

"That damn Cynthia," Diana Moody said. "I never thought John should marry her."

John had sent the children to visit his mother during Easter vacations until Diana's health began to fail. Surprisingly, Sam always went. Diana still saw him as the little boy she hadn't liked who had won her over in a cemetery. She was mad for him, no matter his flaws.

Diana was ridiculously fragile these days. She didn't care about much anymore, other than her grandchildren. She wished Arlyn hadn't passed on so young. Every now and then she dreamed about the day she found Sam hiding in the backseat of her car. She dreamed about watching him climb that big tree while his mother was at home dying.

"I'll go pack up a basket of food for Sam," Diana said. "I know what he likes."

While Diana went down to the kitchen, Meredith and Blanca filled a duffel bag with clothes.

"I don't want to live here if Sam's not here," Blanca said. "I'll run away."

"Sam's almost a man. He needs a place of his own. Maybe he'll straighten out if he's in a different environment." The parrot was squawking like mad. "Shut up," Meredith said.

"Get out!" the parrot told her.

The bird had a mournful voice and was used to being ignored; no one but Sam listened to him. Connie's vocabulary hadn't progressed much; he had only a few random words to repeat: *Hey, Awesome, Get out.* Much to the dismay of Dusty the basset hound, he had a ferocious bark.

Meredith grabbed sneakers, jeans, and a heavy coat, along with chalk and watercolors. She took Sam's wallet from the desk, and his electric toothbrush. She tossed the parrot's supplies into a tote bag. Blanca had gone to the closet; her head was down. But that didn't cover up the fact that she was crying. Meredith suddenly felt exhausted. She hadn't had time to have a cup of coffee. Her hands were shaking.

"Sam is Sam," Meredith told Blanca. "He'll do what he does and we'll love him anyway. The way we always have."

Blanca nodded in agreement. Her shoulders were still shaking. She wiped her eyes with the hem of her skirt. She hated her dress. She'd been thinking of cutting her hair or changing her name. She was sick of being so good all the time. She was sick of being twelve.

"I'm taking this." Blanca grabbed the old sneaker box crisscrossed with tape and stuffed it into the duffel bag. "He told me he had all his treasures in it."

At the last minute Meredith took Sam's pillow and blanket. Maybe he was cold.

"Good thinking," Blanca said. They looked at the collection of antique knives.

"Let's skip those," Meredith said. They actually laughed then.

When they went downstairs, Diana was waiting with a picnic basket. "Tell him I love him," she said. She had fixed two peanut-butter sandwiches, Sam's favorite when he was a little boy. There was also a box of chocolate-chip cookies, some cans of beans and soup, a bag of rolls, and a large wheel of cheese appropriated from the caterer.

Blanca helped Daniel pack up the car. Meredith happened to spy John Moody out past the swimming pool. "I'll be right back."

Meredith walked past the tents. A dance floor had been laid out over the grass. John was wearing a good gray suit. Meredith had lived with them for almost two years and John Moody was a complete stranger to her. She felt she knew Arlyn better, though Arlyn had been gone for twelve years.

"I'm going to bring Sam some of his belongings. He needs time. I think you should help him out financially," Meredith told John Moody. "If he's desperate for money it will make matters worse."

"Of course."

"I don't think he meant to push Cynthia. Sam isn't like that."

"Should I go with you?"

"Given your fight, I think it's better if I go."

John accepted this. He really didn't know what to feel. He had never hit anyone before, and he'd hit Sam hard. He hadn't known what to feel when Arlie was dying, either. He had come out to the lawn to this exact spot and he'd cried, even though George Snow was sitting at his wife's bedside. Now he stood here again, still lost.

"I don't know what to do," he admitted.

"It's a difficult situation." Meredith looked out past the trees. There was the shape of a woman.

"You see her, don't you?" John Moody said.

"I think I see her because you do. If that makes sense. I see how you miss her."

"I didn't know that would happen. I wanted out of the marriage from the start."

"Do you think it's a time or a place or a person that keeps her here?"

"You're asking the wrong man. I have no idea. To be honest, I've tried everything I could to get rid of her, but she won't go. That's all I know. I know Sam wouldn't have turned out this way if she were still here. If you find him, can you tell him I didn't mean to hit him?"

Meredith went back across the lawn. When she reached the car, she saw that Blanca was in the backseat reading *Magic or Not?* The parrot was in a cage beside her, squawking.

"You are not going," Meredith told her.

Blanca noticed the diamond. "Wow."

"It's not what you think," Meredith said. "We're not engaged. It's a friendship ring. And please put a scarf over Connie's cage so he's not freaking out. Then you need to go back to the house. You're going to ruin that dress."

"I have to make sure that Sam is all right." Blanca took one of Sam's shirts and threw it over the cage and Connie quieted down.

Meredith turned to Daniel. "How could you let her get in the car?"

"I didn't let her. She sneaked."

"I'm going," Blanca insisted. "Our mother would have wanted me to."

"Good try," Meredith said. "You're still not going."

"But she would have. Any mother would."

"She's got you there," Daniel said.

Meredith got into the passenger seat. "I give up. But if the place looks too shady, you're staying in the car."

They drove to New York in silence, listening to the radio. Luckily, there wasn't much traffic. On Twenty-third Street they didn't have a single red light; Daniel drove so fast that Meredith couldn't make out whether or not the tearoom where she'd first seen John Moody was still there. The street where Sam was staying was nice, although his particular building looked run-down.

"It's not shady," Blanca said.

"Maybe I should go in first, make sure it's okay," Daniel said after they'd parked.

"It'll be fine," Meredith said. "Either way, we're going in."

They grabbed bits and pieces of Sam's belongings and trooped over to the dilapidated brownstone. The front door was unlocked; they took the stairs up to 4C and rang the bell several times. A young woman about Sam's age opened the door. She was wearing jeans and a sweater and had short, choppy black hair. She let them in without asking who they were or what they were doing; maybe it was so obvious the girl didn't have to bother. The family bearing belongings. They had the parrot with them, after all, which was muttering under cover of Sam's shirt, *You. You. You.*

The apartment wasn't kept up — there were plates of food around and cups used as ashtrays and clothes and newspapers strewn about — but the space itself wasn't bad. There were two people asleep in the living room, rolled up in blankets. It was impossible to tell their age or sex or even if they were alive. The smell of smoke and sweat lingered.

"How do you afford the rent?" Daniel asked. It was a far better apartment than his place in New Haven.

"It was my grandmother's apartment," the girl who had opened the door said. "Rent-controlled. I lived with her and took care of her. When she died it became mine."

Sam was in the bedroom watching television. He was sitting on the bed, his back against the wall; he seemed nervous and jumpy even before they descended upon him.

"You brought her to this hellhole?" he said to Meredith when he saw Blanca. "Are you nuts?"

"How about a thank-you for dragging all your stuff here?" Meredith said.

Blanca put an armful of Sam's neatly laundered clothes down and scrambled to sit beside him. Sam was pawing through his belongings. "My electric toothbrush," he said cheerfully.

"Is she your girlfriend?" Blanca wanted to know of the girl with the dark hair.

"Her name is Amy," Sam said.

Amy came to stand in the doorway. "I'm rescuing him."

Meredith turned and looked Amy over more carefully. She was slight and wore heavy black boots; her sweater had holes in the sleeves. Her face seemed lopsided. She was a serious person. Not pretty, exactly, but inspiring confidence.

"She thinks she can change me," Sam said, amused. "She doesn't understand that I'm doomed."

"Meredith's getting married," Blanca said. "Look at her ring."

"It's a friendship ring," Meredith told Sam.

All the same, Sam took her hand and studied the ring. "Kind of small," he said.

Meredith noticed the bruise on his face. His father at his wits' end. The pushing match that was bound to come to something, but unfortunately it had come to this.

"I wish you were still at home," Blanca said to her brother.

"You'll have a new sib soon. Maybe it'll be a brother. I can easily be replaced."

"I'll hate it whatever it is," Blanca said glumly. "Brother or sister."

"You sound like me. Stop it. Aha!" Sam had taken the old shoebox Blanca had brought him out of the duffel bag. He set it on his lap. "Good you brought this. Now I can give you something that's meant for you. I was supposed to give it to you when you were grown up, but you're grown up enough."

Blanca sat shoulder to shoulder with her brother as he opened the treasure box. She'd always wanted to look inside. It was a jumble of odd things, letters and photos and little bones.

"My squirrel," Sam said. "William."

"Yuck," Blanca said.

There was a photograph of their mother. Blanca held it up to the light. There were no photos around their house. It wasn't that sort of home. "Look at all her freckles."

"Seventy-four on her face," Sam said. "She told me. She'd counted them." He took out something wrapped in tissue and handed it to Blanca.

"Is this more squirrel bones?"

"Dragon bones. I killed him one night on top of the roof and his bones were made out of stars."

"Very funny," Blanca said. "Really."

Meredith had taken the opportunity to check out the room. There was a pipe and some marijuana on the bureau and several empty whiskey bottles. She opened a drawer. Underwear. Needles. She wished this girl Amy more luck than they'd had in rescuing Sam.

"Stop doing that," Sam said when he noticed her snooping. "You're not in charge of anything here, Merrie."

Blanca unwrapped the folded tissue Sam had handed over. Inside there was a strand of what appeared to be black marbles. She lifted them and found they were surprisingly warm to the touch.

"Mom's pearls," Sam said. "They got dusty."

Blanca held them up and blew on them. The black coating chipped away and flew off like ashes.

"They're so beautiful," Meredith said. "Look at the difference!"

They were cream colored, cloud colored, snow colored.

"Don't cry," Sam warned his sister.

"I wasn't about to." Blanca made a face and stuck out her tongue.

But she did cry when it came time to leave. Daniel slipped Sam a hundred bucks when no one could see.

"Not for drugs. For food."

"I am not a drug addict," Sam said. "I'm a recreational user."

Meredith was making up the bed with Sam's pillow and quilt. The girl, Amy, was watching.

"He told me his mother was dead," Amy said.

"Me? I'm not his mother. His mother died a long time ago. I'm nothing to him."

"You're something," Amy said.

"A well-wisher."

The apartment was dark, shades drawn, but there was enough light coming in to allow them to see one another.

"Me too," Amy said.

It was time for Meredith to leave. She hadn't rescued him, but she'd done all she could. She would just have to live with that. Daniel was in the car waiting. Sam was on the sidewalk in his bare feet, his hair sticking up, cold in just a T-shirt and jeans. Blanca was beside him, her arms looped around him.

"We've got to go," Meredith told Blanca.

"Maybe I won't."

"Yeah, well, you have to," Sam said to his sister. "There are monsters on this street at night."

"Very funny." But Blanca looked around, nervous.

"They eat little girls."

"That isn't funny, Sam!"

Sam hugged Blanca, and watched her get into the car.

"Your father didn't mean to hit you," Meredith told him.

"I know that. He probably never meant anything. It was all unintentional, right?"

Meredith took out the cash John Moody had sent to his son. "He asked me to give you this."

"I don't think so, Merrie. Daniel lent me some money. My father doesn't owe me anything and I don't owe him. That's just the way it is. Give it back to him."

For the first time Sam sounded like a grown-up.

"So you're staying here?" Meredith asked. "You're sure?"

Sam nodded. Once he made up his mind about something, he wasn't easily moved. He'd been that way ever since he'd been a child.

"Then I'll have to accept your decision." Meredith would have done anything to save him. "Whether or not I like it."

"What are the odds I'll survive?" he said.

Meredith knew Sam didn't like to be touched, but she hugged him anyway. He was so thin she didn't expect him to be muscular, but maybe he was stronger than she'd thought. He didn't hug her back but he didn't pull away, either. "I'll miss you," Meredith said.

Sam laughed. "That wasn't the question. I mean it. What's your honest assessment?"

So she gave him the best odds she could. "Fifty-fifty. That's probably true for us all."

Sam nodded, pleased. "I'll take that. That's fine with me."

They didn't go directly home. Meredith made up her mind while they were driving through the Bronx. They went as far as Greenwich, then took the first exit they came to. Blanca was sleeping in the backseat, so exhausted she didn't budge until Meredith shook her shoulder.

"Bee, I want you to be my witness."

Blanca rubbed her eyes. The pearls were warm around her throat. They flushed a faint coral.

"Okay. What's a witness?"

"When we get married we need one special person there with us."

"That's me," Blanca said.

They pounded on the door of the town notary, who was

also the justice of the peace. He came down thinking someone had died. His wife had already begun to collect his black
suit from the closet.

"I'm sorry for your loss," the justice said.

"Oh, no." Daniel was apologetic. "It's a wedding we
want."

They looked rumpled and somewhat desperate, so the
justice of the peace agreed. His name was Tom Smith and
he had performed so many marriages he could recite the
service in his sleep. Sometimes he did and his wife would
lie in bed and listen to him, the whole service through,
comforted that someone could know the words of love by
heart.

After the ceremony the three went to celebrate at a diner
that served breakfast twenty-four hours a day. Blanca
phoned home to let her father and Cynthia know she was
sorry to be so late but she was on her way.

"The party's still going on." Blanca was nearly falling
asleep, exhausted from the day, but thrilled to have been a
witness. "Do I have special responsibilities and duties now?"
she asked Meredith when Daniel went to pay the bill.

"Nope. All a witness has to do is be there and remember."

"Fine," Blanca said. "I will."

They went out into the darkening air. It would rain later;
they could feel it. Already there were beads of moisture
on the leaves and the asphalt. But that was later; right now
the sky was clear and endless. Even though she was over-
excited, and had vowed to herself that she would stay up
all night, Blanca fell asleep the minute they were back on
the road. She dreamed of oysters and of pearls. She dreamed

of men who could fly. She dreamed she was walking down a lane with a woman she didn't know who had something important to tell her but didn't speak the same language. By the time they got back to the house, the anniversary party was winding down. It was late. There were a few guests who had decided to jump into the pool, tipsy and fully clothed.

"Wake up," Blanca heard someone say.

When she opened her eyes she had no idea where she was.

The Red Map

S HE LIVED IN A HOUSE IN LONDON THAT WAS
filled with beetles and books. There was a re-
viewer from the *Guardian* on the first floor, a
history professor on the third, with Blanca, the
proprietor of a bookstore, sandwiched in between. It made sense that a girl who had grown
up in a house called the Glass Slipper would be
partial to fairy tales; her senior thesis at university had been entitled "The Lost and the Found,"
a study of those who managed to find a way out

of the woods and of those who were never seen again, whether they'd been snagged on thornbushes or caught up in chains or stewed into a soup of flesh and bones.

Blanca's personal library was piled into cartons in an unheated glassed-in porch that overlooked a small garden in which a lime tree grew. Her flat was perfect — airy, with large, lovely rooms — but Blanca always felt restless. She'd been a good, serious, worried girl who had grown into a less good, but still worried, young woman. Blanca believed in very little other than the assured cruelty of fate. That had been the theme of her thesis. Lost or found, there was no way to avoid the heartbreak. Glass shattered, bones broke, apples rotted.

Blanca thought she'd found the signifier of her own bad luck when the insects arrived en masse, an infestation of paper-eating beetles, *Paperii taxemi*. All of the flats had to be fumigated; Blanca and the book critic and the professor had sat under the lime tree shivering in the chilly late spring air discussing local restaurants until they were allowed to go back inside their now acrid rooms. It was on this day that Blanca received word that her father had died; the phone rang just as she'd discovered little black and silver balls of dead matter falling out of her books, as though the words had come unglued from their pages.

Blanca had been the sort of little girl who always carried a book with her, but she hadn't become a truly serious reader until the year her brother died, during her junior semester abroad. She'd started on the evening when Meredith had phoned with the horrible news; now, five years later, she still hadn't stopped reading. She'd never gone back to the States, taking an extra year to finish her degree in the UK. Naturally she had a book in her hands when Meredith called this time as well — it was a first edition of Andrew Lang's *Red Fairy Book,* which she'd recently found in a church-fair odds-and-ends bin, water stained, but otherwise in good shape. Of course it would be Blanca's childhood nanny to call with the bad news yet again, rather than anyone in her family. Not that anyone was really left. Not now. John Moody had died on the patio outside his house earlier that day. He had asked Cynthia if she could get him a glass of water; when she returned his head was bowed. It was as though he were praying, Cynthia had confided to Meredith, who now relayed the story to Blanca. As though in his very last moments John had seen something that filled him with emotion, an angel perhaps, right there on the grass, showing the path to the state of grace.

The lawn was covered with mourning doves, Cynthia had reported, eight or ten or twelve. They always traveled in pairs, so silent a person might not see them in the grass until they cooed. Cynthia took this mass of doves to be a visitation from the other side. After the funeral home had come to collect John's body, Cynthia had set out birdseed, but the doves hadn't returned.

"As if an angel would ever visit my father," Blanca said when Meredith passed on Cynthia's interpretation of John Moody's death. "He wouldn't recognize an angel even if it appeared right in front of him and tapped him on the shoulder."

Till the end, John Moody had remained a distant, quiet man. He had never come to visit Blanca, not in all the time she'd lived in London; he'd called only on holidays and on

Blanca's birthday. Actually, Cynthia had been the one to call, then she'd hand John the receiver at the end of the conversation for a few awkward moments. He and Blanca had nothing to talk about. The weather. The news. It felt dangerous to speak about anything that mattered. Blanca could not remember when they'd last agreed on anything.

"It wasn't an angel he saw," Meredith said. "It was her."

They had a bad connection and Blanca thought she'd heard wrong. She loved Meredith Weiss and trusted her to be dependable and steady in times when others were not. Meredith now had four children of her own, all of whom had come to London to visit this past Easter. Blanca adored them all, especially the two eldest, Amelia and Ellis, for whom she'd often babysat during the two years she spent at the University of Virginia. She'd applied there because Meredith's husband, Daniel, taught in the physics department. She'd followed them, yearning for a family of her own, even a pretend one. By then, Blanca's grandmother, Diana, had passed on and Blanca did indeed feel she was an orphan. Some of Blanca's friends at school had assumed that Meredith was her mother, and as much as Blanca had wanted to say, *No, she was our babysitter, our friend, nothing more,* she never told them they were wrong.

Of her own mother, Blanca remembered next to nothing. She had only the stories her brother had told her to remind her that she'd had a mother at all, and of course the pearls she wore every day; Blanca refused to take off the necklace even in the bath. It was her talisman, she supposed, a sign that someone had once loved her.

"I doubt that my father saw anything more miraculous

than the gardener or a dead branch on a tree. And how perfect that my stepmother called you before she called me. Such a close family."

"She was too confused to place an overseas call. You know how she gets. I offered to do it."

"It's not just the phone call. I'm not part of the family."

"Come home for the funeral. I'll meet you."

"I have a lot to do here."

There were the books filled with dead beetles to deal with, after all, and the lime tree, greening in the garden with all the rain they'd had that season, in need of pruning, and the fact that she was broke and might not have enough cash for a plane ticket. A thousand reasons to stay away, and how many reasons were there to go?

"When it happened Cynthia and your father were about to have breakfast on the patio. She went inside to get him a glass of water and when she came back he was gone. All of the dishes were broken in half. The doves were on the lawn."

"So he had a seizure and broke the china. Then the doves came to eat the crumbs. That doesn't mean a radiant angel appeared to him and that all was forgiven."

"I'll leave my kids and fly up to meet you in Connecticut. You don't have to stay at the house. I'll get rooms at the Eagle Inn. You can bring that boyfriend of yours."

That would be James Bayliss, the man Blanca had refused to marry even though she found him consistently interesting. She had hired James to install the bookshelves in her tiny shop, an undertaking begun with the small inheritance her grandmother, Diana, had left her. Blanca was drawn to James, not only because he was tall with dark hair, but also because he had the ability to do real things, things that mattered, ordinary tasks such as lifting boxes and stepping on the squiggly roly-poly bugs that came out of the floorboards. Blanca had fallen hard for James when he made a trap out of a shoebox, string, and some orange cheese to catch the mice that rudely ran about. He didn't even kill them, merely carried them out to the garden.

But the real clincher happened one morning when Blanca spied him on the street, headed for her shop. James had come upon two teenaged boys going at each other in some horrible row. *Get the fuck away from each other,* she'd heard him shout, as he held the bigger fellow off. He wasn't afraid to deal with real and unpleasant matters; should he ever stumble upon a hedge of thorns, he would clearly hack it to pieces and make firewood out of it.

All that day Blanca waited for James to say something about the fight he'd stopped, but he never said a word. Quiet modesty, that was the last charm. Blanca was done for then, head over heels; her only escape would be for him to finish the bookshelves, collect his check, and disappear. But James Bayliss took so long with the work in Blanca's shop that it seemed they'd both go bankrupt if she didn't sleep with him. *All right?* she'd said afterward. They were in her bed. The scent of the bark of the lime tree had risen through the open windows. *Now we're done. You can go home.*

James had refused to leave. He'd made plenty of excuses: his own flat was being painted, his brother had moved in, he'd sprained an ankle. Soon enough he was living in Blanca's flat, about to build shelves there as well. Blanca never imagined going home, but if she had to return to the States she certainly had no plans to bring James along.

"I don't want James in the world of my past," Blanca told Meredith over the phone. "He never needs to set foot in Connecticut."

"You think worlds are divided? Like the levels of hell?"

"I know they are. Plus, I have a business to run."

Nonsense, really. Blanca's shop, Happily Ever After, sold only fairy tales; the entire endeavor was a labor of love, with no profits involved and only a very small possibility of any to come. James had recently built two child-sized tables, then set out chairs for the neighborhood crowd who had become regular customers, most of whom read their chosen stories in the store rather than actually purchasing anything. Blanca would have to sell a thousand volumes of Andrew Lang fairy books, from *Red* to *Olive* to *Pink,* simply to break even.

"Don't you regret not coming to Sam's service?" Meredith said.

"Not for a minute. That service wasn't what Sam wanted. It was what my father and Cynthia wanted."

"You can fly in Tuesday. The funeral is the following morning. Close the shop. I'll make the reservations. If you come, I'll tell you what your father saw on the grass."

Blanca laughed. "How could you know? You weren't there." But Meredith had already hung up the phone and only static remained, the faint watery click of a dead line with no one on the other side.

*   *   *

BLANCA COLLECTED BOOKS FROM THE TRASH AND AT JUM-
ble sales and at church-fair bins the way other people rescued orphans. She kept a stack of books near the tub so she
could read in the bath, even though the edges of the pages
turned moldy. She read on trains and on buses, which often
made her late as she was forever missing her stop. She could
not sit at a restaurant without a book in her hands and sometimes she became so engrossed she forgot her cutlet or her
pasta or her dinner companion completely. A dear friend, a
devoted friend, Jessamyn Banks, who had been Blanca's
roommate during that dreadful term when Sam died, had
gently suggested that perhaps Blanca was creating a buffer
between the real world and the imagined world. In response
Blanca had laughed, something her friends rarely heard.
"Well, good for me. I can't think of anything I'd like more."

For Blanca, worlds were indeed divided. The before and
the after, the dark and the light, the real and the imagined,
the world of books and Blanca's personal history, the lost, of
course, and the found. The attraction of fairy tales was how
aware such tales were of these boundaries — countries were
divided into kingdoms, kingdoms into castleholds, castles
into towers and kitchens. Fairy tales were maps formed of
blood and hair and bones; they were the knots of the subconscious unwound. Every word in every tale was real and
as true as apples and stones. They all led to the story inside
the story.

The fairy tale Blanca was reading on the night of Sam's
death was "Hans the Hedgehog." Unloved children were
everywhere in fairy tales; some survived, others did not.
Hans was a sorrowful creature kept behind the stove be-

cause his father couldn't stand to see his offspring. Hans was not what his father had wanted and so he ignored him, forgetting his disappointment, just as John Moody had forgotten his. Poor Sam had never done anything right in his father's eyes. If he'd had whiskers and a tail it would have been no different, no better and no worse.

It had been years since Blanca had seen her brother; still, the world without Sam was so unreal, so impossible. Could there have been a mistake? It was possible, Blanca knew, for a person who'd been thought to be lost to reemerge from the woods, thorns clinging to his clothes. In Sam's case, however, the woods were everywhere; the thorns cut far too deep. There had been a mountain of stones, too high to climb, and far too many apples with black centers, too bitter to eat. He had never found his way.

All the same, Sam had left a trail — the Icarus paintings, graffiti signed with the mark of a man with wings, chalk and paint artwork that could be found all over New York City. Still, no one could find Sam himself. He'd been lost in a place no one else could get to, a twisted path that led through the air.

Sometimes he called Meredith for money, which she sent to a post-office box in lower Manhattan. He crashed at friends' apartments, showing up in Bridgeport or New Haven or the Lower East Side, and when that didn't work out, he lived on the street. He'd been visiting his old girlfriend Amy in Chelsea, and had been out on the roof having a smoke, when his parrot, Connie, the pet he'd had for so long, had suddenly taken wing. Usually the bird stayed on Sam's shoulder, but perhaps the wind was too high, or the horizon too inviting. Sam chased after, worried that the parrot, unused to flying any distance, might rise for only an instant, then fall to the pavement below.

Instead, it was Sam who did so.

Amy had relayed Sam's wishes to be cremated and have his ashes dispersed over Manhattan, but John Moody wouldn't hear of it. He had decided to bury Sam beside his mother. Spreading someone's ashes over an urban area was against the law; John Moody was well versed in bylaws, rules, and regulations. No matter how Amy had begged, she had no legal rights. She and Sam had never married. His father was his closest kin.

"Do whatever the fuck you want," Amy had said over the phone. She and John Moody had never even met in person. "Make a cake, and blow out a candle, and wish he never existed. You didn't even know who he was."

What had John Moody wished for Sam? Surely, he'd wanted a different sort of son, not one made out of porcupine quills and nightmares and bleached bones. There were times when John wished Sam would indeed curl up behind the stove, to be picked up by the tail, swept into the trash, and forgotten. Amy had been right. He had often wished that Sam would disappear, into thin air as a matter of fact, quietly and cleanly gone from their lives. All the same, it was John Moody, legal next of kin, who drove into Manhattan to identify a body that had his son's face and fingerprints, whether or not he really knew Sam.

Because their father did not respect Sam's wishes and never had, Blanca had stayed in London rather than attend the funeral. She was never going back home. Not ever. She decided that while sitting cross-legged on her dorm-room bed, crying as she read "Hans the Hedgehog." And she certainly was not going to watch them put Sam into the ground. She thought to herself, *If only he'd flown away.* He'd be in the air right now, where he belonged.

Blanca had held her own service on the banks of the Thames. She wrote her brother's name on a small piece of paper and tied it to a stone with a black satin ribbon. She threw it as hard as she could and it fell with a plash, into the deep. She hadn't thought something so small would sound so loud. She half expected Sam to rise from the river after she'd thrown his name in, a damp and waterlogged Sam, conjured from words and tides, ink-stained, re-formed on the muddy banks so far from his home. After that ceremony, whenever Blanca walked through the city, she looked closely at homeless men in dark overcoats like the one Sam had worn in New York in the winter, ragged, gray, sleeves and hem unraveling. She found herself drawn to neighborhoods she usually avoided, rough-and-tumble places near the docks, looking for a man who might remind her of him.

Day after day, she searched for her brother, in her garden, on the road, in her dreams. But Sam was gone. In time, Blanca could barely call up his face. Just the gray coat, his graffiti paintings, the way he had whispered to her the last time she'd seen him and asked how he was holding up: *You don't want to know.*

Blanca had learned from Meredith that the service in Connecticut had consisted of a few words spoken at the gravesite by a minister no one in the family had ever met before. Amy, Sam's girlfriend of so many years, did not attend.

If Sam could have, Blanca imagined that he would have climbed out of his coffin and chased the minister off, throwing spitballs and clods of dirt. Sam had always enjoyed a good scare. He was a connoisseur of the wild scene, the evening of deranged doings, the overdose, the wrong turn, the frightened innocent bystander; he was a believer in art for art's sake, pain for the pure and utter realness of sensation, and he'd always been partial to the raw, the bloodstained, the weightless, the orphaned, the dead, the lost.

Burn me, he would have said. *Set me free. Let me fall from the tallest building, the farthest tree.*

"Tell me about your brother," James had asked when he found a photograph of Sam in her desk — Sam in his threadbare gray coat, his dark hair sticking up — but Blanca had refused. It was the only photograph she had of him, of them together: Sam at seventeen and herself at eleven, a snapshot taken by Meredith on one of their outings to the shore not long before Sam took off for New York. It was windy and their hair was streaming across their faces, their eyes were half closed, and they had big smiles, as though everything were perfect. Maybe it was that one day at the beach, a brother and sister so caught up by the wind it was amazing that they didn't just fly away.

When Blanca thought of her brother she most often remembered him standing on the roof of their house, arms thrown wide. Fearful and fearless. A stork, a stranger, a man desperate for flight. How could she ever explain that to James? *What if the wind came up and took him?* she used to think. *What if he slipped?*

When she was very young she had nearly believed Sam

was capable of rising over the rooftop, just as the people did in the story Sam had told her about a secret race of people in Connecticut who waited for the most desperate moment — the ship sinking, the building burning to ash — before they revealed their ability to fly. Dark wing, gray wing, cloud, and air. Who was her brother, this strange creature who could perch on glass and was never afraid of the things that terrified most people? Blanca had wondered if perhaps Sam had hollow bones, as birds do, and rows of black raven feathers along his spine.

One night, when Blanca was six or seven, and Sam was high on drugs, he'd taken her up to the roof with him. It was before Meredith came to live with them, when they could do pretty much as they pleased. The outing had sounded like fun until they were actually out there. Then Blanca felt panic rise in her chest.

Don't slip and kill yourself, Sam told her.

Blanca forced herself to calm down, and once she had, she felt an odd, dizzying joy. At that moment Blanca understood why people sometimes haplessly jumped from heights; they didn't necessarily mean to smash onto the concrete below, but to soar, to disappear, maybe to find the next world, the one they couldn't quite see.

She never told her father or stepmother or even Meredith about being on the roof with her brother. She never spoke of half of what Sam told her or what she'd seen when she was with him. The times she went by bus with him to Bridgeport and waited in the station while he went to buy drugs. How far out in the ocean they'd gone swimming when Cynthia was too busy with her friends at the beach to notice they were too far from shore; they were bobbing unnoticed, out with the rocks and the seals.

What do you want to do, Peapod? Do we go back to Connecticut or stop right here?

Connecticut, Blanca always answered, and she'd laugh at the disappointment on Sam's face when she decided she didn't want them to drown.

Sam was scary, but he was worth it. When they were children, there was no one Blanca would have preferred to be with, no matter how terrifying his behavior might be. The good times they had were exhilarating — shoplifting candy in the drugstore, jumping off the deck of the ice-cream shop into the soft grass below — but Blanca remembered the other times as well. The nights she heard him crying. At first she thought it was the wind or some animal. A wild thing, trapped behind glass, wounded and in despair. Whatever was inside his room, whatever the sound, it was inhuman, or maybe all too human. It broke her heart.

Though she'd always loved books, the most fascinating stories of Blanca's childhood were the ones she heard when she went into Sam's room, no matter how terrifying they might be. There were tales of stabbing himself with pins in order to see if he could learn to control pain and stories concerned with the statistical probability that the sun would burn up and they would all die of the cold; there were sagas that were really dreams brought on by hashish and cocaine, long and involved and poetic and hopeless. But the best stories were about their mother, how her hair was as red as blood, how she had seventy-four freckles on her face, how she was a ferryboat captain's daughter who believed that people could fly.

And then one day Sam stopped telling stories. It was after Meredith had come to live with them, after the drugs got bad, and he'd been forced to go to rehab. Blanca kept begging him for stories after he came back home from the hospital.

Tell me about the possibility of a new ice age when we all freeze to death. Tell me about birds that can travel six thousand miles and find their way to a place they've never been before. Tell me how our mother could talk to squirrels in their own language.

Don't you understand? Sam said to her then, her once fearless brother, wrecked and blank. *I only have one story now.*

The story was heroin. It was made out of sensation, not words; it was invisible and murderous and unstoppable. Sam disappeared from her slowly, like a snowman melting, until all Blanca had left of him was a pool of freezing-cold blue water, arctic cold, sorrow colored, evaporating with every year. She did her best to hold on to him, but it was impossible, like carrying ice into the desert or making time stand still. After the final fight when Sam moved out, Blanca saw him less and less often. He no longer had a presence; he was like the outline of a person, an absence rather than a full-fledged human being.

Their father refused to speak about Sam, and soon enough the new baby was born, Cynthia and John's new little girl. It should have been a calmer time in Blanca's life, but the happier John Moody seemed with his new wife and child, the angrier Blanca became. As soon as she was a teenager, the good sweet girl she'd been disappeared. Sweetness was for babies, like her little sister, Lisa. Goodness was for the false and the childish. Those days were over for Blanca. What she had inside now was something poisonous and green, just below the surface, beneath her skin.

She missed Meredith, although often when she phoned during the worst fights with Cynthia and her father she couldn't even put her despair into words. She simply called Merrie and cried.

"I miss you, too," Meredith would say. "And I miss him."

It was thoughts of Sam that sent Blanca into despair. She could not look at her father without thinking of Sam. *How dare you forget him? How dare you go on with your life? How dare you think that happiness means anything at all?* One Thanksgiving dinner when Sam's name wasn't even mentioned, when everyone was so joyful and thankful and selfish, Blanca had accused her father of driving Sam from their house. Cynthia had quickly taken her aside.

"Your father did everything for that boy," Cynthia said.

"Such as?" Blanca had been reading at the table. *We Have Always Lived in the Castle.* Blanca already preferred paper over flesh, ink to blood.

"Listen, dear, there's a lot you don't know," Cynthia told her. "There's plenty."

Lisa, Blanca's half sister, was only a toddler at the time, a cheerful pudgy girl sitting at the dinner table, playing with some squishy mashed potatoes. Blanca wished she could make Lisa disappear and have Sam reappear in her place. He'd always hated Thanksgiving. A bullshit imperialist holiday. *This turkey died for our sins,* he would have said to their father and Cynthia. *For your sins, for what you did to me.*

"Like the fact that you're a bitch and you're happy that Sam disappeared so he can't cause you any more trouble?"

Cynthia had slapped her then, and as soon as she did, Blanca knew that was exactly what she'd wanted. Now she could hate her stepmother. Now she had every right.

"I didn't mean that," Cynthia said, shocked by her own actions. "I'm not like that."

"Oh, yes you are." Blanca felt her cheeks burning. There was something pleasurable about seeing Cynthia squirm. Blanca was taller than she was by now. She had no attachment to Cynthia, no reason to let her off the hook. Sam always said if they weren't vigilant Cynthia would come after them with knives. *Oink oink,* he'd said. Blanca had had a fear of carving knives for years. *That's how she sees us, kiddo,* Sam had told Blanca. *Pigs in her sty.*

"You know what drugs did to him," Cynthia said. "Your brother fought whatever we tried to do for him and you know it. Whatever I did was wrong."

Cynthia wasn't young anymore and she'd never been pretty. Not the way Sam had said their own mother was, with her rose-red, bloodred hair. There was no way Blanca was going back to Thanksgiving dinner. She could see through the doorway; her father was wiping mashed potatoes off Lisa's fingers. Blanca actually felt sick to her stomach. She felt weightless and mean and powerful and orphaned.

"Why don't you tell the truth?" she said to Cynthia. Her voice didn't sound the same. It was all that poison inside, all the years when she'd said nothing, when she was such a well-behaved little girl. "You never wanted either of us. You would have been happier if my father didn't have children when you met him. You probably didn't wait for my mother to die. I'll bet you and my father were already sleeping together while she was struggling for her last breath."

"Did Sam tell you that? Because there's a lot more to the story. We waited. We did the right thing by Arlyn no matter what else had happened in this house."

"It's a little late for you to tell me stories. To hell with you all."

Blanca slammed out of the house. She took the train into Manhattan and called Sam from a pay phone, crying. He was still living with Amy then, still reachable. It was a holiday after all, no matter how imperialistic, and she missed him. She was thirteen years old. Tall, grown-up looking, but a child all the same. The noise and crowds of New York scared Blanca.

"I don't go out on Thanksgiving. They fucking kill turkeys and take out their intestines while they're flapping their wings around. Is that what I'm supposed to celebrate? Don't make me do this," Sam said over the phone. He and Amy weren't getting along, and he told Blanca he had to pretend he liked holidays so that Amy wouldn't kick him out again. He sounded stoned. He was thinking too fast and talking too slowly.

"I need you," Blanca insisted.

"You are making a big mistake if you're turning to me."

"You're it for me," Blanca said. "There is no one else."

"Just stay where you are. And don't expect me to eat turkey."

He was late, naturally, but at last he arrived. He'd come to meet her in a coffee shop across the street from the train station, his hair unwashed, wearing that filthy gray overcoat he'd come to favor, which made him look like the sort of person no one wanted to sit next to. As Blanca told him how terrible things were at home, Sam played with his silverware, stabbing the tips of his fingers with a fork. The pupils of his eyes were so big his eyes looked completely black. Like a well into which you drop a stone that is never seen again, like the water down below, dark and motionless and so very still. Even Blanca could tell he was high on heroin. He did this thing where he scratched at his face and wasn't aware that he'd started to bleed. Little drops of blood fell on the plastic tabletop, and still he didn't notice a thing.

Crying is what they want you to do, Sam told her that day. *Tears leave a permanent mark. If you cry, people like Dad can find you whenever they want to. You'll never be able to hide. Don't you get it?*

Blanca had missed him so much she couldn't bear it. She didn't understand what he was talking about; all the same, she made herself stop crying. He was right about one thing: it was a stupid waste of time. Sam ordered toast and black coffee. He laughed and said he was on a diet, though he was bone thin. There were abscesses on his hands and arms. *Check it out, Peapod,* he whispered to Blanca. He opened his coat and there was Connie the parrot, dozing in an inside pocket. *No pets allowed,* Sam said.

He stroked the parrot's green feathers and spoke to it in a guttural, nonsensical language he said was Birdish, words Blanca couldn't possibly decipher. He was hushed and paranoid and brash all at the same time. There were things in this world that Blanca couldn't be expected to understand; things he couldn't tell her.

Someday you'll get it, he said to her. *It all adds up to the same thing. All that shit about math? It's a load of crap. They want you to think things make sense if you break them down, but they don't.*

Sam only stayed twenty minutes. Amy was waiting for him at home and she was getting fed up with his antics. *She thinks I'm unreliable,* Sam said, and he and Blanca both laughed. *Unreliable* had been a vocabulary word this term, and Blanca knew its meaning only too well. Sam was in such a hurry that he didn't take a single bite of his toast. Blanca had a hot turkey sandwich in front of her, but she couldn't eat. Maybe Sam was right. Maybe that turkey had died for her sins. Sin of omission, sin of jealousy, sin of girls who were not as sweet as they seemed.

When Sam left, Blanca realized that she was freezing. She'd rushed out of the house without her warm coat, and had only a heavy sweater. She couldn't wait to get out of New York. Blanca paid the bill, and she took the train back to Connecticut. When she got to Madison, she sat on a bench in the station until it was nearly midnight. Then she walked home, slowly down the lane. Oak tree, lilac, shadow, lawn. There was frost on the grass, and she was shivering by now; still, she waited on the patio until all the lights in the house were out, until she could let herself in through the back door and go up to bed without having to see anyone.

She saw Sam less frequently after that, and each time was more difficult. Cynthia was right about the drugs; they'd taken hold, they were all he cared about, it seemed. His temper was dreadful. He got into fights with people; he was arrested for causing a public disturbance and for defacing public property. What was inside him was now outside, in the paintings of winged men he left all over lower Manhattan. Men with huge wings were falling into hell, set on fire, turning to ashes. They called him Icarus, and he signed his graffiti with a *V,* the shape of a bird in a child's painting.

And then, when Blanca was fourteen, Sam disappeared for good. She went to the apartment he'd shared with Amy and they were both gone. The landlord let her in and the place was horrid — a large birdcage had been left in the center of the room, a fetid, filthy mess filled with torn-up newspapers that spilled out from between the metal bars. There were mattresses on the floor and used needles in the bathroom and forgotten rancid bits of food everywhere. But the walls were brilliant, covered by Icarus paintings, alive with color. For years afterward Blanca searched lower Manhattan; she lied to her father and stepmother and took the train in at every opportunity, desperate to find Icarus paintings, the sign that Sam was still alive. She'd see his artwork every so often, usually rising through a fresh coat of paint on the brick wall of a deli or the side of a bus. Still, the Icarus paintings were recognizable through the whitewash with what were now familiar themes: in his vision those

Connecticut men who were said to fly away from disaster couldn't escape; they were all caught in a web of horror.

Once Blanca left a missive of her own, in an alley off Canal Street where she'd found the image of a man wrapped in thorns. She couldn't make out the signature *V,* but she thought the painting was Icarus's. It had to be. The look of ecstasy on the man's face: the dusting of scarlet chalk over paint. Blanca took a black Magic Marker from her backpack and wrote her name and her phone number on the wall. For months afterward there were crazy calls to the house. Nasty, filthy messages, but none of them were from Sam. He would never have done that if he'd called. He would have said, *Don't slip, don't take chances, don't bother with me, let me burn, little sister, just let me fall.*

Perhaps someone else might have turned to what family she had, chosen to befriend the little sister who was there rather than remain allied with the brother who'd disappeared. Not Blanca. She had vacated. Even when she was home, she wasn't there. She spent weekends at friends' houses, spent summers as a counselor at various camps, visited Meredith during school vacations, signed up for ballet, soccer, the school newspaper, anything to keep her out of the house. At night Blanca often sat out on the lawn until everyone else was asleep. She looked at the stars, but she couldn't bear to look at the roof. He wasn't there. What was the point?

The Glass Slipper, though still lauded in the Sunday sections of the local newspapers and design magazines, was certainly not Blanca's home. Nothing belonged to her. Nothing was worth caring about. Even when she found Lisa in her room, dressing up in her clothes, face streaked with Blanca's blush and mascara, Blanca did nothing more than turn and walk out. *Take it,* she thought. *Take it all.*

"I'm sorry," Lisa had called after, but her tone was angry, almost as though she'd been the one whose belongings had been sullied. Lisa was a tadpole of a girl, tall and awkward with big blue eyes, clearly her father's favorite. John Moody, who'd barely been home when Blanca and Sam were growing up, now attended all of Lisa's parent-teacher meetings and piano recitals. One year he took Lisa to Disney World during Christmas vacation, leaving Cynthia at home to keep an eye on Blanca. This was during the time of the bad Blanca, the one who was never home, who slept around, the sour, green-with-jealousy teenager who felt she was an orphan. The cold, harsh girl who got out of Connecticut as fast as she could, first to college in Virginia, then to London. The one who was never going back, the one who picked beetles from in between pages until her fingers were stained with their blue-black blood, like ink she couldn't rinse off, not if she washed her hands a thousand times.

JOHN MOODY DIED IN THE YARD OF THE HOUSE HIS FATHER had built, that award-winning design made out of right angles, glass, and sky. It was a house John hated, but could not leave, because of its architectural value and history, because he had grown up there, but mostly because he had become a captive of his own failure. Every day when he awoke in his father's house, John was reminded that he himself had never accomplished anything as worthwhile. All of his work was derivative — a reaction against his father's actions. If questioned, John would have denied that he believed in predestination, he would have said he thought fate was a muddled stew of half-beliefs and wishes and that people made their own destiny. Yet here he was, stuck, unable to change something as simple as his address. It was as though John Moody's life had already been written in some great book in a language that was impossible to erase. Scrawled in blood-ink, invisible ink, life-and-death ink. Unwavering lines of print.

The only time John had veered from the path before him was that one instance when he'd gotten lost. It had been so misty and foggy, the entire trip over on the ferry from Bridgeport had seemed like a dream. A person could wind up anywhere with a single step on a night like that; knock at a stranger's door, fall into bed with her. Even a man like John could shift so far from the path he was on he might never get back where he should have been in the first place. His real life. The life that was meant to be and had unraveled because of a single night, a wrong turn, a girl with red hair standing on a porch.

What if he'd done what he'd set out to do, become the young man who went to study in Italy? Would that path have revealed a different self? A loving person, a good father? Or maybe those choices would have made no difference. In the end, perhaps he was who he was regardless of any other possibility. John carried his mistakes with him until he was nearly too weighed down to remember what might have been. The children from his first marriage had flown away like birds. What were birds to him? Creatures that hit against the glass roof, dirtied the windows, unwelcome, untrustworthy beings. There were no pictures of his first wife in his house, no mark that she'd ever existed, and yet he saw her when he came down to the kitchen in the dark, early morning. He saw her on the lawn in the evenings. John Moody spied her whenever he took a plane, up in the clouds or there beside him in the very next seat. John really didn't believe in such things — spirits, specters. Yet there she was, Arlyn Singer, exactly as she'd been when he first met her. She never spoke, only gazed at him. Maybe she wanted something from him, but he had no idea what it might be. She wore the same white dress of some thin fabric he could see right through. In the beginning he thought he was going mad; he went to psychics and psychologists, but in the end he accepted the fact that he was a haunted man.

Arlie wouldn't just leave him and let him get on with his life. Did she want him to suffer? After all, where had he been when she drew her last breath? Next door with Cynthia? Walking across the lawn? In his office, eyes closed, hoping for sleep? He no longer expected sleep and hadn't for years. He avoided it, dreaded it; sleep was blank space in which he drifted unprotected. Whenever he did finally manage to sleep, John had a single recurring dream. He was walking through the Glass Slipper; all of the rooms were dark. He went along a glass hallway, never reaching any destination. He woke up feeling lost, gasping for air. He was always on the verge of discovering something, but at the very last minute, he couldn't find his way.

In the last weeks of his life John had felt tired and his heart hurt, but he paid no attention to his health. Never had.

He was busy, with work, with his family. He'd been teaching his daughter, Lisa, to drive. She was a darling girl but a terrible driver. During those last two weeks of his life they went out to practice several times; once, when they were halfway to Greenwich, he became so rattled he'd asked Lisa to pull over. He'd gotten out and stood there shaking by the side of the road. He simply had no idea where he was. He started to flag down a passing car, convinced they were miles off track.

Luckily Lisa had a good sense of direction. She was a practical, no-nonsense girl. She got out and led him back to the car.

It's okay, Dad, she'd said to him. *I know where we're going. We're almost home.*

He'd sat in the passenger seat, his long legs folded, weakened somehow, more quiet than usual, not bothering to criticize Lisa, even when she nearly went through a stop sign. When they got home, Lisa told her mother about her dad's odd behavior. Cynthia wanted to phone the doctor, but John insisted he was fine. He wasn't. He sat beside the sliding glass doors; there was his first wife out by the pool, naked, pale as milk, the way she'd been in the kitchen the night he'd met her. John felt drawn to her again. He went outside. His heartbeat quickened.

Cynthia had been a good wife to him; he'd been lucky that way. He'd fallen into an affair with her, terrified by Arlie's illness, by death itself, by his own children. Frankly, the woman next door could have been anyone and he would have knocked on her door in the middle of the night, begging for comfort, desperate for companionship. Considering all that, the marriage had worked out fine. But now he found himself pulling away. It was Arlie he wanted. He noticed the mourning doves that had collected on the lawn.

Earlier he'd seen ashes on the kitchen countertops; he'd noticed cracks and chips in all the dishes. He felt as though something wanted his attention. He went up to Sam's room, closed and locked for years, took the key and went inside. He sat on the edge of the bed. There were ashes in here, too, as though they would never get Sam out of the room: cigarettes, needles, sour-smelling laundry. Sam was gone, yet in some ways he remained. There was a bag of his clothes in the closet, things Arlie had bought, sweaters and overalls. There were his drawings still on the walls.

The odd thing about identifying Sam's body wasn't that Sam had seemed like a stranger, but that in death he'd somehow been returned to John. He looked exactly as he had as a little boy, back when they lived on Twenty-third Street; a good, serious child John hadn't bothered to make time for. Arlie had adored Sam; John himself couldn't understand the ferocity with which she'd loved him. He'd been a terrible father and maybe he had no right to mourn, but he sat on a bench outside the morgue and wept. John hadn't known he could make those sorts of sounds. He hadn't known he could feel anything for his son. He hadn't been certain he could feel anything at all.

When he left the morgue, he made his way to Sam's last address on Tenth Avenue. Were there belongings John needed to pick up? Was he supposed to have a key? Should he talk to the super? This was the building from which Sam had fallen. The hallways were dark and there were smudgy paintings and chalk drawings in the stairwell, disturbed black and red and blue inkblots of men and birds and clouds. John Moody was never supposed to be in this hallway or have Sam as a son. He was never supposed to get lost that night.

It had been nearly eleven years since Sam first disappeared. The horrible truth was that John had been happy that he was gone. He'd never spoken it aloud, but he'd been relieved. Out of his hands; not his problem; far better this way. Now he was exhausted from walking up four flights of stairs. No one had ever cared about this building. It was lightless, ugly, a concrete box. It was everything John Moody had worked against in his life: disorder and despair. But this was the place. This was his son's last known address, so he knocked on the door. It was iron; it hurt his hand. He had a racing thought — *I could still get away.*

A boy of ten opened the door. John Moody recognized him. The boy was Sam, but that was impossible.

Sam? John said.

My father's gone, the boy told him. *I'm Will.* He was a serious fellow, very much in need of a haircut. *Do you want to come in? My mother will be back soon.*

Sam as he might have been, without that look in his eyes, that boneyard, black night, uncontrolled look. Just a little boy.

No, I think I'm at the wrong place. Wrong address.

John Moody hurried off. Two steps at a time. He quickly hailed a cab. He already knew he would keep the boy a secret, even from himself. What wasn't spoken of soon disappeared, at least on the surface, enough to let him get by. What he didn't think about, he wasn't responsible for. Instead, he went for long walks. He was distracted. He attended Lisa's piano recitals. He talked to her guidance counselor about which college would be best and went over her schedule and class selections, but all the while he was lost. He thought about that hallway in New York more than he should. He had conversations with a grandson he didn't even know. John began to keep a tape recorder in his pocket. Cynthia recorded not only his daily appointments for him, but directions on how to get there as well. John was that confused.

But he remembered to go to the cemetery once a month. The old cemetery, Archangel, where Arlie was. No one had to tell him to do that; no one even knew that he went. He parked and looked at the big tree, a sycamore, he thought, not that he knew much about trees. It had a mottled peeling bark. John knew glass and steel. He knew what it felt to be hollow inside. He had missed Arlie all this time. He had a photograph of her in his wallet; he'd snapped her picture on the ferry one day when she insisted they go back so she could see the house where she'd grown up. Arlie was wearing a white dress that was unsuitable for the weather, but John had bought it for her as a gift. He wasn't a man who thought about gifts, but when he'd seen the dress, he'd known it was right for Arlie. The sky was dark and threatening and for an instant John worried that his wife would be carried off by the wind.

Don't be silly, she'd called to him. She was holding on to the railing. *I'm not going anywhere.*

The day before he died John had trouble breathing. He went outside to get some fresh air and there Arlie was, surrounded by mourning doves. He thought perhaps he had taken the right path all along. Maybe he was meant to get lost that evening, meant to find Arlie in the kitchen, meant to be a father to Sam, his only child with her. He knew that. He knew why George Snow had sat at Arlie's bedside, not that he loved Blanca any less for it. He didn't even blame Arlie. Not one bit. He'd gotten lost, that was the problem; he hadn't been there for her and he'd never been the sort of man who could ask for help.

"I really think you should try to get more rest," Cynthia said on the night before he died. He was logy, distracted.

"She was absolutely naked in the kitchen," John Moody said.

"Who?"

John took hold of himself. "Some movie. I saw it on TV last night. They have nudity."

"You shouldn't be up watching TV so late," Cynthia said.

On that night John Moody did as he was told. He fell asleep and began to dream that he was walking down the hall. This dream was different from the usual one. He heard something breathing; he smelled smoke. There was soot on the floor. He came at last to a room he hadn't known was there, in the very center of the house he'd grown up in. The room he'd always been looking for. The door was closed but he could hear something flying around inside. It hit against the wall with a thud; there was the sound of wings beating. Like a heart, just as regular, but louder, so loud he could feel it inside his own head.

The key to the room was made out of glass. It cut John's hands and made him bleed. The blood itself had a steady rhythm, as it dropped onto the floor. Something was flying around in the dark, something large and dark with leathery wings. It had talons. It had been there all along. It had broken all the glass, the ceiling, the windows; glass was everywhere, like falling stars.

John lit a lantern. All at once he saw the truth. It wasn't a bird trapped inside the room; it was a dragon. Red and wounded, wings beating. A dragon in his very own house.

John Moody held the glass key in his hand even though he continued to bleed. He could hear himself breathing, his sleeping real self. But his dream self couldn't catch his breath. He didn't dare move. For here was the problem, as it always had been: he didn't know if he was supposed to kill the dragon or rescue it.

John had a headache when he woke in the morning, and decided not to go to work. A rarity, and cause for concern. Cynthia phoned the doctor to make an appointment as she was fixing his breakfast. Best to be safe rather than sorry. They weren't young, after all. They didn't always agree, but she was a good wife, and he a good husband. She made up a tray: fruit, eggs, decaffeinated coffee with skim milk.

When John came downstairs he was still in his bathrobe. He said he couldn't breathe; he needed a bit of fresh air.

I'll bring you some water, Cynthia had said. *We can have breakfast outside.*

After he'd gone into the yard, Cynthia watched John sink into one of the patio chairs so he could look out over the lawn. He loved that view. He was a handsome man, even now, and Cynthia appreciated him. *He's finally resting,* she thought, but that wasn't it at all. John Moody was waiting, and in no time she was there. He could see her clear as day. Her long red hair, the thin white dress he could see through. She was perfect; he'd forgotten that. Surely, he understood why he'd stayed.

When he had woken on a strange couch in a stranger's house all those years ago, he'd quickly sat up and put on his shoes. John Moody wasn't some fool ready to be waylaid. He got his car keys and found a map on top of the desk in the parlor. There was the route he was supposed to take, a thin line of color cutting across the North Shore of Long Island. Easy enough. Easy as pie. But then he heard something that caught his interest. A sound he couldn't ignore, like wings flapping, or fabric slipping off a woman's shoulders. Twenty steps to the kitchen door. The carpet was worn, the floors wide yellow pine. How could he ever have forgotten how much he had wanted her? His hands were actually shaking when he pushed the door open. Big, white hands, clumsy, young, a man in search of what he wanted. Here was the path, the future, his destiny. Italy was nothing compared to her. Everything that might have been fell away.

He stared out at the lawn and understood himself at last. A dozen mourning doves. Pools of dark shadows on the lawn. She was gone, but he didn't need her to remind him anymore. The way she had turned to him. The way she walked to him. The way he was waiting for her.

He remembered everything now.

A RED MAP ISN'T EASY TO FOLLOW. ANY DOCUMENT MADE of blood and bones is tricky. Wrong turns are easily made, and there are often piles of stones in the road. A person has to disregard time and sorrow and all the damage done. If you follow, if you dare, the thread always leads to whomever or whatever you've forgotten: the little girl lost in the woods, the hedgehog, the strand of pearls, the ferryboat, your own father.

Every traveler needs a warm coat, walking shoes, a bottle of water, a watch that can be trusted, an honest man, and a mirror that reflects back truthfully. James Bayliss drove Blanca to the airport. He was angry, but most people wouldn't have been able to tell. Blanca, however, could. She knew James well enough to notice that his shoulders were a bit higher than usual, tensely held, and there was more silence; his work boots were especially heavy on the gas and the clutch. James was pissed because Blanca wouldn't let him go with her. It made no sense to him at all.

"Don't be mad. You're not missing anything. It's a reprieve, really." Blanca was traveling light — one small carry-on case filled with black clothes, shampoo, books. "James, please," she said when he didn't answer. James was searching out a space even though she told him not to bother with the car park, just to drop her off. "Right there," she said, pointing out the departure section. "They're not even technically my family," Blanca insisted. "They're all semi-relatives. My real family is dead."

"You don't want me to go inside the terminal with you and wait?"

"Well, why would you want to do that?" Blanca said. "You can't go with me to the gate. It's a waste of time."

"I want to. That's the point, Blanca."

"Well, that's just stupid," Blanca said.

James nodded. There it was, a jab at the fact he hadn't gone to university. "Exactly."

"I don't mean stupid in that way."

"No, you meant it in a positive way."

They both laughed at that, even though this moment seemed as though it might be the end of them. They said good-bye on the sidewalk outside the British Airways terminal. It was noisy and crowded. James didn't make a move toward her, just stood there and handed Blanca her overnight case. It was awkward. James had played semi-professional soccer when he was younger and now someone recognized him and patted him on the back. That happened often, strangers coming out of nowhere to address him.

"I'll be back in no time. I promise." Blanca hugged him, then stepped away. He hadn't hugged her back. "This isn't about us. It's about going home."

"You can't keep dividing your worlds." James kept his hands in his pockets "It's all one big rotten mess. We're either in it together or we're not."

Blanca simply wanted this journey over and done. She could come back and fix things with James. Her life was here, after all. She checked in and waited in the lounge; when her flight was called, she boarded, took a sleeping tablet, and closed her eyes. She was asleep in no time. She dreamed of a swan out on the lawn of her father's house. It moved with difficulty, slow, exhausted, then it lay down in the grass. It was giving birth, and it labored horribly. The delivery was sudden, pouring out of the swan with the great force of birth — a full-grown duck encircled by a thick, mucusy casing. As she woke, Blanca thought to herself, *But swans lay eggs.*

It was dark and they were halfway across the ocean; Blanca's head filled with the droning of the jet's engines. She thought of the way James had stood there on the sidewalk. She thought of the many ways love could hurt you. She was not an open person; she knew that. She'd assumed James had known that about her as well.

Blanca rented a car at Kennedy and drove to Connecticut; because she wasn't sure she remembered the way, she'd had the rent-a-car attendant go over the map several times. Still, she was nervous as she drove. She felt panicky, imagining she was on the wrong side of the road; she felt confused and out of sorts and she hadn't even bothered to comb her hair. When she got off the highway, most of it came back to her. Turn left, and there was the market. Turn right, and the road led home.

There had been a brief, uncomfortable phone conversation with her stepmother. Thank you, but no, she wouldn't be staying at the house, but would instead be at the Eagle Inn, just on the other side of town. Meredith had already made the reservation. When Blanca pulled up, she remembered the inn, a white house with a stone foundation and patio. The school bus had taken this route, but Blanca had never looked much beyond the hedges.

She parked and walked down the path. There was the sound of bees and of traffic on the road. Blanca suddenly wished she'd brought something other than black to wear; she was broiling. How humid summer was here. The air was sticky and it was difficult to breathe. Blanca was wearing a long-sleeved blouse and a pair of corduroy slacks that should have been packed away for the summer.

The owner of the inn was a local woman, Helen Jeffries, a recent widow herself, who seemed to know the Moody family. "I'm so sorry for your loss," Helen said as she checked Blanca in and handed over a key. "Your father was a lovely man."

Blanca went up the carpeted stairs and found her room — a bed with a dust ruffle, a view of the lawn. She thought about the swan she'd dreamed about on the plane. The inn wasn't air-conditioned and she felt feverish. There were no private bathrooms, so Blanca went down the hall to wash up. The dress she'd brought to wear to the funeral was wool, totally inappropriate for the weather. She'd forgotten what June could be like here. She'd roast, she'd burn, she'd burst into flames as she stood at the gravesite.

Blanca ran the cold tap and dashed water on her face. If she opened her eyes would she be back in her flat? If she blinked would she be in her driveway, where the lilacs grew all those years ago?

There was a knock at the bathroom door.

"Don't use up all the water!"

It was Meredith, teasing her. Blanca opened the door and they embraced.

"Let me look at you."

Meredith still saw Blanca as the ten-year-old girl she'd first come to babysit, even now, when Meredith's own youngest child was nine and her eldest thirteen. Merrie had been in Connecticut only a few hours, but she'd already phoned her kids; she missed them terribly despite their racket and their constant demands. She could not imagine what it was like to leave your children behind for good, to know you wouldn't see who they grew up to be. Well, here Blanca was — if only her mother could see — a beautiful woman with a life of her own.

"You're gorgeous, even if you haven't combed your hair," Meredith said.

"God, I'm dreading this." Blanca was wearing heavy black boots as well. Where had she thought she was going? The frozen tundra? Some arctic location where workers had to chip away the ice with picks in order to bury a man?

Meredith was wearing a pale gray suit with black trim and a black silk blouse. She'd been married for fifteen years, was the mother to four children; she had gone back to graduate school and now taught English in the local high school. Meredith was far too busy to come to a funeral for a man she hadn't seen in years and hadn't even liked to begin with. She looked into Blanca's face. She thought about her first day with the family: Sam on the roof, so dangerously close to falling. Blanca running down the driveway.

Meredith's time in Connecticut had allowed her to learn who she was and what she wanted. Just last night in bed, for instance, Merrie had turned to her husband and asked if when he died he would promise to come back to haunt her.

"Why would I do that to you?" Daniel had long given up thinking about spirits. He was the head of his department and he concentrated on the real world now.

"Because I'd want you to."

Daniel laughed. "You wouldn't want that."

Meredith had circled her arms around him. She'd never

in her life thought she would love anyone this deeply. "Yes, you must."

"So that's it, Merrie. That's why people are haunted."

It was a discussion they'd been having since the night they first met, back when Meredith claimed the house in which she worked was haunted. What kept a spirit tied to earth? Love or hate, time or desire?

"People are haunted because they want to be," Daniel said.

Meredith was missing her husband. He was right about ghosts. She would want him to haunt her; she'd never want to let him go. "You'd better get a move on," she told Blanca. "We have to leave in ten minutes."

"Why do we have to leave so soon? The cemetery's right down the lane."

"No. It's farther."

"Isn't it the one with the big tree? Archangel? Sam took me there once to visit our mother's grave. He didn't have a license but he hijacked Cynthia's car. It was late at night and there was a full moon and I was terrified."

"It's a different cemetery, Bee. One Cynthia has chosen."

"Ah. He's not being buried with my mother." Blanca felt her face flush. She had been here for only a few hours and was already furious. "And not with my brother, either. Well, of course. It makes sense. He certainly wouldn't want to spend eternity with my mother or Sam."

They went out to the car Blanca had rented. Meredith had come by cab, but now she insisted on driving; at least she knew which side of the road to drive on. Blanca brushed her hair in the car, brusque, wrenching strokes. She still had beautiful pale hair, but she quickly wound the length of it into a knot before savagely running a clip through it. She looked out the window as Meredith drove. They merged onto the highway and traveled past two exits, then found their way along the back roads. There was to be a graveside service at the cemetery; already there were so many cars Meredith had to park outside the gate. Blanca rummaged through her purse for a little black knitted hat. Perfect for Antarctica. Sweat was running down her back and her wool dress itched. Thank goodness for the cool strand of pearls around her throat. She and Meredith walked down a cement path.

"Do you know why I came to work for your family?" Meredith asked as they walked.

"Because you were a masochist?"

Meredith laughed. People at the graveside gathering looked around as they approached.

"Well, yes. I suppose I was. I took the job because I saw your mother's ghost."

"Look, Meredith, I don't believe in any of that. When you're dead, you're gone. So maybe it doesn't matter whether or not my father and mother are buried together."

"Your father had gone to a psychic. I was at a party for my college roommate and I saw her. She had long red hair. She was wearing a white dress. I had the feeling I was supposed to follow her home."

"That's how you made your decision? God! I thought you were the sensible one in the household."

"It was a good decision."

Meredith hugged Blanca. She thought of Blanca as her

first daughter, her practice daughter. "I saw her in the house, on the lawn, on the roof. Your mother was there the whole time."

"What do you think she wanted? Don't ghosts always want something? To right a wrong? To change the past? To get even?"

"I used to think ghosts wanted to be remembered, that they refused to be put into a drawer like a pair of old stockings. Maybe she was looking out for you and Sam, but I think it had a great deal to do with your father. He was seeing her on the lawn the day he died."

"You can't know that," Blanca said.

"No, but I believe it."

Blanca didn't know anyone at the gravesite except for Cynthia, who was wearing a black silk suit and a hat with a small veil. And there was Lisa; it must be her, a girl of sixteen with honey-colored hair, weeping. She was hardly recognizable; the last time Blanca had seen her half sister she'd been a child, not a leggy teenager.

The Connecticut heat was overwhelming. In truth, Blanca wished James were there. She liked the way he felt beside her, even when he didn't speak.

"I wish I'd seen my mother," Blanca said. "I don't even remember what she looked like."

"You were too young to remember. I've come to believe that spirits don't choose whether or not to remain. They stay because the living won't let them go. That was why your father continued to see her."

"Are you saying it was my father who was holding on to her? He didn't even want to be buried beside her."

They had reached the mourners and several people greeted Blanca as though they knew her, offering condolences. Perhaps she had known them once, when she was a girl, but now they were just a dizzying collection of strangers. Meredith pointed her in the right direction and Blanca approached her stepmother.

"Cynthia," she said tentatively, as though she didn't quite expect to be recognized.

"Oh." Cynthia lurched forward and hugged Blanca. She'd obviously been crying for days. "I can't believe he's gone."

"No," Blanca agreed, shocked by how frail Cynthia seemed within their embrace. When they backed away from each other, Blanca realized how much older Cynthia appeared, even with the veil hiding her face.

Blanca nodded at her half sister. Lisa stared at her.

"I think I'll go stand over with Meredith," Blanca said.

Cynthia didn't seem to notice as Blanca slipped away. By now Blanca's pale skin was blotchy. Even the pearls she wore — usually so cool and refreshing against her skin — burned like little coals. She remembered now that the pearls had been black when she first saw them, covered with ashes.

The service began and Meredith took Blanca's arm when Cynthia and Lisa began to sob. They were wailing, joined in the deep sound of grief. The minister spoke so softly Blanca could barely hear him. There were robins on the grass and the hum of a lawn mower somewhere far away. Her heart hurt against her ribs.

"We will miss him," the minister was saying. Blanca heard that part at least. "Now and forevermore."

There was to be a luncheon held at the house, but Blanca

wasn't ready for that yet. She needed time to catch her breath. So what if they'd be late? Let people talk.

"Let's just drive," Blanca suggested.

They rolled down the car windows and let the air whip through. Blanca unlaced her boots and took them off. She took off her stockings as well. When they stopped for gas, Meredith got out and bought two bottles of soda; they drank them in the gas station lot. A bit more time. A few more minutes before they had to face the Glass Slipper. Blanca's bare feet were burning from the hot asphalt, but she didn't care. At least she could feel something. By now people would begin to wonder what had happened to them.

"I want to rip off my clothes," Meredith said of her silk suit. "I didn't think it would be so hot up here."

"I want to rip off my skin."

They both laughed and then Blanca started crying, all at once. She'd thought she would never cry again, but here she was, in tears.

"Oh, Blanca," Meredith said. "I'm so sorry."

"I'm supposed to go and mourn with them and I don't even know them. I wish Sam was here. I mean, what kind of person am I? I can't even cry for my father."

"You are crying," Meredith said.

They got back in the car, but instead of turning left toward the house when they got off the highway, Meredith made a right and headed along the town green.

"Where are we going?"

"You said you wanted Sam."

When Sam had sneaked Blanca up onto the roof of the Glass Slipper when she was a girl he'd told her that when walking on glass, bare feet are always preferable. They don't slip and slide as much as shoes, plus you can feel the icy cold through your feet, up inside your bones.

Try it, Peapod, he'd said.

But Blanca had been too afraid to unlace her sneakers.

"I do want Sam," she said now.

Meredith drove to the other cemetery, the one with the big tree and the iron gates, the one Sam and Blanca had run off to the night Sam stole Cynthia's car. He'd driven eighty miles an hour and Blanca had been terrified, but she never once told him to stop.

This is how it feels to fly, Sam had told her.

Meredith and Blanca circled around the cemetery, lost. Every path looked the same, ivy and hedges and long, blue shadows. And then Blanca recognized the big tree.

"There it is!"

They parked, then walked toward the graves. The grass was soft and cool under Blanca's bare feet.

"Sam climbed way up that tree when we snuck out here one night. It was pitch-dark and I couldn't see him. I was terrified. I didn't know how I would ever get back home if he fell and broke his neck."

"You would have managed," Meredith said. "You were that sort of child. Practical. Smart."

Indeed, Blanca had always been self-reliant, but all her confidence had disappeared. If it had been confidence in the first place and not just a thin veneer of bravado to cover up her fear. It was cool here in the cemetery, and the grass was wet. The dampness and cold were rising up through Blanca's feet, into her bones. It had been much easier to mourn her brother from a distance, there on the banks of the Thames. That had been paper and stones and water, not flesh and blood. *What you don't see, what you don't know, what you don't feel.*

"Let me take a breath." She was so dizzy. She counted to fifty and back down to one.

Meredith waited. There was no rush, after all. She knew what this felt like, to walk across the grass toward someone you'd lost.

"Okay," Blanca said after a few minutes.

But it really wasn't. The closer she came to the graves, the more stones there were in the ground. She wished then that she had kept her boots on. She wished she'd stayed where she'd been, with her books and her beetles and her lime tree in the garden; a place where there were no stones at all, only moss, the sort that is so soft to walk over you might think you were far above the earth and all its rocky paths, some-place in the clouds, where the temperature was cold enough to turn breath to ice crystals, even on a hot June day when the leaves were falling off the willows, curled at the edges, dry as dust.

WILL ROTH WAS TURNING SIXTEEN. HE HAD ALREADY AR-ranged his own birthday party. He was like that, clear-headed in the face of disaster, joyous in times of good fortune. Will was a planner, a doer, a guy his friends could depend upon. On Will's birthday, his classmates would be treated to bowling, pizza would be ordered, and a good time would be had by all. Will had been saving money for months and had enough to pay the bill in case his mother was short on cash, but as it turned out he needn't have bothered. His mom had come into an inheritance. Her parents had died and now Will and his mom were rich, more or less. Well, at least they weren't poor. They had been on welfare for a year or two, and Will had lived with his grandparents when he was too young to remember while his mother was recovering from her misspent youth. Misspent except for him. Love of her life, child she couldn't believe she was lucky enough to have. Her only family now.

Amy had used her inheritance to buy a condo right down the street from her grandmother's rent-controlled apartment, the one Sam had gotten them kicked out of when he fell asleep and started a fire one night. She paid all their bills, got Will a skateboard, bought herself a new wardrobe and went back to school. Since then Will's mom had become a substitute teacher in a private school in Brooklyn. She taught biology and earth science. Will, on the other hand, was an artist, as his father had been.

Death wasn't all bad, Will saw that now. You lost things, you found things. His grandparents, for instance, continued to give even after their death; they'd provided for Will, even had a college savings account in his name. He had loved his grandparents and had spent summers with them out on Long Island; he'd had more time with his grandparents than most kids did because his mother was so young, seventeen when she had him, and his father, well, his father wasn't reliable. Will knew this early on. That was probably why Will still was so careful with money. He was careful all the way around. He knew the way things could get away from you, right out of your hands.

His parents sometimes lived together and sometimes didn't and in the end his father sort of disappeared. But his dad always came back, at least for a while, and Will's mom always let Sam crash with them, even when they'd pretty much broken up for good. She let Sam's parrot stay as well, as long as there was newspaper spread out under the metal stand they brought out from the closet when such visits occurred. Will understood how kind his mother was; she hated that parrot, and he hated her right back. *Get out,* he would cry whenever Amy came near. *You,* he would croak accusingly.

Whenever Will's dad was there, he was vivid, like a splash of color. Sam painted the walls of the bathroom one day and let Will help until they were both human swirls of color, covered with oil-based paint that lasted for days and wouldn't wash off. Sometimes when Will's dad visited, his parents would end up fighting; his mother would cry and she'd say, *Why can't you just grow up?,* and then Will would feel responsible. He'd feel bad for liking the time he spent with his father, who didn't even make him wear shoes. Sometimes the concrete was hot and burned his feet. Sometimes there was ice and snow and he wished for a pair of boots. But Will never complained to his father. He was grateful for whatever he got. He grew up to be a steady, practical kid, dark-eyed with chestnut hair, tall and lanky and serious.

"What about Dad's family?" he'd asked his mother, and she'd answered, "The parrot is his family. He had a sister once, but I don't know what happened to her. It's mostly the parrot." Then she added, "And us."

One night when Will and Amy were walking home from grocery shopping, a gray rainy night when the air smelled like sugar and ashes, Amy suddenly stopped and dropped her packages in the street. For a minute Will thought she was having a heart attack, but no. His mom was looking up. There was Will's father on the roof.

"Be careful who you fall in love with," Will's mother had told him then. *Ashes, ashes,* he'd thought to himself. *There was no place to go but down.* "Anything you fall into can't be good. Remember that."

Will's mother had short black hair and she wore jeans and T-shirts when she didn't have to go to work. She had a tattoo of a rose on her shoulder that she wished she'd never gotten.

"From the time of my idiocy," she told Will. "And don't you even think about getting one. You're underage."

Will understood that his parents had used drugs, that they'd fallen in love without thinking about consequences. Will saw that his mother had pulled herself together, but his father never had, and so Will didn't expect anything from Sam. Sometimes his mother would be ranting about how irresponsible his dad was, but Will took that as a given, the way some birds are blue and some are black. His father was himself, nothing less and nothing more.

There had been a few bad incidents. Sam occasionally showed up at Will's school, and that was always a disaster. Back in first grade, the police had been forced to eject Sam. Or at least that was their story. Will would have been able to talk his father down when he was high; he'd done it before. *We'll take two steps, we'll make a run for it, we'll hide in the subway, the stairwell, the basement, the coffee shop.* Sam was paranoid. Will had learned that word when he was very young. He knew what was going on when Sam stood on the sidewalk in front of the school shouting that someone wanted to kill his son; that danger was everywhere. Will went to the window and watched them take his father away. When you yelled or screamed or shouted it only made things worse. He wished he could write out a list for his father: *crouch down, keep your arms loose and to the sides so they don't break like twigs, don't struggle.*

They got Will's dad down on the ground when he wouldn't cooperate; one officer sat squarely on top of him, the other cuffed his hands behind his back. There was blood on the sidewalk, or maybe it was paint. Will's father was a great artist, though he never got paid. Will hoped the officers wouldn't hurt his father, that they'd understand who he was. Will's dad had his own belief system. He believed in evil people, maps made of tears, cities of white powder, tents constructed with needles. He believed there was a heaven; it was right above the everyday realm, it had to be. This couldn't be the real world. Not this terrible plane of existence. Not this world they were walking through.

Will's dad suffered, he ached, he hurt. He did bad things like steal; he was a slave to heroin. Will understood what drugs did to you; they took you apart bit by bit until only your heart was left. Still, no one else's father cared enough to run up the school stairs shouting about evil kidnappers; no other dad was brave enough to be dragged away, shoved into a patrol car, handcuffed, arms bent into wings, looking back through the window of the car, desperate to protect the son he loved.

And then Will's father died. No warning, no reason. It was just a regular day and Will was in his room. He was doing homework, writing a paper on the great religions of the world, when he saw something go past the window. He had the craziest idea — that the sky was falling, the world was ending. Maybe the city was under attack. It had happened, and it could happen again. His father had told him he'd been so close to Ground Zero he'd been covered with ashes; he'd kept a jarful in his backpack to remind him how near the end might be. Maybe it was happening now. Tenth Avenue turned into a war zone. Maybe pieces of the sky were crashing onto trucks, buses, sidewalks, wounding anyone foolish enough to venture out.

What would he do in the few minutes allowed him if this truly was the end of the world? Not homework. That was certain. Will went to his desk and he wrote, *I love you,* although to whom he was leaving this message he wasn't sure. It just came to him. A message to the universe, to everything that had ever been and wasn't anymore. Every day, every moment, every molecule.

Someone was pounding on the front door and Will heard it open. Then he heard his mother sobbing. It didn't even sound like her. The sound was like glass; too broken, too torn apart for the human throat. He stayed where he was, listening to himself breathe. Something bad was happening out there. Then there was a knock at his bedroom door. His room was small, fashioned out of two closets with the wall between them taken down; it had a window and a great loft bed. Will was sitting at the desk beneath the loft, looking at what he'd written. It didn't even look like his own hand-writing. All at once, he wondered if perhaps it wasn't a mes-sage he had left, but one that had been delivered to him. His mother opened the door. Will was ten at the time, but any-one would have guessed he was older. He looked up at Amy. And then he knew it wasn't the sky that had fallen.

The next day, his mother went to see her doctor for some pills that would help her stop crying. Overnight, she looked her age, or maybe she just grew up the rest of the way, fast. She'd met Sam Moody at the bus station on Forty-second Street when she was fifteen. It seemed a second ago, sitting there with her back against the wall, wearing army boots, a green plaid skirt, a sweater she'd stolen from Lord & Taylor, thinking about getting a tattoo on her shoulder, thinking what it might be like to fall in love, crazy head over heels in love. That was when he sat down beside her, just like that, as though she'd called him to her. Sam smiled at her, and she wondered if this was how angels made themselves known to those on earth. They sat down beside you and changed your life. Sam said, *Hey, you want to get high?* Amy had taken his words to mean *You are so beautiful I am undone by you.* After his death, it was the other way around. She was undone by him completely. He'd been sleeping on the couch, half living with them, half disappearing. She counted on Sam's unpre-dictable nature, a funny way to chart your life. But he had always come back. Until now. Maybe that was the reason Amy couldn't stop crying; in losing Sam she'd lost herself, the girl she used to be, the fearless one who fell in love at Port Authority without the slightest bit of hesitation.

When Amy went off to her doctor's appointment, Will made himself lunch, but then he couldn't eat. His stomach was all jumpy. He had weird thoughts ricocheting through his head. He kept expecting his father to knock on the door, and for everything to be the way it had been. He'd never told his mother, but he knew where his father had lived when he wasn't with them. Sam had taken Will there once, and even Will could tell it was a dump. They had to go in through a basement door, then up some metal stairs. People were staying in rooms that had no doors. Will and Sam went up and up to the top floor. Sam had his parrot with him; it was a small parrot that fit inside his coat pocket. His family, his confidant. Sometimes Sam talked to the parrot, and people on the street backed away.

Pick a door, any door, his father had said, once they'd climbed as high as they could go. But of course there were no doors, only open, filthy rooms. There was bedding and clothes on the floor and water leaking from the pipes. There was the smell of mold and of urine.

Wherever you want to go, Dad.

Well, you're the first person who's ever said that to me. His father had sat down on the floor, right there in the hall. Will had sat down across from Sam. He knew that no one else's father would bring them to a place like this, but his father couldn't be anyone but himself.

You can get hurt here, Dad, Will had said. *I don't want that to happen to you.*

Now on the day after the accident, not long after Will had made the sandwich he couldn't eat, a man Will didn't know came to the door. There was a knock, and for an instant Will had the crazy hope his father had returned, even though he knew it couldn't be. Will went to answer; a tall man in a gray suit was in the hall. The man was older; he seemed tired, as though he'd climbed a million steps. He looked familiar, but Will couldn't place him.

The man called Will by his father's name.

My father's not here, Will said. *Do you want to come in? My mother will be back soon.*

The man said something Will couldn't make out, then turned to leave. Will had gone out after him, but the man was already down the stairs. Will wondered if their visitor had been a friend of his father's; he seemed choked up and lost somehow. Will went back into the apartment and looked through the window. The old man wasn't out there, but Will saw something green out of the corner of his eye.

Even now, more than five years later, Will saw it sometimes. A flash of color and feathers. The parrot that got loose the day his father died. And he wasn't the only one. People in Chelsea saw the parrot on rooftops along Twenty-third Street; there were those who swore they'd spied it in the hallway of their apartment building, sleeping in vestibules on snowy nights, sitting perfectly still on window ledges, or roosting on water towers.

Parrots, Will knew, could live past a hundred, like Winston Churchill's famous pet. For a long time Will left out traps on the roof of their building, tins of seed and grapes and carrots, all beneath a laundry basket set to fall upon the creature should it alight. He caught a rat, and two pigeons and a dove, and then he gave up. He stopped taking the subway to Brooklyn and Queens, where there were reports of wild parrots roosting. The one time he spotted a nest, the birds inside were red, nothing like his father's parrot. All the same, he still looked at the sky. He did it all the time. Some of his friends called him the Stargazer, not that you could see stars in Chelsea; but it was true, he was always looking up. It was in his nature to be hopeful, but not to be a fool.

His mother had told him it was an accident, and Will acted as though he believed her. He was that kind of son, and Amy was grateful to him. She thought Sam knew what a great kid they had. In spite of everything, they had brought something good into this world. Maybe that was their destiny, their combined task, a boy like Will.

Now, it was Will's birthday. He was about to turn sixteen, a year older than Amy was when she made her life-changing decision in the bus station. Will was much purer than she ever was. Much more centered. Almost six years without his father. Hardly a little boy. Every spring Amy and Will rented a car and went up to the cemetery in Connecticut where Sam was buried. He wanted to be turned into ashes, but he and Amy had never married and she had no legal rights to make a decision like that; Sam's father saw to that, even though he never saw to anything else, least of all his son.

When they had first visited Archangel Cemetery, Amy had suggested Will leave a stone; that's what Jews did to remember their dead. That's what they did when they visited his grandparents' graves on Long Island. And so every year Will left a stone for his father, and not just any stone. It was always one he'd spent weeks searching for, a perfect stone, one his dad would have appreciated. There was a white one that he'd found in New Hampshire, where they were vacationing with some guy his mother thought she might marry, but it didn't work out. There was a green stone from Cape Cod, a black stone from Central Park, a bluish swirly thing he had uncovered under a pine tree while walking with his grandpa on Long Island, a chunk of granite from the sidewalk on Tenth Avenue. The last one he'd found was silver, shiny, discovered on the floor of the Museum of Natural History. Maybe it was something important that had rolled out of an exhibit, a moonrock, say, or a prehistoric piece of petrified wood, or maybe it was trash dragged in on the bottom of someone's shoe. He thought his father would appreciate its mystery. He thought his father would love it best of all.

"I wish Sam could see you now," his mom said on the day of Will's birthday. "So grown up." All his buddies had come over and they were gathered around the table. Will had ordered six pizzas with everything. Will went over and hugged his mother and she started crying for no reason.

"I'm an idiot," Amy said, wiping at her eyes, laughing. All of the wildness she'd had as a kid had been drained out of her. Now when she thought of the person she'd been, the things she'd done — hitchhiking across the country, living in strangers' apartments, all those drugs, pills she took to make her smaller or larger, anywhere but where she was — it was like remembering a long-lost sister, one she hardly knew. A crazy kid. That wild girl. Whoever she might have gone on being if she hadn't gotten pregnant with Will.

"You're just overprotective," Will said. He knew his mother was a good-hearted, well-meaning person. Maybe she wasn't always right about things. She wasn't an idiot, that much was obvious. It was just that sometimes there were certain things she didn't want to know. About his father, for instance. Falling off the roof. That's what she wanted to believe. That day when Sam had taken Will to the run-down building, the one with no doors and a staircase to nowhere, the one where he lived when he wasn't with them, when all he could think about was drugs; they'd sat there knee to knee in the hallway, on the dirty floor. Sam had leaned very close to his son. For someone who wasn't very clean, he smelled good. He smelled like fresh air and green grass.

You can't go with me, he'd said to Will. *You know that, right? Nobody can.*

Maybe it was an instant, maybe it was well planned out, maybe it was his dream come true.

I've got to get there by myself, Will's father had told him that day in the hallway.

Someone downstairs was drunk or stoned and screaming but Will and Sam had both ignored the ruckus. Will had nodded; he understood. Some people had choices and some people didn't. He knew that then and he knew it now, as he led his group of friends down the stairs, all of them whooping, stomachs filled with pizza, happily on their way to Will's birthday celebration. Another year most gratefully spent in this world.

*   *   *

BLANCA HAD GONE TO THE HOUSE FOR THE FUNERAL luncheon, but Meredith had been driving then. Now Meredith had left, back to her own family, and navigating alone the next day was a trial. Blanca was lost in no time. She tried to follow the route she'd once known so well she could find her way in the dark, flying along on her bicycle. But everything seemed changed. Trees had been cut down, new houses built, roads had been extended to sweep through developments that had once been nothing more than meadows; everything seemed to be on the wrong side of the road.

Blanca was to meet with her stepmother and half sister and her father's attorney, David Hill. It was still hot and she had bought an outfit for the occasion in the Dress Shack in town, along with a pair of white flip-flops and some summer clothes. Her hair was loose and she wore her mother's pearls, cool drops of salt and stone. James had phoned the inn twice, but both times Blanca had been out when he called. She felt isolated and abandoned; all the same, she hadn't phoned back. She was in a bubble. All alone. She drove to her childhood home with the windows down so she could spy the street signs; still she was over an hour late. Blanca dreaded the meeting. It was one thing to avoid her father all these years, another thing altogether to go home and not have him there.

The Glass Slipper, when Blanca came to it, was bright, blindingly so on this summer afternoon. Blanca parked her rental car and walked up to the door. The drive was still made of little white pebbles, round stones that crunched under Blanca's flip-flops and threw her off balance. Today, John Moody's will would be divulged. Funny, Blanca had never thought of the second meaning of the word: what he wanted, desired, yearned for.

When she opened the door, Cynthia hugged Blanca and drew her into the hall. It was the only dark, windowless place in the house.

"This is not a happy day," Cynthia said.

"No."

Had the house always had an echo? As they walked down the hallway, there was the *slap slap* of Blanca's flip-flops against the wood and the brisk clip of her stepmother's heels.

Lisa and the attorney were waiting in the living room. It all felt very formal. Too formal for a loose dress and white flip-flops. They all said good morning, except for Lisa. She was still tall and awkward, washed out with grief. She looked at Blanca, then quickly looked away.

"Let's get to it, shall we?" the lawyer said. "As you can imagine, John left the house and half of his estate to Cynthia. The other half of the estate has been divided equally. It's quite a good amount. A third to Lisa and a third to Blanca."

"There are only two of us," Lisa said.

"Who is the third person?" Cynthia asked.

David Hill handed Blanca a manila envelope. "You're supposed to take care of it. Your dad asked if you would."

"There must be some mistake," Blanca suggested.

"No mistake."

Cynthia and Lisa were quiet, but they shifted closer

together. Surely they were thinking the same thing. Why Blanca? Did John Moody have a cause they didn't know about? Perhaps he'd paid the expenses for his first wife's aged aunt in a nursing home? Or was it something worse? A mistress or a love child?

"You can open it here or privately," David Hill said. "However you wish to handle it. Once the estate is settled, bank accounts will be set up for all three individuals. Lisa also has a separate college fund, which at this point will be more than enough for any further education."

Blanca slipped the envelope into her purse. He'd stapled it closed, then Scotch-taped it. There was some sort of meaning in all those measures. *Don't let the cat out of the bag. It bites, it scratches, it eats mice whole, tail and ears and all.*

"You're not opening it?" Lisa leaned forward. She was wearing the same black blouse and skirt she'd worn to the funeral. She was tall like John Moody, but she had her mother's delicate bone structure. It was an odd combination; difficult to tell if she was fragile or strong beyond belief.

"Maybe later," Blanca said. "I don't think this is the best time."

"We have a right to know who this other person is," Lisa said to her mother. "Don't we?"

"I thought we'd have lunch." Cynthia stood and suggested they follow her into the kitchen.

"Mom! Blanca wasn't even here to visit Dad. She never came back."

"She was here before you were born," Cynthia said. "I learned everything I knew about babies taking care of her. She was only eight months old when I moved in. So hush."

"Gee, Cynthia, I never knew you had so much concern for me and Sam."

You moved in for convenience' sake, Blanca stopped herself from saying. *That way our father didn't have to sneak across the lawn in the middle of the night.* Blanca felt especially cold. Maybe it was the pearls at her neck. Maybe it was the way Lisa was glaring at her. Cynthia, on the other hand, chose to ignore her comment.

"I made egg-salad sandwiches," Cynthia said. "Dave, are you staying for lunch? I've got Bloody Marys, too."

"Wouldn't miss it," David Hill said.

The attorney was a big, friendly man with whom John Moody had played golf for thirty-five years. A widower who was more than happy to have an egg-salad sandwich and a good Bloody Mary and was already trailing after Cynthia.

"Well, you got what you wanted," Lisa said. "You upset my mother."

"Did I?"

Blanca felt a bit of remorse; Cynthia had been married to her father far longer than her own mother had been. Blanca now remembered a ballet performance that she'd practiced for nonstop. She was six or seven. After a while Sam knew half her routine and did it with her on the lawn, in the living room. She'd had a horrible brief thought: *I hope he doesn't come to the performance and ruin it.* Before they left for the performance, Cynthia had pulled her aside. *Don't worry,* she'd said. *Sam's asleep. He won't be there.*

"I'm sure you're thrilled that my dad left you more than he left me," Lisa said.

"Actually, he didn't. You'll inherit whatever your mother

got and this extra third goes to someone else, not to me. So you're wrong there, Lisa. Get your facts straight."

Lisa came right up to her. For an instant Blanca thought her half sister might haul off and hit her full in the face. She deserved it, really.

"What did I ever do to you?" Lisa said.

"Nothing."

"You never even talked to me! You acted like I wasn't here."

"Actually, I was the one who wasn't here. Or so I prayed."

"It doesn't really matter. I was his favorite," Lisa said.

At that moment, Blanca hated her own sister. She was jealous of this leggy, unhappy girl her father had indeed loved.

"Well, hurray for you," Blanca said coolly. "You should have that written on your own gravestone: *Daddy liked me best.*"

"Why should he have loved you? He wasn't even your real father."

Lisa had bitten-down cuticles and there was a line of blood under each nail. She was the nervous type. Down the lane someone was mowing the grass; there was the muffled whir of the motor. Blanca felt sick. Everything stopped right then.

"You knew that, right?" Lisa was studying Blanca for a reaction. Lisa herself had heard it from a friend's mother; as it turned out, many people in town had figured out Blanca's parentage. When Lisa had come home to ask her own mother if it was true, Cynthia had clammed up; then Lisa had known for certain. Now she dug deeper, looking for a nerve. "I mean, everyone knew."

"I made a good decision not to have anything to do with you," Blanca said. "You were a miserable child."

Not at all true. Lisa had been a placid, willing-to-please girl who would have followed Blanca anywhere, had she but been allowed. Still, she deserved to be slammed if she was going to start telling lies.

"Your real father was a janitor or something in town," Lisa said. "He sold dogs."

All at once, Blanca felt some sort of truth; she saw it in Lisa's face. *This is bad. Stop talking to her. Walk out the door.*

"Ask my mother." Lisa looked pleased with herself. "Ask anyone. It's true."

"Lisa!" Cynthia had come looking for them. She had a tray of celery and olives. Her face was blotchy. Lisa ran to her mother.

"Tell her."

There were cumulus clouds today and they were racing across the sky. Anyone could look up through the atrium in the living room and see them, faster and faster.

"Yes, tell me," Blanca said. "Go ahead."

"Blanca, she's a child."

"Don't make me out to be a liar!" Lisa said. "Tell her!"

"Yes, tell me, Cynthia."

Cynthia looked apologetic. Blanca stared at her step-mother, shocked by her hesitation.

"Cynthia!"

This might be true, Blanca found herself thinking. *He wasn't even my father.* She felt a line of sweat down her back, even in her summer dress, even though the house was air-conditioned.

"Are you going to tell me?"

When Cynthia said nothing, Blanca grabbed her purse and went out. The birds in the hedges were deafening. There was a jet overhead. She couldn't hear anything. Her ears actually hurt. Cynthia came out after her. Blanca turned to face her.

"It was George Snow. Your mother was in love with him. But your father was John Moody. Make no mistake about that. And he loved you."

Blanca turned her back on her stepmother and went around to the rear of the house, following the stone path. It felt as though there was glass inside her lungs. Had it ever been so difficult to breathe? Her summer dress was too hot. Her skin was on fire.

There was the patio where John Moody had died. There was the lawn where Blanca had danced with Sam one evening. Where she'd watched him shoot up drugs on the night Meredith first brought Daniel to the house and found them sitting at the table in the dark. *It doesn't even hurt,* Sam told her. *One pinch and it's all over.*

Fuck it, Blanca thought. Nothing was what it seemed. Not even her own blood and bones. This was where the red map led, to a place she'd never imagined, to the house where she'd grown up, to the center of who she was. Blanca put her purse on the edge of the patio and walked to the pool. Green and cool. Meredith told her once that she'd found the truth about herself in a pool, floating in the dark water. Blanca slipped off her white flip-flops and sat beside the edge. It was the last day of something. She might never come back here. More than anything, Blanca wished she could remember her mother. She unclasped the pearls from around her neck and held them in the water. If she let them slide into the pool, would they float or fall? Would they spell out the name of her mother's true love, her blood father, or would they simply drift, then fall to the very bottom, like stones?

She opened her hand and let go. The pearls immediately began to sink; in no time they were submerged. Blanca dove in after them, still wearing her new dress. Amazing how quickly you could lose something. Blanca made her way across the very bottom of the pool, forcing herself to go on though she had barely any air left. She groped along the concrete until she had the pearls in hand, the only thing she had left, the one remaining piece of evidence that there was something that was solid and real and worth searching for.

BLANCA WAITED TO OPEN THE ENVELOPE UNTIL SHE WAS IN the yard behind the inn. It was early evening and the sky was hazy and pink. She had taken off her soaked dress, hung it in the bathroom to dry, then put on shorts and a T-shirt. Her hair was wet and smelled like chlorine. She still felt chilled. The shadows in Connecticut were so deep and blue that the temperature could change drastically in a few moments. Blanca placed the envelope her father had left for her on the wrought-iron garden table and watched some bees in the rhododendrons. *Loves me, loves me not.* She was glad to be alone. Everything was so green. Everything smelled like grass.

She had absolutely no idea what was in the envelope. It could be anything at all, a snake, a ruby, an admission of guilt, a key, a lump of coal. The letter was handwritten, dated nearly five years ago, not long after Sam's death. John Moody had kept it in his desk drawer, and then a few months before dying, he'd sent it to his lawyer's office. On his last day on earth the fact that the letter existed brought him comfort, as he'd hoped it would. He imagined it inside his head, the envelope, the thin paper within, the blue ink, the words he'd written.

There was something else inside. Blanca pulled out a photograph of her mother. The photo was faded and worn; John Moody had kept it in his wallet for thirty-seven years. Arlie was on the deck of a ferryboat, her back against the railing; she was smiling at the camera, her red hair flying out behind her, wearing a white dress. She was seventeen, young but brilliant with her huge smile. On the back of the photo, in ink, John had written *Arlie on the ferry, the day after marrying me.*

Blanca opened the letter. She felt as though she were unwrapping skin from bone. It crinkled and she thought of the sound of fire.

I should have spoken to you, but I don't think I knew how. I wanted to tell you about George Snow.

While she was at the cemetery with Meredith, Blanca had noticed three graves beneath the tree. Her mother's, with its small square marker set into the ground, which Blanca remembered. Sam's, with only his name and dates of birth and death, meant to be plain as well, but decorated instead with a hodgepodge of stones, as though the earth he rested in knew Sam needed more than a slab of gray granite.

Look, Blanca had said to Meredith. *Sam would have loved this. Rock art.*

The third grave was in the rear; Blanca had quickly decided it belonged to another family, set close by circumstance. She had ignored it. Now she realized why her father had been buried elsewhere. Another man had taken his place.

Young men are stupid, and I was stupid for a long time. Your mother turned to George Snow. He never married and had no other children. He died three years ago — leukemia. I went to see him in the hospital and I brought photographs of you. He asked if he could keep them.

I told him he'd be proud of you. He said he already was. He'd gone to dance recitals and school assemblies; he'd followed your life. I didn't tell you because I was afraid I would lose you. I'm sorry I was a terrible father.

You seemed to have understood Sam, so maybe you will find it in your heart to understand me, too.

Sam has a son. I saw him one time. I want to leave him what I leave to my daughters. On the back of this letter you'll find his address.

This is something I never told anyone: I wasn't with her when she died. I was out in the yard. The sky was blue and the weather was fine. I couldn't believe she was really going. I refused to believe it.

George Snow was upstairs in her room and I could hear him crying. A man I didn't even know. But when I looked up, there she was, standing in the grass with me. In the same dress she wore in the photograph. She didn't say a word, she never did, but I knew what she was saying to me: Let me go.

I tried, but I couldn't. I didn't realize until that moment when I saw her. It was her all along. She'd been the one, and I'd never known.

I tried to do what she asked, but I couldn't do it. I never let her go.
Your Father

BLANCA SAT AT THE TABLE AS THE EVENING GREW DARKER. There was a party going on inside the dining room of the inn. Someone had graduated or gotten engaged. She thought about George Snow in love with her mother. She thought about her father writing a letter and keeping it in his desk for years. She thought about Sam on the roof and John Moody standing on the lawn, lost.

When she went upstairs Blanca burned the letter in the bathroom sink; it left a pale blue film on the porcelain, which she then had to scrub. She didn't want anyone to be hurt by its contents. No wonder it had been stapled and taped: this letter was not for Cynthia's eyes. She and John had had a good marriage, and some things were better left unspoken. People had been hurt enough. Blanca kept the photograph, though. She slipped it into her wallet.

She thought she remembered George Snow sitting in the back row at the ballet school performances. A tall, blond man who applauded for her. Perhaps she should have been angry that she'd been so misled; instead, she found herself missing John Moody. Even if he had been a terrible father, she missed him more than she ever would have imagined, here in Connecticut, a place she'd avoided for so many years.

That night as she was packing, there was a knock on her door. Lisa. Blanca stood in the doorway, surprised.

"I would understand if you didn't want to invite me in," Lisa said.

Lisa didn't have her driver's license yet; she'd walked several miles to reach the inn. Now she stood scratching at her mosquito bites. She looked younger than sixteen.

"You wanted to hurt me and you did," Blanca said. "Since it's done, you might as well come in."

Blanca went back to her packing. There really wasn't much. She hadn't expected to stay here any longer than absolutely necessary.

Lisa followed her inside the room. She was cautious; she smelled like citronella and smoke. "You're leaving now?"

"I'm going to New York tonight. My plane takes off the day after tomorrow. To tell you the truth, I just want to get the hell out of Connecticut."

"Me too," Lisa said sullenly. She dropped into a wing chair and pulled out a pack of cigarettes. "Mind if I smoke?"

"By all means." Blanca got a water glass from her bureau to use as an ashtray.

"He didn't love me best," Lisa said. "I think that was the meanest thing I ever said."

"No, telling me he wasn't really my father was probably meaner."

"You're right. Maybe I just wanted your attention."

Blanca laughed. "You got it." Lisa took a deep drag of her cigarette. "That's bad for you," Blanca told her.

"Did Sam smoke?"

"Sam did whatever was bad for him."

Blanca pushed the water glass toward Lisa, who took one

last drag, then stubbed out the cigarette. Lisa pulled her legs up and sat on them. She was tremendously self-conscious about being so tall. "Everybody just took off and disappeared. It was just me and the dog. Which was really supposed to be your dog. That George Snow guy gave him to you, but when you went off to college you left him so I pretended he was mine. I loved him. Do you even remember his name?"

"Of course I do," Blanca said.

"Dusty." Lisa started crying. She put her hand over her mouth so she wouldn't sob.

"I know his name. I just forgot for a minute. What happened to Dusty?" Blanca asked.

"He died eight years ago. See what I mean? You never even thought about us."

"All I was thinking about was getting out."

"I think about the same thing! I hate that house. It's like a birdcage. Thirteen months till I escape to college. And four days. But that's only if I attend graduation. I presume Cyn would have a shit fit if I didn't go."

They both laughed. Lisa used the bottom of her T-shirt to wipe her eyes and blow her nose.

"Oh, lovely," Blanca said. "Miss Snotty."

"I tried everything to get your attention when I was little. You were so uninvolved. You were so mean."

"I was heartbroken."

"Sam. You missed him." Lisa looked around the room. "Do you have a minibar?"

"Am I supposed to let you get drunk?"

"You're not that kind of sister?"

"Not usually."

Blanca had bought a small bottle of vodka in town. She poured a little into two glasses.

"Oh, my god." Lisa wrinkled her nose after a tiny sip. "Don't you have some soda we can add to it?"

Blanca went to the bathroom and added tap water to Lisa's drink. She remembered wanting to be grown up, thinking it would make a difference.

"What are you going to do with your inheritance?" Lisa asked as she took tiny sips of what was now mostly water.

"Pay off my debts. Maybe buy my bookstore free and clear so I can go bankrupt all on my own. And if I have anything left over, buy as many things made out of cashmere as I can afford. You?"

"Medical school."

"Frivolous type, eh?" Blanca was done packing. She finished her drink, then zipped up the suitcase. "Sam had a son. That's who the last third is for. I didn't want you to think there was any great mystery."

"I barely remember Sam. I think I saw him twice when I was a baby. I'm glad that's who the money's for."

"Maybe I was a shitty sister," Blanca said.

"Take out the maybe."

Blanca sat down on the edge of the bed. She was more like John Moody than she ever would have imagined. "I'm sorry."

"Well, fuck you," Lisa said. "You left me and the dog. You probably wouldn't have known if I had died eight years ago, either."

They started laughing and couldn't stop.

"At least I know your name," Blanca joked.

"Oh, yeah? What's my middle name?"

"What's mine?"

They got hysterical over that one.

"Okay," Blanca said. "I'm sorry."

"Good. I want you to be." Lisa leaned forward in her chair. "I'm sorry, too."

Lisa carried the suitcase for Blanca, who had her purse, and the damp summer dress she'd gone swimming in rolled up in a laundry bag. Blanca had paid for the night, but she was leaving anyway. She gave Lisa a ride home. They both used to fly down the same lane on their bikes, years apart.

"I like it here in the dark," Lisa said, her nose up against the window.

"Sam liked the dark," Blanca said.

"Would he have liked me?"

"God, yes. Sam would have let you have that whole bottle of vodka."

Without even trying Blanca found the way; a right and a left, then past the hedge of lilacs. *They smell like our mother,* Sam used to tell her. She could smell them right now.

"Thanks," Lisa said when they got to the house. "When I walk in the dark I always walk into spiderwebs. I'm afraid of spiders."

"Afraid of spiders." Blanca took note. "I'll remember that."

"FYI, my middle name is Susan. Named for my maternal grandmother."

"I don't have a middle name. I think my mother forgot to give me one."

"How about Beatrice?" Lisa said. "I had a pet mouse named Beatrice. Then your nickname can be Beebee."

"Meredith used to call me Bee."

"See, it's a perfect name."

"Cynthia let you have a mouse?"

"She didn't know."

They both laughed then.

"If I come to London, I'll look you up." Lisa opened the car door, but before she got out she asked, "What are you going to do tonight? By the time you get to New York it will be midnight."

Not the best time to be rapping on a stranger's door.

I'm lost. Open the door. Tell me where I am.

"You can stay here," Lisa suggested. "No one would bother you."

Blanca was touched. Lisa was just a kid. She wasn't so bad.

"Maybe I'll just park here awhile. Take a walk around for old times' sake."

"Okay." Lisa got out. "Bye, Beebee," she said.

"Bye, Lisa Sue."

Blanca watched Lisa run up the steps and go inside. It was an especially dark night. No stars at all. Or maybe there was a cover of clouds. Blanca got out of the car and walked down the driveway, then to the lawn beyond the pool. The grass was so soft; she slipped off her flip-flops and sank down into the grass, just for a minute. Silvery clouds were moving through the dark sky. *Beebee,* she thought. Meredith would get a kick out of Lisa's nickname for Blanca.

Blanca closed her eyes. Just for a minute before she got back in the car. Without wanting to, she fell asleep quickly and deeply; she dreamed of the swan. It was beside her in the grass. In her dream, Blanca opened her eyes. This time the swan had a clutch of eggs, luminous, moon-colored. They looked at each other, and even though one was a woman and the other a swan, they could understand each other. Not through words; it was more basic, more intense than that.

Don't fly away, Blanca thought in her dream.

But the swan rose up, her wings enormous, up into the dark night. There were the eggs, left in the grass. Blanca had no idea who they belonged to. She had a feeling of panic — *How will I take care of them? What will I do?* But when she looked closer, she saw they were only stones. Perfect white stones. Nothing more.

Blanca awoke early, arms and legs stiff. The lawn was wet and her clothes were damp; her hair was threaded through with stray bits of grass. She stood up. Mist was rising from the ground. The sky was the color of pearls. She thought of George Snow sitting in the back row of all her dance performances. She thought of John Moody writing her a letter. She thought of James Bayliss breaking up a fight between boys he didn't even know.

It was so early there wasn't much traffic on the highway, but Blanca got lost in the city. She circled Union Square, then took Broadway downtown, before she finally made her way to Twenty-third Street. She searched for a parking space, finally finding one on Tenth Avenue, a few blocks from the address her father had written down.

She thought about what she would say to Sam's son when she met him. *My mother was a ferryboat captain's daughter. My father was a stranger. My brother was the person I loved most in this world even though I always knew I would lose him.*

She should have needed to be buzzed into the building, but someone was coming out and Blanca managed to catch the door before it closed. The hall was black and white tile and it echoed. It was a walk-up, so Blanca started up the stairs. When she got to the fourth floor, she spied 4B, the apartment where Sam's son lived, but she kept going up. Another floor, and then another; to the very top. She wanted to see where it had happened. The door to the roof was locked, but when she pushed against it she could see a bit of blue. Maybe that was enough. It was what Sam had seen, after all. The same sky. All his life he'd been thinking about that race of people in Connecticut who could fly only when circumstances were dire. At the very last moment, when there was no hope and no possibility, they rose up from the sinking ship, the burning building. Their mother's father, the one who'd died when Arlie was only seventeen, swore he'd seen them, high above Long Island Sound. They looked like birds, but they were not. They were something else entirely.

He jumped out of desperation or he fell by accident, but maybe he'd had hope as well. Once upon a time, in a place not far from here, someone who was lost was found. Someone who was sinking rose into the clouds. Someone fell in love. Someone was saved. Blanca went back down to the fourth floor. She couldn't remember the last time she'd felt anything resembling happiness. Here she was, all by herself on a singular morning. She let everything go as she stood in the dark hallway; she let it drift away like ashes on a windowsill or birds on a ledge. She thought of Icarus and of the glass house where they'd grown up; she thought of her mother in a white summer dress. It was hot and humid and the sky was still dark at the edges, riotously blue in the very center. She had no idea where she was or how she'd ever get home or if she'd go back to London or if she was in love or even if there was someone inside the apartment who would open the door for her.

All the same, she rang the bell, and then she waited for whatever would happen next.

ABOUT THE AUTHOR

ALICE HOFFMAN is the bestselling author of seventeen acclaimed novels, including *The Ice Queen, Practical Magic, Here on Earth, The River King, Blue Diary, Illumination Night, Turtle Moon, Seventh Heaven,* and *At Risk;* the highly praised story collections *Local Girls* and *Blackbird House;* and eight books for young readers. She lives outside Boston.

Reading Group Guide

Skylight
Confessions

a novel by

Alice
Hoffman

A conversation with
the author of *Skylight Confessions*

Alice Hoffman talks with Allen Pierleoni
of the *Sacramento Bee*

"I write from such a subconscious place, it's almost like the elements of a dream," said the novelist Alice Hoffman on the phone from her Boston home. "I don't understand what it means until I'm done. Sometimes I still don't understand it. That's where the readers put things together more quickly than the writer does."

Hoffman is being modest again. Her well-crafted, fast-moving tales are lecture-hall examples of structure, plot, and imagery. Just ask anyone — except maybe Hoffman herself.

Hoffman just published her seventeenth novel for adults (she's written eight books for young readers), *Skylight Confessions*. It's a rich, heavily symbolic story of family relationships, bad choices, love gone wrong and right, and how, despite everything, we still can salvage redemption of a sort.

This being a Hoffman novel, there's magical realism sprinkled throughout like pixie dust, along with the sense that we're at least partly inside a fairy tale. A ghost is involved, of course, one that breaks dishes, leaves trails of soot, and haunts one character in particular.

Hoffman, fifty-four, grew up on Long Island and earned degrees in English and anthropology from Adelphi University there. Later, she graduated with a master of arts degree in creative writing from Stanford University. She and her husband, Tom (a former teacher turned writer), have two sons, eighteen and twenty-three.

You wrote your first novel, Property Of, *when you were twenty-one and attending Stanford.*

I'd never heard of Stanford until [an Adelphi professor] got me a fellowship to go there. I was a working-class girl who never thought about going to college at all. I got a job at the Doubleday book factory on Long Island, and I worked until lunch and quit. Something had to be easier than factory work, so I signed up for a college course at night.

Is your family anything like the one in Skylight Confessions?

No, I write to create something different. Fiction writers are writing either to write about their lives, or they're writing to create a different reality. Even though all of my characters contain bits and pieces of me, they're not me.

You're big on ghosts, and there's one in Skylight Confessions.

I think what happens with ghosts is they haunt people who won't let them go. In the book, what it means to be haunted is that you take your past with you. Unless you learn in some way to deal with it and let it go, it's going to haunt you.

The ferry-boat captain tells his daughter about a race of people who have wings and can fly away from impending disaster. In one way or another, most of the characters in Skylight Confessions *metaphorically fly away but later end up having to confront their issues.*

You can have a fantasy about being able to run away, but if you do, it's not necessarily a positive thing. You really have to stand and face whatever it is. There's no way to fly away from it. That's what the book is about.

Certainly the children and teens in your stories have a hard time, due to the behavior of the adults in their lives.

That's true. As adults, we know that we mess up things. Children don't really know that until they're adults themselves. A lot of this book is about surviving tragic circumstances. At the end, though, I hope there's a feeling of hope.

The last line is: "... she rang the [door]bell, and then she waited for whatever would happen next." That sounds like hope.

Yes, but doesn't that also feel like what we're all doing all of the time? We have to.

Most of your books impart lessons to young adults. What wisdom did you share with your own sons?

I hope what I showed them is that if you want something enough, you can make it happen. Also, I hope I showed them that whoever you are, you have to be true to yourself.

Another theme in your stories is one of seemingly ordinary lives that turn out to be surprisingly multilayered.

I do like the idea that people are not always what they seem to be. I grew up in a neighborhood where every house was exactly the same, but there was a sense that you didn't know what was going on inside the houses.

One of the reasons I saw the world that way was because I was a huge fan of *The Twilight Zone*. Rod Serling was a genius who influenced a whole generation. A lot of his stuff was so political and social and ahead of its time, and so much about how you think something is one way but it's really another.

Then there's Ray Bradbury, who is so positive. After 9/11 I was extremely blocked and thought I'd never write again.

I was thinking about the books I had loved as a kid and was somehow smart enough to reread *Fahrenheit 451,* and it made me remember how incredibly important books are and allowed me to write again. Ray Bradbury had a huge influence on my life.

Many of your books hark back to fairy tales and fables, magic and the supernatural. Why is that?

Because I think that's the most interesting part of literature. All those things are what literature is made out of — folk tales, fairy tales, fantasy. For me, realism isn't that interesting. I'm much more interested in mythic, psychological literature.

Like fairy tales, which dwell on the worst parts of human nature.

Yes, they're brutal and raw. They originally were part of the oral tradition of women telling stories to children. They were moral stories that dealt with the psychology of childhood. As a kid, I loved them because they weren't sugar coated. When you're a child and you read gruesome stuff about families and parents and being lost in the woods, you feel the emotional truth of it.

What are you working on now?

A new novel that's going to be out next year. I'm starting to do the serious revisions, which is the part I hate. It's about three different weddings and three different love affairs.

Is there a common thread that runs through the fabric of your books?

I always feel like I'm writing a message, but I don't know what that message is until I'm done with the book. But I think the message has to do with having hope. It's a message [that says]: "You have to go on. These are the possibilities and you can survive." I think that's my reason for writing.

As a writer, you assume many guises.

That's the great thing about fiction: You get to live all these different lives that aren't yours. It's almost like being an actor, where you put on all these different roles and become other people. I wrote a book called *The Ice Queen,* about the survivor of a lightning strike. I knew so much about lightning and weather then, but now I don't remember a thing. [Becoming an instant expert] is just for the period of the book, and then I go on to the next thing. It's not me, it's not my life, but I get to kind of experience it.

Last question: If you were interviewing yourself, what would be the last question you would ask?

I would ask, "Are you happy that you spent your life as a writer?"

That's a key question.

I think about it all the time. I've spent so much of my life being in other worlds, and I have to say I don't think there was a choice; it's who I am. And if that's true, then I have to be happy about it and feel really lucky that I got to do it.

The complete text of Allen Pierleoni's interview with Alice Hoffman originally appeared in the *Sacramento Bee* on Monday, January 29, 2007. Reprinted with permission.

Questions and topics for discussion

1. There is much speculation by characters in the novel as to whether John and Arlyn were fated to find each other. Do you think they were destined to be together? Or do you think that Arlyn was meant to be with George Snow? Would Arlyn ever have met George if she hadn't first fallen in love with John?

2. Arlyn's hair is described as being several different shades of red in the book, from fire-red to blood-red. How do you think these varying descriptions affect the way you perceive Arlyn in these scenes?

3. Why is it significant that the Moodys live in a glass house, and that the design of this house is the crowning achievement of John's father's career?

4. Why do you think Arlyn haunts John Moody for so long after her death?

5. After Arlyn's death, John and his son, Sam, manage to clash on just about everything. Is there anything besides Arlyn that you think these two have in common?

6. Birds make notable appearances in several scenes in the novel. Identify a few such scenes and discuss the role that birds play in the story.

7. Arlyn passes on to her children specific items that they wear like talismans: Sam gets her gray coat and Blanca her pearls. In what ways is each of these gifts appropriate for its recipient?

8. "Sam Moody wasn't like other people. The things he thought most often about were dishes, bones, vases, model planes, buildings made of blocks — things that could be broken" (page 44). What do you think this passage says about Sam's personality? To what do you attribute Sam's addiction to drugs?

9. Discuss the role that Meredith, as an outsider to the family, plays in the novel.

10. How do you think Blanca's life will change after the novel ends? What do you hope will happen for her? What effect will the revelation of her true father's identity ultimately have on Blanca?

The Foretelling

A novel by Alice Hoffman

Rain is a girl with a certain destiny, living in an ancient time of blood, raised on mares' milk, nurtured with the strength of a thousand Amazon sisters. A girl of power, stronger than fifty men, she rides her white horse as fierce as a demon.

But then there is the foretelling. *The black horse.*

In truth, Rain tastes a different future in her dreams. She is touched by the stirrings of emotions unknown. She begins to see beyond a life of war . . . and wonders — about mercy and men, about hope and love.

"Hoffman's prose eloquently expresses the beliefs and rituals of a lost civilization and offers a sympathetic portrait of a young leader who chooses kindness over cruelty."
— *Publishers Weekly*

"A subtly inflected characterization . . . holds the center of this high-action survival and battle drama."
— *The Horn Book*

"A spare, compelling coming-of-age story."
— *Kirkus Reviews*

Published by Little, Brown and Company

Available wherever books are sold

Incantation

A novel by Alice Hoffman

Estrella de Madrigal thought she knew herself: daughter, granddaughter, dearest friend. But truth is rare in this cruel and unforgiving century in Spain, when Jews who refused conversion to Christianity risked everything — love, life, family, faith.

Then: a startling discovery shakes Estrella's world to the core. Emerging from a cocoon of secrets, new love burns brightly, but betrayal unleashes a monstrous evil upon her. Estrella must find the strength — despite grave consequences— to become the person she is destined to be.

"Riveting." — *School Library Journal*

"Hoffman tears a horrific page from history and melds it with mysticism to create a spellbinding tale." — *VOYA*

"Alice Hoffman's books of magical realism and even more magical language have great appeal to teens. . . . Her signature lyricism is much in evidence." — *KLIATT*

Published by Little, Brown and Company

Available wherever books are sold

ALSO BY ALICE HOFFMAN

The Ice Queen

"A moving tale of love, loss, forgiveness, and spiritual renewal, *The Ice Queen* is one of Alice Hoffman's finest novels."
— Dorman T. Shindler, *Denver Post*

"Magic with intermittent flashes of reality. . . . The transformation of a woman through passion is at the heart of *The Ice Queen*."
— Anita Sama, *USA Today*

"Stunning. . . . An electrifying novel. . . . Hoffman explores the consequences of both magic and lightning with luminous clarity. It is a stunning feat."
— Melissa Mia Hall, *Chicago Sun-Times*

"Nothing less than stellar. . . . A lush tale of loss and redemption. . . . Whether evoking the sultry landscape of southern Florida or the layers of ice around the librarian's heart, Hoffman reminds us how little distance there is between magic and mundane."
— Amy Waldman, *People*

"Alice Hoffman sets in motion another of her modern-day fairy tales, and in so doing she mesmerizes the reader. Clear your calendar before picking up *The Ice Queen*. You will get nothing else done during the day or two it will take you to finish this fluid, lovely novel."
— Lisa Jennifer Selzman, *Houston Chronicle*

Back Bay Books • Available wherever paperbacks are sold